WHO KILLED HARLAN PARKER?

WHEN SMALL TOWN JUSTICE MEANS ONE
LESS LAWYER

JOHN CAUDILL

BY *HIDDEN LETTER PUBLISHING*
Louisville, Kentucky
Who Killed Harlan Parker © 2018 by John Caudill

Work included also by *Hidden Letter Publishing.*
Every Life a River © 2017 by John Caudill
Her Silhouette © 2018 by John Caudilll
Gum Pond Road © 2018 by John Caudill
The Glutton's Punishment © 2018 by John Caudill
River Queen Maiden © 2019 by John Caudill

For my father, James Reid Caudill.
The best trial lawyer in this town, and the next.

Prologue

A liar sleeps eternal
Inside a steel cold keep
A Lincoln and a lawyer
One-hundred-nine feet deep

Among forsaken pieces
Upon its limestone floor
A crypt with tinted windows
And space where once a door

Gaze upon the fortunes
Of one who found great wealth
By serving ends of justice
That only served himself

Just follow Bubba's junk
Where they roll tide roll
Down to the murky murky
Just off Gum Pond Road

1

QUARRY LAKE

The old Gulf station in the forgotten town has been closed and boarded up for years, just like the Seven-Eleven next to it and the laundromat next to that. Bitty, Alabama is a two-minute pass through on a county road where the only intersection has a traffic light that never turns red because there's little traffic and no good reason to stop there. There are only three reasons you would find yourself in Bitty: you were unlucky enough to be born there, your car broke down on the way to someplace way better, or you didn't want anyone to know what you're up to.

Sparks fly through the old service station's interior like fireflies in June as a man in a wetsuit steadies the flame of a welding torch against a driver's side door hinge of a 1981 Lincoln Town car. Hip hop graffiti covering the cinderblock walls fades in and out with the cobalt flame. The car isn't a classic and the man has no designs on making it one, but he must work quickly to finish the job and be three hours north in Summerville, Kentucky before the sun rises.

In three days, Harlan Parker, the richest and most crooked lawyer in Summerville, will have his case called on the docket in Crawford Superior Court. His client will be present in the courtroom, but Parker will be uncharacteristically absent. Judge Mac Renfro's assistant will call Parker's office asking where he is, and an associate will be sent scrambling across the street to cover the hearing.

Tori Stevens, Parker's paralegal, will call his condo but get no answer, then try his private cell that will immediately patch to voicemail. Parker has been divorced for twenty years, never remarried, and never had kids. At least none who'd claim him. His law firm, Parker, Barnes and Jeffries, is the closest thing to family he has, but only one of financial convenience. None of them associate with him outside work. They will have no idea what's happened to him, either.

By 10 a.m., Stevens will start cancelling his Monday appointments, and after not hearing anything from Parker the rest of the day she'll cancel Tuesday's as well.

Forty-eight hours will pass and Ridley Barnes, Parker's junior partner, will call a friend at the police department and ask them to discretely comb the area for Parker. But the police are aware of Parker's reputation as an epic philanderer, so they won't take Barnes' concerns seriously, at least not initially. They'll look for Parker's car at the parking lot of the Blue Jay Inn, then the Stoney River Motor Lodge and every other seedy hotel in town without any luck.

By Wednesday afternoon after Parker's a no show for three more court appearances, wild speculation over his whereabouts will go into full throttle. A couple of lawyers will feign concern publicly, but for the most part Parker's disappearance won't be a source of anxiety or despair but only one of morbid curiosity and fodder for the local Bar.

Parker is not only the wealthiest lawyer in town, he's the most despised. Half of the businessmen in Summerville and most lawyers in the area have a story over the past twenty plus years about how Parker's swindled them out of a case or client. The chatter will be neither flattering nor sympathetic.

I think Parker was probably sleeping with some
hooker he's represented and his heart just exploded.
Clicked out mid stroke. Ha!

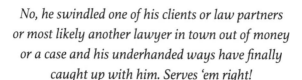

*No, he swindled one of his clients or law partners
or most likely another lawyer in town out of money
or a case and his underhanded ways have finally
caught up with him. Serves 'em right!*

*No, some good ole' country boy that Parker took
to the cleaners in a divorce case caught him alone
somewhere and put a couple of slugs in him.
I'll bet you dollars to dimes that some hunter
will stumble across his no-good carcass next spring.
If anybody had it coming, it's Harlan Parker.*

But the ten attorneys at Parker, Barnes and Jeffries will be angling for their own survival. From their perspective what happened to Parker will be far less concerning than what will happen to them and his clients if he doesn't show up. Parker was the economic engine that made the firm go, its only trial lawyer and the only one among them with connections strong enough with the judiciary to make indictments and lawsuits go away. Without their rainmaker the rest of the lot are nothing but street lawyers walking, soon to be fending for themselves, scratching out a living at a fraction of the one they've enjoyed under Parker.

Within a couple of months, the firm will disband, and they'll have to move out of the nicest office space on the downtown square into far more modest surroundings. The firm's cash cows will scatter to the wind, including the lucrative small businesses and well-heeled criminal clients Parker has represented on healthy retainers for years.

Within six months the coffeehouse which occupies the space next to the firm will knock down the wall between them. It will annex the firm's vacant first floor office space and transform it into a popular

gathering spot for college students enjoying flatbread chicken pani-
nis, tomato bisque and hazelnut lattes.

When Parker is out of the way, other lawyers in town will be in
line to inherit a healthy share of Parker's civil and criminal clients.
Men whose marriages ended because Parker was sleeping with their
wives will suddenly flash big grins at work for no apparent reason,
while others will gleefully skip down the street and fist bump
complete strangers at the gas station over the very notion that
someone did him in.

The fact that few will care about what happened to Parker just a
few weeks after he's gone missing is something the man with the
welding torch is counting on.

After several minutes the hinge gives way and drops the door to
the ground. A crash reverberates inside the empty structure. But it's
just past midnight, so no one is around to hear it. The man flips up
the glass faceplate of his welding mask to get a better look at his
handiwork. He thinks about how suspicious he'd look if anyone saw
him driving down the highway without a door. But that is highly
unlikely. Bitty, Alabama is well past its heyday. No one lives within a
half-mile of the place. The man only has a few minutes' drive to the
car's destination.

He hoists the detached door off the floor and places it in the back
seat, then walks to the trunk and pushes down on it, trying to assure
himself it won't easily pop open. Under the rear bumper tiny drops of
blood begin to drip to the grimy concrete floor.

A couple of days before the man was in the pasture of a resting
corn field in rural Crawford County jump-starting the rusting sedan
before driving it 80 miles to Johnson City, Tennessee. He paid $250 to
the first mechanic he could find to make the car serviceable enough
to travel just a few hundred more miles. The late Friday evening
journey from Summerville to Bitty was its last.

He rolls up the overhead garage door and pulls out of the gas
station heading down the highway. The cool early morning air
rustles through the door opening against his face. It feels soothing,
even calming, after the heat of the welding torch. After a few

minutes he is on Gum Pond Road approaching the entrance of Quarry Lake.

Once a limestone rock quarry, the expansive gash in the Alabama countryside has been transformed into a lake after years of collecting rainwater trickling down from higher elevations. For decades it has served as a popular fishing and swimming hole for locals. And because the lake is over 100 feet deep, it is an ideal location for novice scuba divers to hone their skills without having to drive six hours to the Gulf Coast.

The quarry's murky depths also make it an ideal dumping ground for things people don't want to be found. Its bottom is littered with appliances, vehicles, farm equipment and all manner of junk. But a few years ago, after a couple of teenagers drowned attempting to swim across, the owner closed the lake to the public and posted no trespassing signs throughout the perimeter of the property. The only vehicle entrance is blocked with a twenty-foot cattle gate padlocked to a fence post.

The barrier provides little resistance to anyone with a bolt cutter. The man clips the lock and drives the Lincoln through the entrance. The oversized heap rattles, creaks and moans over the uneven Alabama clay as it ambles down a narrow passage for several hundred feet leading to the lake. The man begins to question why he had selected the car in the first place, but he quickly abandons the thought. He isn't there to drive off-road.

He pulls to stop a couple of hundred feet from the water and jumps out, retrieving the detached door and carrying it to the lake. The strange conflation of vinyl and steel isn't as heavy as it is awkward. Then, with the spinning motion of a hammer thrower at a track and field competition, the man hurls the door into the water and watches. It floats on the surface for only a couple of seconds before vanishing. Because the lake is so deep, he figures that it would take a couple of minutes for an object the size of the Lincoln to hit bottom.

The man pulls out a glow stick and bends it, which makes a crackling sound as it creates a luminous green light. He'd already determined where to climb out of the quarry, a ledge about 150 feet to the left of where the car would enter the water. He walks over and places the glow stick there. The light would be necessary to guide him back to land after he pulls and pushes his way from the sinking car. If he lost his bearings, he could swim in wrong direction and be in big trouble. Now that the door was gone water would rush into the car quickly, causing it to sink much faster. But the opening would also make it much easier for him to get out, that is, now that he didn't have to push open a door against rushing water.

It isn't the man's first trip to the place where people were left for dead if they weren't dead already. He knew it well enough to understand he couldn't just put the car in neutral and roll it into the water. That might work at a large pond or lake but not here. A rock quarry doesn't have a muddy bank that declines gradually into the depths, but a limestone edge cut at a 90-degree angle, dropping off precipitously for over 100 feet. As the front wheels pass over the water, the car's undercarriage would hang up on the bedrock and it would move no farther. Then the man would have to leave the car hanging over the edge of the water. The next morning someone would find Harlan Parker, and then things would quickly start to unravel. The man isn't going to take that chance. He has no choice but to drive the Lincoln into the lake, and with some speed at that.

The day before he'd stashed a pickup truck deep in the woods about a mile from the quarry. There would be no bus ticket from Huntsville to Nashville to Summerville to show he was in the area. Nor would there be a witness to say they picked up a hitchhiker on I-65 North near exit 22 in the early morning hours of October 6th and drove him a couple hundred miles before dropping him off near the Kentucky-Tennessee line. Within 30 minutes he is at the truck changing out of his wetsuit into dry clothes. In four hours he will be back in Kentucky home in bed and no one would know he had ever left.

2

THE EDUCATION OF A SOCIOPATH

Summerville is a quaint little town in central Kentucky in the heart of the Bluegrass region. Its countryside is filled with beautiful horse farms, distilleries and hidden marijuana groves. Though Crawford County must claim its share of cultural troglodytes, there are significantly fewer of them when compared with the rest of the state. Socially Summerville would be described as welcoming and inclusive, and it's ahead of the curve in how it educates its youth and relaxes public policy to improve the welfare of its residents.

One example is an unwritten policy referred to as, *don't ask, don't smell.* Laws prohibiting the growth and sale of marijuana are not enforced by local or county law enforcement. The result is that Crawford County has the lowest number of meth labs and opioid deaths per capita of anywhere in the state. State and federal law enforcement also stay away from Crawford County because its distilleries, horse farms and marijuana trade also make it the wealthiest county per capita. Money talks, so they let what happens in Crawford County stay in Crawford County.

Crawford's education system is based upon the principle that the worst thing a school can do for a kid is create an environment where they peak in high school. In 1981, the school board came to this conclusion after receiving recommendations from a task force comprised of members of the business community, marriage counselors, developmental psychologists and corrections officials who examined student traits that correlated most to difficulty adjusting to life after graduation. And the results were surprising, to say the least.

They found that post graduate quality of life had less to do with academic achievement that the level of social or athletic attention someone experienced during high school, and, even more surprising, there was an inverse relationship between the two. After a comprehensive review of every school sponsored program, the task force identified the following students as those at the highest risk of becoming dysfunctional adults:

- Starting quarterback and the captain of the football team.
- State champions and all-state selections in revenue sports.
- Class president.
- Cheerleaders for all male sports.
- Kings and queens of homecoming, sweetheart ball and prom, runner ups and their dates.
- Students who attended a minimum of 90 percent of all school sponsored dances with an actual date, which was defined as another student who either provided or received a boutonniere.

*Students who attended dances in groups of three or more were shown not to exhibit socially deviant behaviors post-graduation.

Socially and athletically elite students far more than any other were statistically shown to exhibit an inability to cope in the adult world, including struggles assimilating into the workforce and forming healthy, lasting relationships. But most concerning was a direct correlation between these students and behaviors consistent with antisocial personality disorder.

They engaged in egocentric acts that failed to consider the feelings or rights of others. Behaviors associated with unethical, manipulative and impulsive actions. They were much more likely to engage in deceitfulness at work, like repeated lying or stealing, and they were far more likely to end up in prison because of fraud or some other disregarded legal boundary. These students were far more likely to use their charm and charisma to manipulate and harm others without any remorse for their victims. In short, the task force found that high schools in their current form were nothing but petri dishes for the development of sociopaths.

So, the school board eliminated football, basketball and baseball teams and cheerleaders. There would be no prom, no homecoming kings or queens, no selections of most popular, or cutest couple or other such nonsense. There was no more student government. Why provide students interested in politics a training ground for sociopathic behavior when they would eventually get there on their own?

There were no school sponsored dances, which resulted in a significant increase in disposable household income for parents in Crawford County who were now not spending money on their daughter's expensive evening gowns.

While the school board was in a *less now means more later* mode, they also imposed a conditional ban on tattoos, body piercings and wearing trousers below the waistline. Crawford schools said that if you want to look like a criminal, you must first be convicted of a felony before earning the right to do those kinds of things. The school board ultimately mandated that Crawford County High and Summerville High keep their students miserable for at least 50 percent of the academic year.

However, while sports, cheerleading, and dances were prohibited, participation in cross country or band became mandatory, as studies showed that students engaged in these activities were far more miserable in high school and far more successful after it.

Drama was not mandatory but encouraged, as administrators viewed pathological honesty as one of the greatest barriers to adult happiness. Telling your boss or spouse that new suit or outfit looks fantastic when it makes them look twenty pounds heavier may be a lie but necessary to achieve the greater good of preserving your marriage or job.

Despite all the success that came with initial reforms, the school board sought to do more than simply eradicate the seeds of sociopathic behavior. Crawford was the first high school district in the United States to develop a curriculum on narcissism. Although not all narcissists are sociopaths, it is generally accepted that all sociopaths are narcissists, so the board decided to give its students the tools to identify and cope with both. This was not only done to reduce the number of innocent victims beguiled into sociopathic relationships, but to reduce the number of students who were just full of themselves.

So, they conducted a national search seeking the best candidate to oversee its visionary program. The qualifications listed in the job description included expertise in antisocial personality disorder and a strong teaching background. When all the interviews were done, the board tabbed Western Kentucky University Associate Sociology Professor, Marshal P. Wilt. What made Wilt especially attractive to the board was his groundbreaking work in criminology.

The 33-year-old teacher is a lean, gangly man with premature grey speckled black hair, traditional black-rimmed eyewear and a thick mustache. He has a distinctly midwestern, nasally accent and walks with a stick that looks like a billy club with two dozen keys dangling from it, though no one is quite sure why. And he talks exactly how you'd expect a homicide detective to because his unspoken dream is to one day be one. It's the reason Wilt was willing leave a college teaching position to work at a high school. His destiny wasn't to work in academia his whole career but to eventually put his knowledge into practice on the mean streets of Summerville.

When he ran across the job opening posted in WKU's student newspaper he quickly researched nearby Summerville and determined that it was the ideal place to transition from teaching to law enforcement. Although there were no openings in the police department when Wilt took the high school job, he was more than willing to bide his time until one came open. Like every other challenge else

Wilt takes on, he teaches with extraordinary passion and intensity, demanding the most of himself and those around him.

MONDAY 10:15 AM, January 4, 1982

The school theater with stadium seating has a capacity of over 300, and it's almost a third full on the first day of spring semester for the most popular class at Summerville High. Narcissism 101 is taught in the Drama Department for good reason. Narcissists are natural actors with the ability to morph into any one of multiple personas to appeal to whoever they're interested in.

Mr. Wilt is leaning against a bar stool with his arms folded as his vision oscillates between his watch and theater doors. A grimace flashes across his face as the last students file in to take their seats, barely beating the third period bell. There's a quote written on the portable blackboard behind him.

> *I think you're absolutely amazing!*
> *Yours truly,*
> *A Sociopath*

When everyone is seated, Wilt steps off the stool to address the class.

"At this very moment, there are at least five sociopaths sitting in this room."

The theater erupts in laughter, but Wilt isn't laughing with them. He waits for a couple of seconds for the uproar to subside, then continues.

"Sociopaths are people who will beguile, deceive and manipulate to take everything you have, and they're so good at it you'll never see it coming, that is, until it's too late. They're sitting right next to you in class. They're your boyfriend, girlfriend, best friend and co-worker. In the beginning, they make you feel like the most special person in the world. They overwhelm you with love and attention. They're the ones who know how to say just the right thing at just the right moment."

"When you go out into the workplace someday, they'll be the one schmoozing your boss and winning her over to take your job. In the end, after they've got every thing they wanted out of you, it will be as if they're a completely different person. Because they were never who they pretended to be to you. It was only a very convincing act to get what they wanted. The smiles, the attention, the contrived flattery was never about you. And whatever you had of any value before you encountered them isn't yours anymore. It's theirs. Your money, your career, a connection you had with someone else they wanted while pretending to want you. They have everything, that is, except you, left disillusioned and broken in every way imaginable. And while you're left reeling, they're on to the next unsuspecting opportunity."

No one in the class is laughing now. Instead, the room is filled with a muffled chatter of concern.

Kelly Wright isn't saying anything, because there's no one close enough to say anything to. She's seated alone, in the front row. She's the student who takes up residence front and center for every class, usually taking copious notes. We all know her. She raises her hand at least once every day to ask a question and the first to answer when the teacher poses one. Kelly's looking around the room with mild concern, but with even more suspicion. She raises her hand.

Wilt flips a wrist in her direction. "Yes, Ms. Wright?"

"Mr. Wilt, how am I supposed to know if I'm going out on a date with a sociopath?"

"Well, it's ironic that you would ask that question, Ms. Wright, because that's the first exercise we're going to do today."

Wilt grades his students on their ability to deal with a narcissist through an exercise in which they are interacting with one. The student is placed into a scene with another student playing the role of a narcissist and expected to work their way out of it without becoming a victim. The role playing not only simulates social situations, but professional ones as well, along with a wide variety of other scenarios where the student might cross paths with a sociopath.

Wilt came up with the idea as a graduate student at WKU and even published an academic paper on the technique. He's found it to be a very effective tool to help the student identify and deal with sociopaths. In Wilt's exercise, the role of the narcissist plays is critical, and after just five months at Summerville High, he's discovered a kid in the Junior Class who he believes to be the most gifted student at playing the role of anyone he's seen.

His name is Harlan Parker.

There's a very simple reason why Harlan was so good at role playing. For Harlan, the school board had acted too late. By the age of 16, his moral compass was irreparably broken, his interpretation of Rorschach ink blots indelibly formed, and the once malleable clay of his emotional makeup was now as firm as concrete. Going into his junior year, he was the football team's starting quarterback and a consensus preseason all-state selection. Alabama, Notre Dame, Georgia and Penn State were just a few of the schools wooing Parker. But after football was canceled and his family too poor to move him to another school, the interest from college football's big boys faded, leaving Parker only one scholarship offer his senior year: Division III, bottom-feeder, Summerville College.

He enrolled with his hometown school but quit the team midway through his sophomore year when it became clear that the student body and community were far more interested in showing up for poetry night than attending football games. Parker never forgave Summerville High, Summerville College or its creative writing program for denying him a shot at football glory. He made an unspoken vow to one day exact his revenge. Sort of like *Revenge of the Nerds*, just replacing the pocket calculator with a jock strap.

Even in high school, Harlan's gravitas is so considerable you can smell it the moment he walks into the room. And it's with such bearing that 16-year-old Harlan completely fools his teacher into believing that he's nothing but a bright kid with uncanny acting chops. It never dawns on Wilt that there's a very dark reason why Harlan is so charming to everyone he encounters. And the day Harlan confides in his teacher that his secret dream is to one day be an actor, Wilt is so moved by the personal reveal he resolves to go out of his way to help Harlan develop his gift.

But for Kelly Wright and most every other girl at Summerville High, Harlan's gift of gab is developed more than enough. His chiseled six-foot, two-inch frame and blonde, Samson-like locs would make Harlan persuasive if he never uttered a word.

Wilt walks over to Kelly. "Ms. Wright, because you're so timely with your question, you can participate in our first exercise."

Kelly asks, "What role am I playing, Mr. Wilt?"

Wilt turns to the rest of the class. "Well, that depends on you. Just as it is for each of us every day, you can play the role of someone who is paying attention to who they're interacting with, or you can play the role of a victim." Wilt then looks around the room.

"Harlan, get up here and show us what a real predator looks like!"

Wilt gives the signal to a student backstage to cut the lights in the gallery. A minute later, Kelly is standing on stage as Harlan enters stage left.

"Hey Kelly, how's it going?"

"Good Harlan, thanks for asking. What's up?"

Harlan smiles, then drops his eyes to the floor, shuffling his feet for a moment before looking back at Kelly.

"Saw you at the park yesterday. What's the name of that cute little puppy I saw you walking around with?"

Kelly flashes a big smile. "Oh, that's my English Terrier, Flash. He's my bud!"

"Well, I think Flash is about the coolest dog I've ever seen. Used to have one just like him. Called him Surf, because of his wavy black hair. My parents gave him to me for my 12th birthday. I think I was the happiest kid in Summerville."

Kelly curiously turns her head. She really was at the park yesterday, and she's not one bit bothered by the fact that he noticed. She likes it so much she instantly loses herself in Harlan, completely forgetting she's on stage and role playing in front of 100 classmates.

"I just love that name, Harlan. Where's Surf now?"

Harlan turns his head away for a moment, as if trying to fight off tears. He looks back at Kelly.

"Well, a couple of years ago my little brother left the back door open and Surf got out. Was a quick little guy. Ran clear out of sight. Looked for him for a month, but never found him."

Kelly's genuinely moved by this sweet, vulnerable Harlan she's never seen before. She steps closer and places her hand on his shoulder.

"Oh, Harlan! I'm so sorry to hear that! Is there anything I can do? Anything at all?"

Wilt sounds a detached bicycle horn, stopping the exercise.

"Ms. Wright. I regret to inform that you've been ensnared by a sociopath!"

The class again breaks out in laughter.

Kelly turns to smile at Harlan as she's snapped back into reality, but she could care less she just failed the exercise, thinking to herself:

If this is what a sociopath looks like, then sign me up!

Harlan was so good at role playing, Wilt talks the principal into allowing his star pupil skip gym class and role play for classes he wasn't even signed up for. Because of Wilt, Harlan continues to develop his gifts of charm and persuasion for much of his junior year and all his senior year. By the time he graduates from high school, he's already taken the art of deception and manipulation to a level few approach.

As for Wilt, by simply trying to help a young man develop his acting talent, he's done the very thing he was brought to Summerville to prevent, only far worse. He's unwittingly created an elite, highly functioning sociopath, a colossal miscalculation Wilt would come to regret for the next three decades.

While some sociopaths often struggle to form healthy relationships and otherwise function normally in daily life, others are successful in business and politics, climbing high on their respective professional ladders. The only difference between them is being more adept at disguising their disorder. When Harlan Parker got his law license it was a perfect career for his sociopathy. He was a natural at using charm to manipulate and deceive and knowing when to ignore the rules to gain an advantage.

There is a common joke among lawyers throughout the Summerville Bar that is revealing about Parker's reputation: Parker had died and was standing in a long line at the pearly gates when Saint Peter came up to confirm his identity.

Excuse me sir. Are you Harlan Parker?
That's correct.
Then you need to move to the line for spirits age 90-100 years old, sir.
But I'm only 50 years old.
Well, your billable hours indicate you're at least 98.

Most lawyers bend the rules from time to time: citing a case with a fact pattern that isn't remotely close to the one they're litigating, slightly altering a fact during closing argument that wasn't established during trial or using the opening statement to do an opening argument. When it works such is considered no more than gamesmanship or good lawyering. But Parker's tactics went far beyond crossing the line, oft times enough to result in suspension, disbarment, and even prison – if not for his uncanny sense of when to try it.

Parker always knew what channel to go through to bribe a juror or witness, when to alter the date of a document or fabricate it from whole cloth, or how to make a key piece of evidence disappear.

The more success Parker had through cheating, the greater it enhanced his bearing to get the close calls that can often make the difference between winning and losing, which only emboldened him to make arguments and pull stunts most lawyers would never even attempt. There were times in the middle of trial when Parker prevented damning evidence from being introduced against his client by approaching the bench and saying he'd never received it, even though he had, sometimes successfully keeping it from the jury.

He'd withhold evidence that was clearly discoverable seemingly without consequence. He'd convince the court to compel private information about his opponent's client which should not have been disclosed. He'd slip in unauthenticated documents at trial or was allowed to present expert testimony from witnesses not close to qualified to give them. He'd rarely Bate stamp documents he disclosed to his opponent, or he'd assign numbers with gaps and out of sequence to leave himself the option to claim he'd provided critical evidence when he'd never done so. On the rare instance such an issue got to an appeals court, most of the time they were considered harmless errors, though they were anything but.

As the years passed, Parker's underhanded ways made him a wealthy man. But for all the success, he made lots of enemies along the way. And for one, it would prove to be just too much to get over the antics of Harlan Parker.

3

THE ANGRY HUSBAND

M onday *8:30 am, October 9, 2017*
In the week following Harlan Parker's disappearance, events transpire fairly close to how the man at Quarry Lake had envisioned.

Judge Mac Renfro is presiding at Crawford Superior Court. Standing six-feet, six- inches tall, Mac Renfro would have been an imposing figure even if he'd never been a judge. But he had little choice. His father, grandfather and great grandfather had occupied the same seat he did and rattled the same gavel going back four of the last five generations. The name Renfro was engraved into the annals of legal legend and lore not only in Summerville but throughout Kentucky. Counted among Renfro's ancestry were members of the federal judiciary, the State Supreme court, U.S. Attorneys, a U.S. Senator and even a Governor.

However, Renfro had surpassed them all. He distinguished himself serving in the 23th Infantry Regiment in the Vietnam War and most notably during the battle of Canyon Vietnam. U.S. forces had engaged the enemy for weeks attempting to take and retake a plateau which could only be reached by climbing a 150-foot canyon wall. At the base of the canyon, Renfro threw himself on a live grenade to save the lives of a dozen soldiers. And he was far from finished. With shrapnel imbedded throughout his lower left leg, he threw a fellow officer over his shoulder and carried him over ten miles to get life-saving medical attention through a jungle crawling with Viet Cong guerrillas. But his valor came with a heavy cost: Renfro had to have his leg amputated just above the knee.

For bravery and courage far beyond the ordinary, Lyndon Johnson awarded Renfro the Medal of Honor, the highest award given to someone serving in the U.S. military. He returned to Summerville after the war, earned his law degree and practiced law in Crawford County.

After he won his first election by a three to one margin, few ever dared to run against him again. He's sat on the Crawford Superior bench for over twenty years and is known for his no-nonsense demeanor and keeping his court docket moving forward.

If you have a case in his court, you'd better be ready to have your arm twisted to settle it. Renfro has a reputation for completely ignoring rules which forbid judges from participating in settlement negotiations, keeping lawyers in his chambers late into the night to strike a deal. He never talks about the war, his many military honors or his lost leg, and he doesn't have to. His awkward gait lumbering up down the hallway and straddling up the steps to take his seat on the bench reminds every one of the sacrifices Judge Renfro made for his country.

Judge Renfro looks about the room for the parties and their lawyers to approach the bench as he calls the next case on his docket. "The next case on the docket is Braden vs. Braden, set for a hearing on an Emergency Protective Order issued last week, I believe."

Brock Braden and his lawyer, Dan Jack Gray, approach. Braden is a local contractor and the owner of Lonesome Pine, the finest golf course in the state. He also has the distinction of driving away more wives than anyone in town. Today he's in court to defend against accusations by his fourth and most recent wife, Christa, that he's physically and emotionally abusive. She's requesting that Renfro issue a restraining order to keep Braden out of the house and from having any direct contact with her.

Dan Jack Gray has been Braden's criminal lawyer for about ten years. Like his father before him, Gray has steered Braden through various scrapes with the law, mostly related to Braden's well-known drinking problem. Public intoxication, driving under the influence, and threats made against his former wives and girlfriends after having too much to drink are just a few of the offenses listed in Braden's rap sheet. And Renfro has just about reached his limit with him.

Christa Braden is the former lead meteorologist at Louisville's WLOV, affectionately dubbed as 'the sunshine girl' by her viewing audience. Channel 7 had ruled local ratings for years by dominating the 18 to 60 male demographic. Every testosterone-laden man in the region tuned in nightly to see Collinsworth stand in front of the national weather map in skin-tight dresses, turning and posturing at every opportunity as she went on and on about jet streams and high-pressure systems. To her audience, the temperature outside never really mattered because the forecast was always hot at WLOV. She was always very dramatic and entertaining during her nightly weather segment, and especially so when the station cut in on regular programing to report a tornado warning or heavy snow. She came by it all quite naturally. Her high school senior class voted her to be the person most likely to appear on a reality TV show.

Her 30-month marriage to Brock was longer than he'd lasted with any of his previous three wives.

Christa approaches the bench without her lawyer, Harlan Parker. Judge Renfro addresses her. "Good morning, Mrs. Braden. Have you spoken with Harlan this morning?"

"I've texted him a couple of times, your honor, but he hasn't gotten back to me just yet." Christa looks over at her husband, scowling. "Something isn't right. I've got a very bad feeling about this, your honor. My husband has threatened to kill Harlan more times than I can count. He's insanely jealous of him!"

"Right, Christa! It's far more likely that you sent him into cardiac arrest when you were repeatedly consulting with him in his condo. I'd go check there first. You'll probably find him there, clicked out in bed or on the floor!"

Dan Jack tries to calm the storm. "Brock! Can you please ratchet it back a few notches! My apologies, your honor. Things are very emotional for them right now."

Renfro has had enough of the dramatics. There are at least a hundred other people in the courtroom waiting for their cases to be called, and he needs to maintain control of his courtroom. "Now, I know these things are stressful, but you better calm down or you're both going to sit in jail a few hours until you do. I'm sure Harlan is on his way. He has three cases on the docket this morning. It's not like him to be late for an appearance without letting us know." He looks to his assistant. "Thelma, can you please call over to the Parker firm and get someone over here to cover the case? We don't have time for these antics."

Thelma goes back into chambers and calls Parker firm and is patched through to his paralegal, Tori Stevens. "Morning, Tori. It's Thelma, over at the courthouse. Harlan has three more cases on the docket this morning set for arraignment. Judge just called the Braden case. Can you please let him know?"

"Yes, ma'am. He usually goes straight from home to court on Monday morning. Haven't been able to reach him this morning myself. I'll send someone right over to cover for him."

"Thanks, Tori."

Tori calls Parker's condo with no answer and then calls his cell phone with no answer.

Ridley Barnes walks into the office returning from court in Cousin, Kentucky, the county seat the next county over, about 25 minutes from Summerville.

Tori seizes on his arrival. "Good morning, Ridley. Have you heard from Harlan today? The judge is looking for him."

"I'm looking for him myself. He texted me last night asking me to cover a court appearance in Cousin, but when I showed up for court, he didn't have a case on the docket there."

"That's odd. Harlan didn't have a case scheduled in Cousin today!" Tori walks into the lobby and meets Maggie West and her adult son, Riley. They're scheduled for 10:00 am meet with Parker to go over final draft of Mrs. West's revised will. The 73-year-old widow is wearing her best dress and even went to the trouble of putting her hair up in a beehive for the appointment with her lawyer. As with many locals of West's generation, a visit to the lawyer's office wasn't a casual affair, but an opportunity to present the best version of oneself. She's rarely been out of the house in recent months, still grieving the death of her husband. But her oldest child, Riley, was considerably better off financially than his siblings and he had insisted that they inherit his share of their mother's estate.

"Good morning, Mrs. West. Harlan is a little under the weather today. I'm afraid we'll have to move your appointment."

"I hope it's nothing serious?"

"That's very sweet of you, but nothing some fluids and a day's rest won't fix. He'll be fine. How does Friday work for you?"

Mrs. West pulls out her calendar.

WEDNESDAY *8:15 AM, October 11, 2017*

After two days pass without any sign of Parker, Ridley Barnes believes it's time to contact the Summerville Police Department. "Hello, Chief Justice. It's Ridley Barnes, from Parker, Barnes and Jeffries. I'm sure you've heard by now that Harlan's gone missing."

"Yes, we've heard the scuttlebutt down at the courthouse. Do you have any idea where he could be?"

"None. Harlan didn't divulge much about his personal life to his co-workers, I'm afraid. Kept it pretty much to himself."

"Well, you'd be one of the few!" The Chief laughs. "All kidding aside, I'll have a couple of guys on patrol go around to the parking lots of Harlan's favorite—motor lodges and talk to a couple of the dancers at Cork and Cleavage he's been known to be with." Cork and Cleavage is Summerville's strip club. Justice breaks into laughter again. "He drives that metallic blue Beamer sedan as I recall. If we come up with anything, I'll let you know."

Barnes isn't amused with Chief Justice's brand of levity, but he doesn't let on in his tone of voice. "Thanks, Chief. I only ask that your department use the utmost discretion at this point. Harlan has some very nervous clients right now asking a lot of questions, and I'm running out of answers. If word gets out that his disappearance is being investigated, they'll bolt to another firm and we'll soon be out of business."

"Understood, Mr. Barnes. You can count on us to handle this quietly with the highest degree of professionalism. I'll be in touch." The instant Chief Justice hangs up he starts laughing loudly. "Just got off the phone with Harlan Parker's law partner. Haven't seen him in five days. Looks like somebody finally gave Parker his comeuppance!" He yells across the squad room full of people. "Lisa, print out a public service award certificate and leave the recipient's name blank for the time being until we find out who did it!"

Laughter fills the room.

Chief Justice starts assigning duties to his patrolmen. "Ross, go check all the fleabag hotels west of Center Street. Hines, you check the parking lots of everything east. Look for a seven series Beamer, metallic blue. Jones! Find one of our confidential informants from the Cork and Cleavage to discretely ask around to see if anyone over there's spent time with Parker in the last week. And everybody here, keep things quiet, for now."

But a canvas of Parker's local haunts doesn't turn up anything. While most in local law enforcement believe Parker is just on another extended weekend of debauchery, one man believes Parker is dead, Detective Marshal P. Wilt.

After three years at Summerville High, the law enforcement door finally opened for Wilt. The Chief of Police was so impressed with Wilt's investigative acumen, he promoted him to Chief Homicide Detective within 18 months of graduating from the police academy. He's been on the force over thirty years and though he's less than two years from mandatory retirement you'd never know it by any letdown in his workload.

His marathon stints of undercover surveillance continue for days on end, outlasting the endurance of officers half his age. His relentless interrogation of murder suspects until they break is legendary. Wilt badgers, even manhandles suspects if necessary, and if they invoke their 5th amendment right requesting an attorney he'll ignore it or incredulously treat it as if it were a request for carry out from a five-star restaurant. He'll go for days living off nothing but vending machine snacks and Marlboros until the job is done. Nailing bad guys is Wilt's poetry and he has no time for crooked defense lawyers, sanctimonious judges or the blowhard half-wits that local politicians appointed over him to run his department.

Wilt could be included on the long list of persons in Summerville who loathe Harlan Parker. Parker had beaten him out of more convictions than all other criminal lawyers in town combined.

Whatever affection Wilt had for schoolboy Harlan as his teacher immediately evaporated the first time Parker cross examined him in a murder trial a few months after passing the Bar. It was a case where Parker convinced a jury to acquit his client, a cold-blooded killer, letting him walk out of the courtroom only to look back at Wilt with a big grin on his face. But it would only be the first in a long line of cases Wilt would build with painstaking effort only to be undone by the unscrupulous tactics of Harlan Parker. The student that Wilt had once taken under his wing to nurture and encourage to be an actor would return to Summerville with a law license and become Wilt's professional nightmare.

When Chief Justice announced the missing-persons case, Wilt laughed just as loudly as everyone else.

But for what he lacks in compassion for the would-be victim, he more than makes up for with the intrigue that came with the challenge of figuring out who was behind it. If someone had killed Parker it would certainly be the greatest challenge and achievement of Wilt's career to solve the case.

His initial dilemma is what to do if he did, because he could envision himself slamming the suspect into a wall as he cuffed and booked him for murder just as easily as shaking their hand to thank them.

But there is one thing Detective Marshal Wilt is sure about; There would be no lack of suspects with a motive to kill Harlan Parker.

4

THE LAW PARTNER

Wednesday 11:00 am, October 11

Wilt's first order of business is to interview Ridley Barnes, Parker's law partner and the person who filed the missing person's complaint.

Ridley Barnes isn't a trial lawyer, and he'd never been particularly good at legal research or writing, either. You'd much more likely find him at lunch networking over midday cocktail than see him in front of a judge.

Barnes isn't a legal beagle as much as a butterfly. He is the guy with a law license who doesn't really practice it and mostly makes his money from kickbacks he receives from lawyers he refers business to. And if someone referred something to him, he'd just get another lawyer in the firm to handle it and take his cut later. He spends his workdays on the phone nurturing professional connections with his peers with local gossip and his evenings at funeral homes, bars or Bar functions mining for cases only to dole them out to someone else.

He made a pretty good living for someone who never darkened the door of a courtroom, good enough that Harlan Parker put his name on the letterhead and gave him an office from which to project the image of a courtroom lawyer.

And he certainly looks the part. He is the best dressed attorney in town, seen frequently at the Preppy Peacock, the Summerville lawyer's downtown clothier, standing in the three-way mirror trying on the latest, greatest fashion trends. If you look across the square at some distance to see a man with a loud sport coat and pastel shirt with fancy bow tie, you'd immediately know it was Barnes. And although he didn't struggle with either short or long vision, he wore round framed glasses with fake glass lenses because it makes him look lawyerly.

But for Barnes, it isn't just about appearances. It's about feeling like a lawyer. Fashion is the means through which Barnes convinces himself he is a real lawyer, even though he rarely does lawyerly things.

When Parker disappeared, the job of giving the appearance of calm to anxious clients falls to Barnes, at least for the first couple of days.

Harlan is just taking a couple of days off.
Needed some rest. Nothing serious. No worries.

∽

Harlan had a sudden death in the family. An uncle
in California. Harlan often spoke of him fondly.
Was a significant influence I understand.
He'll be back in no time. I can assure you
that you'll be the first to know.

∽

We regret any misunderstanding or inconvenience
that Harlan's missed court appearance caused.
Unfortunately, it was simply mis-calendared by
one of our staff. I can assure you that PB&J has
your matter under complete control.

Barnes is Parker's law partner in name only, which means he owns no equity in the law firm. Parker was the sole owner of the firm and the rest make a living based on what they bring in for themselves and what Parker threw their way. While referral fees are considered a violation of ethics rules of any state Bar, it is a violation that's never enforced and widely ignored. Most lawyers would expect anywhere from 10 to 25 percent as "referral fee" while some lawyers would take nothing in return. Parker always required a kickback of fifty percent of the fee charged for any work he referred.

Wilt enters the front door of the Nahm building, where Parker's firm is located. Built ten years before the Civil War, the red brick, three-story structure styled in the Greek Revival tradition has been the crown jewel of Summerville Square for generations. And why wouldn't it be? It had been the 19th century residence of the Nahm family, one of the more prominent merchants in Summerville, who forged a commercial empire with a half dozen general stores throughout central Kentucky. People traveled in horse and buggy from miles around to buy all manner of produce, dry goods and merchandise: milk and bread, hardware, handmade toys and apparel, and even corn cob dolls. Like many other downtown architectural wonders that have faded into disrepair and obscurity over the decades, its fate was to be converted to a haven for predatory lawyers like Harlan Parker.

The elevator door opens to a lavish second floor lobby draped in cherry paneling and appointed with shining burgundy and light brown leather couches and chairs. An oak coffee table covered with vintage magazines from *Life, Time and The Saturday Evening Post* sits in front of a burning fireplace framed by a mahogany mantle.

Over it is an oil painting of a far younger, thinner and follically enhanced Harlan Parker holding an opened American Jurisprudence book in a law library. Although he'd lost all the hair on the top of his scalp by the age of 30, it didn't stop Parker from directing his portraitist to engage in some revisionist history by including copious amounts of mane where little existed. On the left side of the room is a seldom used spiral staircase leading up to the third floor where Parker's office is located.

At the opposite end of the lobby is a leggy, forty-something receptionist with a platinum blond pixie cut. She's wearing a navy, single button skirt suit so exquisite you'd just as likely envision her at a black-tie gala, that is, if she wasn't answering a phone at a law office. Her elegant appearance is only surpassed by a deep, alluring voice that reeks of sensuality and projects precisely the professional, high-end image Parker has created for his law firm.

Because of Parker's absence, she's on the phone trying to coax another potential new client into an office visit with another lawyer in the firm.

"I can assure you that the rumors of Mr. Parker's demise are just that, unfortunately spread by others trying to take unfair advantage. Mr. Parker's out of pocket for only a few days, but we have some of the most highly regarded legal minds in the region who will be more than happy to fill in until he returns."

But it's clear from resigned expression that comes across her face the prospective client isn't buying it and has no interest in seeing anyone but Parker.

"I understand completely sir; best of luck in your search for counsel." She hangs up the phone and exhales forcefully. Then she looks up and discovers Wilt. "May I assist you, sir?"

"Detective Wilt, ma'am. I'm here to meet Mr. Barnes."

She pages Barnes, who quickly emerges from the hallway to meet Wilt. As Wilt and Barnes shake hands, Barnes looks very lawyerly and concerned. "Good afternoon, Detective."

Wilt likes to start his interviews striking a thankful tone to encourage the witness to divulge as much information as possible.

"Good afternoon, Mr. Barnes. I appreciate you taking the time out of your schedule to speak with me. I know it must be a hectic week at your law firm."

"I should be thanking you, Detective. We appreciate any assistance you can provide. And yes, it is. We're very concerned about Harlan. It's not like him to just drop off the face of the earth like this."

Barnes ushers Wilt back to his office. Wilt notices that Ridley Barnes' office is a lot like Harlan Parker's, elegant, trendy and just shy of pretentious.

Barnes gestures to an oversized stuffed armchair upholstered in paisley. "Please, Detective, make yourself comfortable. I'm willing to set aside as much time as it takes to aid your investigation."

Wilt sits on the very edge of a chair that dwarfs him. "Can you recall where you were the last time you saw him?"

Barnes sits at his gleaming mahogany leather top partner's desk. "It was at the firm, last Friday morning. We exchanged a few words as we passed one another in the hallway. Just small talk about what he was doing for the weekend."

"And what did he say, Mr. Barnes?"

"He has a rather lengthy trial scheduled to start next week. He indicated he was going to be working at the office."

"What is this trial going to be about?"

Barnes smiles. "If we have our way, there won't be a trial, but I take your point, Detective. However, it's an open and shut case as far as I'm concerned. A doctor we've represented for years was sued for malpractice. Harlan was convinced he could get Dan Jack to settle before trial."

"Then the office of Blue and Gray is representing the Plaintiff?"

Barnes' expression grows just a touch condescending. "Sure. If Dan Jack knows anything, it's how to pick the wrong end of a lawsuit." Even though Barnes wouldn't know where to begin to evaluate a case, that doesn't stop him from tapping into Parker's success to project his own competence.

Wilt redirects the conversation. He's not here to listen to a lawyer talking smack about the competition. "What kind of a relationship do you have with Mr. Parker?"

"We're friendly enough, but we don't hang out outside the office or exchange Christmas cards, Detective. I would describe my connection with Harlan like I would describe it for the rest of the lawyers in this firm: Socially awkward and professionally convenient."

"Do you know of anyone who had a problem with Mr. Parker?"

"Problem could mean anything from a momentary irritation with Harlan to smoldering resentment to homicidal rage."

"Let's go with smoldering resentment, then."

"Again, you're going to have to be more specific, Detective. Are you talking about people who work in the office, outside the office or clients?"

"Let's start with people in the office then."

"Well, I can say with confidence that everyone here wanted to kill Harlan, that is, at one time or another. But you could only count on one hand the times that we had homicidal thoughts about him all at once." The corners of Barnes' eyes crinkle at his little joke.

Wilt flashes a wry smile, refusing to be drawn into Barnes' attempt at sarcasm. Instead he responds with some of his own. "It's certainly good to know that we probably won't be indicting twenty-five people in a murder conspiracy."

Wilt thinks Barnes is making things more difficult than necessary, and he muses why?

> Do you have something to hide or are you just a prick
> by nature?

Wilt changes the tone of the interview.

"Where were you last weekend, Mr. Barnes, starting with Friday evening?"

Clearly caught off-guard by the intimation, Barnes turns his head slightly and smiles in return. His back stiffens as he digs his fingers into the upholstery-padded arms of his chair.

"What exactly are you getting at Detective? You wouldn't be suggesting..."

"I'm not suggesting anything. I'm asking you a direct question you should have no trouble answering. It was less than a week ago. No need to take it to heart, Mr. Barnes. At this point in the investigation I have to see everyone with a more critical eye. Where were you and who can verify your location?"

Barnes sits back in his chair trying to appear nonchalant but failing at it badly.

"But of course. No offense taken, Detective. Friday evening, I was in Louisville at Jack Fry's, the restaurant, sharing a couple of drinks and pleasant conversation with no one in particular. She didn't provide me her name. It wasn't the kind of interaction that required a formal introduction. I paid my tab in cash, so I'm afraid you'll just have to take my word for it."

"What about the rest of the weekend, Mr. Barnes?"

"Kept to myself around my townhome, Mr. Wilt. I can provide you names a couple of neighbors I spoke with in passing, if you need them."

Barnes goes on to say that he had last heard from Parker was at 8:34 pm, Sunday, October 8th. Barnes received a text from Parker asking him to cover a court appearance at 8:00 am the following morning in Cousin, Kentucky, a town 25 minutes from Summerville. "But when I asked Tori about it, she knew nothing of it, and if she doesn't know, the case doesn't exist," Barnes says, frowning in a very lawyerly way so that his brows furrow over the top of his glasses. "For the life of us, we can't figure what Harlan was thinking."

"Tori? Tori Stevens?"

"Yes."

"May I have a copy of that text, please?"

Barnes prints out a copy of the text and gives it to Wilt in addition to Parker's cell number. He indicates that Parker used an android smartphone, which means that Wilt would be able to retrieve Parker's text conversations, even those he'd deleted.

As he's leaving PB&J, Wilt gets a call from dispatch that Parker's car has been found in the carport of Parker's condo.

Word of Parker's likely demise travels throughout the local Bar and beyond. For the competition, Parker's A-list clients are suddenly up for grabs. The kind with steady work that paid by the hour with the means to do so. Parker's rivals waste no time trying to take advantage.

~

CRANSTON AND CLARKE are a five-lawyer outfit just off the square with a focus on commercial litigation, and now that Parker is out of the picture, Tom Cranston decides to make some door calls on some of Parker's better clients. Riley Router Manufacturing is first on his list.

"It's very unfortunate to hear about Harlan. Like everyone else, we're praying and still holding out hope for a miracle. Just checking to see if you need anyone to step in, just for the time being of course, until Harlan returns, God willing. Just know that Cranston and Clarke are here if you need a contract, a non-compete or just sage advice from a firm that's been providing counsel to the business community here in Summerville for over three decades." He hands out his business card. "Just wanted you to know, Mr. Riley, that we're just a phone call away."

"I think we're fine for now, but thank you for your concern, Mr. Cranston."

"And I think you'd find our hourly rates very competitive with other firms in the area."

"Harlan is still our lawyer, Mr. Cranston. He's only been missing about six hours. We're still hoping for the best. But we'll certainly keep that in mind. Thank you."

"Well, of course. Not to jump the gun here. But technically no one's seen him for three days. Not sure if you were aware of that? Personally, I have serious doubts you'll ever see him again, alive that is. Truth is that half of Summerville wanted to kill him! You wouldn't want to give your rivals a competitive advantage when you have other legal talent readily available to you. That's all I'm saying. Just know we're also accessible on the weekends when most firms aren't so accommodating."

"Thank you, Mr. Cranston. Unfortunately, I have a meeting to catch, so if you'll please excuse me."

~

WEDNESDAY 12:34 PM, October 11

Wilt drives over to Parker's residence at Park West, a sprawling one-level condominium complex adjacent to Highland Acres, Summerville's largest public park. The high-end development wasn't designed for the resident who seeks social interaction but privacy, so there are no elevators or common walkways to cross paths or have chance encounters with its residents. Each unit can only be accessed through its own designated carport, which is secluded from view or access of any other condominium. Wilt knows it would be a waste of time to ask if anyone had seen Harlan Parker.

Wilt also knows Park West's manager, Bud Bowman, well enough to get into Parker's garage to see his BMW but there is no answer after knocking on the door to the condo. There's no sign of forced entry and the BMW looks spotless to the naked eye.

Wilt's first and most obvious conclusion is that Parker has died, clicked out of natural causes inside his condo. A heart attack, a stroke, an embolism are the likely culprits, not an angry husband or disgruntled client. Less likely but still possible is a drug overdose. Parker is known in the legal community and law enforcement circles to have snorted cocaine at social gatherings with businesspeople, lawyers and other companions. But Wilt hasn't heard about Parker being involved in anything of that sort for several years.

At this point, the facts as Wilt knows them are:

- Parker has been missing since Friday.
- Parker has missed seven court appearances without explanation or notifying the judge.
- The only vehicle in Parker's name is still at his residence.
- Parker isn't answering his phone or his front door.

Based on such information, Wilt all but eliminates foul play. And once Wilt comes to an opinion, he isn't in any mood to waste any more time on the matter.

Wilt wants in the unit ASAP to confirm his instincts and he isn't above painting a darker, more sinister picture to get there. He rejoins Bowman, who's been waiting outside the carport.

"He's obviously in there, Bud. And make no mistake about it, he's dead. Face down in a pool of blood, most likely."

Bowman, if not tall in stature, is a stout man wearing the same crew haircut he had in his senior yearbook picture in the 1970s. Always one to project matters in a positive light, Bowman's mother would gloss over her son's pumpkin-shaped frame by frequently boasting on his handsome looks: "You know, Buddy would have been a very successful big and tall clothier model but for his height."

The keys to Parker's condo dangle off a hook latch on Bowman's belt. But Bowman gives no sign that he's going to use them. He's clearly perplexed by Wilt's statement particularly considering the detective has been on the scene less than five minutes. "How can you be sure about that, Marshal?"

"Because of over thirty years investigating death scenes. If you had any idea how many doors that I've knocked on of someone reported missing with their car still in the driveway. His dead body has fully defecated and otherwise discharged the entirety of its bodily fluids, Bud. And it's been decomposing in there for several days, at a minimum."

Bowman continues playing devil's advocate. "But not answering the door doesn't necessarily mean he's been murdered. Maybe he's got a honey bear with him in there and just wants to be left alone for a few days."

Wilt has heard enough of the point, counterpoint. "If someone has in fact murdered Harlan Parker, critical evidence of that crime is evaporating with every moment that passes. As such, under the auspices of the Summerville Police and the citizens of Summerville proper, I order you to open this door and allow me to investigate this crime scene."

But Bowman is more concerned about what the ownership would do to him if he let a cop in Harlan Parker's residence and it turned out that he wasn't dead but on a trip. Then Highland Park West would send him on a one-way trip, home. "I don't think so, Marshal. If you're wrong and Harlan's on a little getaway somewhere for a few days he will sue my employer the day he returns, and they'll drop me the day after. You're going to need a court order if you want in this condo."

Wilt exhales in frustration and stares at Bowman for few seconds before pulling out his phone and calling Jim Lesousky, Crawford County's District Attorney. Lesousky is a career public servant. Wilt and Lesousky have been working together so long they instinctively know what the other's thinking, sometimes rendering the effort of words unnecessary.

"Jim. This is Marshal. I'm over at Park West at Harlan Parker's condo. His car is in the carport and I think he's in here. But Bowman says we're going to need a warrant to find out."

Lesousky promptly calls Judge Renfro. Within an hour, Wilt serves Bowman with a search warrant for Parker's residence and vehicle.

Wilt's new partner Wesley Andrews arrives on the scene. Andrews is a five-year veteran of the beat who, in the eyes of the police chief, shows enough promise to promote to the rank of associate detective. The baby-faced 28-year-old understudy is of average height, clean cut with wavy brown hair and blue eyes. His athletic build belies the fact that he never played or had interest in sports growing up. Wilt isn't so sure Andrews has got what it takes to be a detective, but he's the heir apparent so Wilt's going to take the kid under his wing and help him any way he can. Andrews usually keeps his opinions to himself, deferring to Wilt, for whom he has immense respect.

Bowman opens the door to let Wilt and Andrews in. "Can't be too discreet, you know. Have a heart. Management would have my head if word got out that police are rummaging through a unit and treating it as a death scene."

Wilt ignores Bowman, walking past him and into the condo. Out of the corner of his eye he notices Andrews on his heels pulling on latex evidence gloves. Wilt redirects his vision down the hallway in front of him. The last thing he wants to do is step on any evidence.

But he has nothing to worry about. Parker's condo appears clean and undisturbed. Harlan Parker isn't there. Nor is there anything to indicate a struggle. Wilt and Andrews proceed to Harlan Parker's bedroom. They find an unmade bed and a couple of shirts and socks in the bathroom and on the bedroom floor.

The only item of significance in the condo is Parker's cellphone which is still on his nightstand. Wilt walks over to the nightstand and puts on his evidence gloves as he turns to Andrews. "Okay, Andrews. There's no Parker. No forced entry or anything to suggest a struggle. What do you think?"

Andrews follows Wilt's line of reasoning easily. "But he left his phone here. You wouldn't think a guy with that many clients would go someplace without his phone?" Andrews is still green enough that he phrases his observation as a question rather than a statement.

Wilt drops the phone into an evidence bag. "Correct. He wouldn't have. That's because Parker didn't leave it here. His killer did, wanting us to find it. He wants to play a little game with us. Hide and seek. Catch me if you can. What we're clearly dealing with here is the twisted machinations of a sociopath. We'll have the phone checked for fingerprints and for its location settings."

"Oh, I see. Might give us an idea where Parker was murdered." Andrews had accepted Wilt's supposition as soon as Wilt had voiced it.

Wilt sealed the evidence bag. "Or where his killer wants us to think he was murdered. This is officially a homicide investigation."

5

THE LONESOME PINE

ednesday 2:05 pm, October 11

Wilt and Andrews leave the forensics team to scan Parker's condo for prints, DNA and other evidence that might indicate who else was at the residence. When they return to the police station, Christa Braden is waiting for them, clutching soiled tissues now black with the mascara she's wiped off her face. She demands to speak with them immediately. "He's lost it! He's crazy. I'm telling you he murdered Harlan!"

Wilt and Andrews soon situate her in an interview room with a cup of coffee, a bottle of water, and another box of tissues. "Your chief of police thinks I'm hysterical. Wouldn't you be hysterical if you were about to be murdered by your estranged husband, just after he murdered your lawyer? You don't get it! Brock's not the kind of man who's going to be told where to live or who he can and can't talk too. And he's not going to stop with Harlan. You've got to do something."

In a twenty-year span, Braden Excavation & Paving went from a one-man operation with a compact utility vehicle digging out goldfish ponds and swimming pools to the largest road contractor in the state of Kentucky. They employ over 300 people and earn annual revenues exceeding $50 million.

But several years ago, Brock Braden had stepped back from road contracting and passed the business to his son, Braxton. This allowed Brock to pursue his ultimate dream: building a PGA grade golf course with a residential real estate development at the southeastern corner of Crawford County.

He hired the foremost golf course architect in the country for the project and spent over 120 million to sculpt the Crawford's pristine countryside into Lonesome Pine. The original name was intended to be Pine Valley, but a dyslexic heavy equipment operator mistakenly bulldozed the property's only swath of pine trees. Only a single tree was spared.

But it was magnificent, a 240-foot white conifer which lorded over Braden's golf masterpiece at the bend of the course's final hole, a par five, 580-yard dogwood. The tree was so large and picturesque, the course designer had contoured Lonesome Pine's last and signature hole around it. It was not only the course's namesake, it was its most distinctive feature as seen from the clubhouse and the trademark displayed on its golf balls, clothing line and club letterhead.

It was Lonesome Pine's version of Augusta's Eisenhower tree. To make sure Lonesome wouldn't meet the same fate, Braden installed a $50,000 electric heating system throughout the tree to defend it against ice storms. During special events and the holiday season, it was decorated with lights of all patterns and colors. The grand conifer was emblematic of everything that was Lonesome Pine. From the day it opened, it was hands down the best golf course in the state and in play as an attractive venue to host the U.S. Amateur and major golf championships.

Braden earned his fortune the old-fashioned way, giving kick-backs to state transportation officials to win road contracts worth tens of millions of dollars. And if anybody got in his way, word was that Braden wasn't above putting a contract out on them. One of Braden's upstate rivals, Abner Fields, went missing a few years back just as Braden was moving massive patches of earth around to build his golf course.

Rumor among well-heeled Pine membership was that Abner was

buried just off the 18th fairway under the thick bluegrass. Local duffers even dubbed the hole Abner's Revenge for its treacherous knee-high rough that spelled certain doom for any golf ball that found it. Even if the legend were true, Braden didn't have to worry about anyone going out there to dig around. The local and state police had been in his hip pocket for years, including the county sheriff and chief of police, both avid golfers and honorary members of Lonesome Pine.

But for all his millions, life was far from perfect for Braden. As brilliant as he was at business, his personal life was a biohazard, most of all, his failed marriages. Each one had started out like a fairytale, only to deteriorate into a sea of acrimonious brutality. Braden's downfall was he only courted women who possessed the kind of dangerous beauty that turned heads and stopped conversations when she walked by. And she was always someone who desired expensive things without the means to acquire them on her own, typically a woman in the mid to late twenties, ten or even twenty years younger than him.

Braden flashed his wealth like a peacock fans its feathers and sure enough, the next time you turned to watch her walk down the street she was on Braden's arm. At first, every one of Braden's wives had been wonderstruck enough by his money and success and look past his narcissistic and paranoid ways. What woman looking to significantly improve her prospects wouldn't be drawn by the trappings of money of a hugely successful bachelor like Brock Braden?

But the initial allure always faded and the advantages that came with wealth were always overshadowed by his dysfunctional personality. And though most men would fall for the kind of beauty each of Braden's wives possessed, it attracted male attention so frequently it became a narcotic their vanity couldn't get enough of. So sooner or later, each of them would look elsewhere to find it. And there was always another guy that had more to offer, if not financially, then emotionally, and most the time, physically. For Brock Braden, the other guy always seemed to be Harlan Parker.

Christa was the type of woman who still wore intentionally

distressed blue jeans into her mid-thirties. For certain women, life ends, at least socially, by age 40 so they simply refuse to acknowledge aging beyond that point. But it's a mindset that works for some better than others. For a while longer, it was working for Collinsworth. Now fearing that time was running out to cash in on her looks, Collinsworth eagerly accepted Braden's invitation to take her on a private tour of the club. Three months later they were in Belize tying the knot. And just like that, her weather girl days at WLOV were over.

When Christa and Brock moved into their new 8000 square foot home at Lonesome Pine, it was the perfect opportunity for Christa to fall in love with the sport of golf again. Christa had also been an avid golfer in college, but she hadn't done much since. So, she was a frequent visitor to the driving range and of course very popular with club staff.

At 30 months, Brock and Christa's marriage lasted 29 months longer than anyone had predicted, but only because Christa had figured out how to be there for Brock without being with him. She texted him throughout the day, every day, telling him anything necessary to keep a smile on his face from afar.

"Brock, that haircut makes you look twenty pounds thinner!"

"It's uncanny how the new Jag takes ten years off of you, dear!"

To compensate for her not being around, she sent him selfies to him several times a day. Face selfies, butt selfies, side-boob selfies, photos of her on the golf course or shopping or at the day spa. In time, her virtual presence came to replace the physical one. A lot of effort went into it, so much you could argue that Christa more than earned the extravagant lifestyle that came with being married to Brock Braden.

It was designed to give Brock the impression she was doing anything but sleeping with other men. Her strategy worked beautifully mainly because Brock was a workaholic and spent 12 to 14 hours a day at the golf course. By the time he got home, Christa was usually just returning from a round of golf, or a grocery run or dinner date with friends. Their shared time at home was rarely longer than an hour or two, which for Christa, could easily be taken by a bubble bath or her meditation time that was critical for her life balance and overall well-being.

Then it was lights out. After just three months of marriage, Brock relented to Christa's request to sleep in a different room because his snoring kept her awake all night. Of course, Brock never realized he had a snoring problem, that is, until Christa brought it to his attention.

"As heartbreaking as it is to not sleep by your side, my first priority is your health, Brock!"

She insisted that he get it checked out by her ear, nose and throat specialist who Christa was also sleeping with. Even though Brock exhibited no signs of sleep apnea, Christa's doc had Brock take a sleep test which confirmed he indeed had moderate sleep apnea. The results were predictable.

"Mr. Braden, if not treated, sleep apnea could result in a stroke, heart attack or even death. But fortunately, we can set you up with one of our CPAP devices."

"CPAP?"

"Continuous Positive Airway Pressure."

That sounded impressive. Brock walked out with the most expensive CPAP machine on the market.

Initially Brock was grateful, even touched that his wife cared so much for him to insist he seek medical treatment.

"Thank God for Christa," he told his friends at the time. "Her insistence that I see a doctor probably saved my life." Unfortunately, it also meant he had to sleep with an oxygen mask, rendering late night romantic rendezvous in the middle of the night with Christa awkward to eventually nonexistent.

By the beginning of year three, unable to find love at home, Brock returned to Cork and Cleavage. At first, he returned home a quiet drunk and went straight to bed. But then he reverted to his old falling down drunk and belligerent ways, referring to his wife as a whore in every synonym in the English language and many others in foreign tongues.

Initially, Christa consulted with an attorney but continued ride the gravy train and put up with Brock's verbally abusive ways, that is, until the last week of September 2017, when she'd had enough. She had no trouble finding a divorce attorney. She had hired Harlan Parker a month before. Brock was served with a divorce petition and emergency protective order (EPO) on Monday morning, October 2, the latter which directed him to vacate the residence. Though the EPO alleged that Brock put his hands on Christa, she made it up to get him out of the house. Braden's reputation for being a hot head and getting physical with his previous wives was well known, so Judge Renfro didn't doubt the accusation for a second.

At the police station, Christa continues to plead with Wilt and Andrews to protect her. "You've got to move me someplace he can't find me, at least until next week." Andrews is curious.

"What happens next week, Mrs. Braden?"

"I'm leaving Summerville, Detective. For good! Can't get out of here soon enough!"

Andrews and Wilt look at each other. Wilt turns to address Christa.

"Why are you in such a hurry to leave Summerville, Mrs. Braden?"

"Let's just say for now that I have a new life plan, Detective. For me, there's no more summer in Summerville!"

"Well, wherever your life plan takes you, we'll need to get in touch with you, Mrs. Braden." As for the witness protection program, we won't be able to do that. It's a federal program and your family court matter wouldn't qualify."

"Then perhaps you can place a couple of big, husky officers to keep watch over me at the house," Christa suggests quickly. She looks up and down at Andrews and flashes a big smile.

"Your partner here looks like he has what it takes to take care of a woman in distress." Andrews smiles back and nods enthusiastically as Christa continues, "And if you want to know where to start looking for Harlan, you'd be wise to start with Lonesome Pine! Remember my words. Harlan's buried somewhere on that golf course."

Andrews blushes, then looks at Wilt nodding his head imploring him to grant Christa's request, but there was no chance.

"I'm afraid Mr. Andrews doesn't do protective duty at this point, Mrs. Braden, but we'll see if the Chief is willing to free someone up for a few days."

Christa suddenly leaving Summerville, after she's just filed for a divorce raises more questions for Wilt and Andrews, but they'll have to wait for now. Wilt gets Christa's contact information and assures her that he'll find someone to watch over her for a few days.

6

THE LAW OFFICE OF BLUE AND GRAY

W hile most people in town could have cared less that Harlan Parker was missing, Granville Pearl isn't one of them.

Granville Pearl is the Imperial Wizard of the Klan's local chapter and owner of Granville Junction, Roller Coaster Paradise, Crawford County's amusement park. Its slogan is prominently displayed on billboards throughout the region: *The roller coaster paradise where every child's dreams come true.* Although he is widely known to be a lily-white bigot who openly discriminates against blacks, rarely hiring them at his amusement park, the only color that matters to the entrepreneur is green. So, of course kids of every race and ethnicity are more than welcome to spend their parents' money at his amusement park.

Parker has been Pearl's lawyer for years and the Imperial Wizard had sought Parker's advice almost daily. It isn't like Harlan not to return his phone calls for several days, so Pearl knows something isn't right before most anyone else in town. If someone's in fact taken out his attorney, Pearl's none too pleased about losing the guy who had saved his bacon more times than he could count. While rumors are spreading all over town about who did Parker in, Pearl doesn't participate in any of it. But he has his ideas. And Brock Braden is at the top of his list of suspects.

Pearl has more than a few reasons not to like him. When Braden was 12 years old, Pearl kicked him out of his amusement park for trying to steal nudes by unscrewing the back panel of a naked lady slot machine. Things only got worse when Braden married his only daughter, Melia, named after his dear Aunt Peromelia. The marriage lasted less than a year, thanks to Braden coming home drunk one evening from Cork and Cleavage and putting his hands on her. Pearl considered getting one of his flunkies to rub him out until Harlan Parker talked him out of it. He opted to pay for his daughter's divorce instead.

Summerville is small enough that word and rumor travels around town quickly. One of Pearl's employees had overheard a loud and obnoxious drunk talking at Deadwood Rose, a local steakhouse, about putting a contract out on Harlan Parker and Pearl feels sure it had been Brock Braden.

But Pearl needs more than that to stick a fork in Braden. And he isn't about to go to the police with any information until it is airtight. He's had his own issues with the cops.

TWO YEARS EARLIER. *Tuesday 8:30 am, November 10, 2015*

It was the first day of trial in the case *Commonwealth vs. Rowdy Johnson*, being held in the Crawford County Justice Center. Daniel Jackson Gray sat at the counsel table going over final details with Johnson before opening statements.

In Crawford County and beyond, Daniel Jackson Gray is just as well regarded in the courtroom as Harlan Parker, only cast from a different mold. He graduated from University of Louisville School of Law and was hired at the nearby U.S. Attorney's Office within a couple of years after passing the Bar. It was as a prosecutor that Gray learned to be a trial lawyer, and a very good one at that.

If the courtroom were a baseball diamond, then Gray would be described as a five-tool player. He is quick and nimble on the base paths, with the ability to suddenly change directions during argument or questioning a witness. And he has a gun for an arm, bringing the heat during cross examination with pinpoint accuracy. He plays defense at a Gold Glove level, known for preparing witnesses with baggage vulnerable to cross-examination and making them virtually untouchable. He could hit for power, going yard by giving a riveting closing argument that spellbound the jury or ask that one question that could win the case. And finally, Gray could hit for average. He is reliable and consistent. You could always count on him to be prepared.

Gray left the U.S. Attorney's Office in his late thirties and returned to Summerville to start his own law practice. From the other side of the courtroom, the notoriety of his trial exploits only grew. Gray is the lawyer who finds light where there is no light. He routinely shreds indictments brought by the government previously believed to be unassailable. The former prosecutor has become the prosecutor's worst nightmare. No witness, piece of evidence or legal argument is safe within the crosshairs of Dan Jack Gray.

Outside of work, he is as affable and gracious as they come. But as he approaches the courthouse, the switch flips. The switch that everyone has; the one that toggles between self-doubt and quiet confidence, or in Gray's case, total invincibility. When he enters the courtroom, he carries himself as if he owns it. And if you happen to be the lawyer on the other side, he owns you, your girlfriend, your future girlfriend, every unspoken fear you ever harbored and every dream you ever had. As the legend tells it, Dan Jack Gray is a lawyer so dangerous that courthouse security has standing orders to keep watch for whenever he enters the building and immediately scan his briefcase, for his questions.

But for all his prodigious achievements in the courtroom, the overall success of his law practice is pedestrian, at best. He simply refuses to do the things other lawyers do to prosper. When it comes to promoting the law practice, he is old school. He disapproves of television and billboard advertising, that is, unless you're attractive, in which case he strongly encourages it.

While other lawyers use spirit animals like tigers or bulldogs to market themselves as fearless and ferocious advocates, Gray frowns on such gimmicks. He believes the best advertisement is a job well done that produces a referral from a satisfied client or an attorney who knows of your work and has high regard for it.

But few lawyers refer cases to Gray. He refuses to split retainers or settlement proceeds, a kickback for referring the case, unless the referring attorney does some work on the case, and he is against networking with peers for referrals. It might compromise his loyalty to a client down the road if he has a case against a lawyer from whom he regularly receives business. Gray does well enough to provide for his family, but he never went to law school to get rich. And no one would ever have mistaken him for someone who did.

Jennifer and Dan Jack Gray had been married 15 years when she passed away of leukemia at the age of 37. Dan Jack never remarried, remaining a single parent to their only child, Savannah.

Savannah was never far away from her father. In grade school, she rode shotgun to the courthouse with him on summer break. As she grew into a teenager, her father demanded much of her, sometimes too much, trying to prepare her to take advantage of life's opportunities. Even though most youth sports were banned by Crawford County schools, Dan Jack introduced his daughter to soccer, fast pitch softball and cross-country believing sports were just as important for girls as boys, if not more so. Dad was at every event, and he took a not so low profile if an umpire or referee blew a call.

But instead of shrinking from lofty expectations or rebelling like many teenagers, Savannah used the humor and wit she inherited from her father to put him in his place. "That was just great, Dad! Thanks for the spotlight! Can you please calm down at the games?"

"That sweeper tripped you, Savannah. It was clearly a yellow flag. You were about to score."

"It's just a soccer game, Dad. You're taking things way too seriously, again."

"Now you're the one who's overreacting. How am I different than any other parent?"

"Dad, If I came home and told you my blood type was B positive, you'd grimace and tell me that you expected an A next time."

As a middle schooler, Savannah spent much of her summer break at the courthouse sitting in the back row of the courtroom drinking a soda pop, watching her father and learning how to be a trial lawyer. And like her father, 15-year-old Savannah was just as forthcoming providing advice, like when they rode home after one of Dan Jack's clients was convicted by the jury.

"You know, Dad. The closing was really good, on balance. I just thought you lost a little bit of your edge about halfway through. Closing is all about taking momentum away from your adversary or keeping it and creating separation. You were really kicking it, but then you kind of stalled a little bit in the middle there. But don't get me wrong. It's not the reason your client was convicted or anything."

Dan Jack just nodded his head, agreeing in jest. "Well, that's a relief! At least I'll always have that! Now I can sleep at night knowing my closing statement isn't the reason Billie Joe is sitting in jail right now."

"Not at all, Dad. That was a done deal the moment you put him on the witness stand."

Despite the occasional excessive enthusiasm from her father, Savannah followed his footsteps into the practice of law.

By her mid-twenties, she had grown into the spitting image of her mother and graduated near the top of her class at the Brandeis School of Law. Soon thereafter, she married her college sweetheart, David Blue, and returned to join her father's law practice despite Dan Jack trying mightily to talk her out of it. She had offers from three of Louisville's top five law firms with a starting salary twice what Dan Jack was able to pay her, but she never considered anything else.

Ordinarily, the first name in a law firm is chosen from the best-known or senior lawyer, but Dan Jack wanted to promote his daughter's profile any way he could. He felt putting her name first would give her a sort of a jump start which could eventually benefit her after he wasn't practicing anymore. Savannah was reluctant to agree to the idea, not having yet earned such an honor, but eventually relented to her father's wishes with the joke that the name of their new law firm would work as long as her marriage did.

But the unexpected benefit from changing its name to The Blue and Gray Law Office was its marketing appeal. The firm began to attract business from a major target market in central Kentucky: the dysfunctional, white, working class male. This is a demographic which is a frequent visitor to the county courthouse. They are charged with assault, illegal firearm possession, driving under the influence, pot possession, violating domestic violence orders and endless other crimes. And it is also a group that overwhelmingly identifies with the South and the Confederacy.

So, in hindsight, the name change turned out being a brilliant move. Blue and Gray became the law firm associated fighting for the rights of the good ole country boy gone bad, the rebel rousing redneck who was unfairly maligned and frequently misunderstood. At Savannah's urging, Dan Jack finally relented, agreeing to a minimal amount of advertising to promote the firm, running a radio spot which proved to be very popular.

Got Court?
Charged with a criminal offense?
Wrongly accused?
The law firm of Blue and Gray will stand and fight for you.
Blue and Gray will help you rise again.

The ad appealed to the like of Rowdy Johnson, so when he was indicted by the Crawford County Grand Jury, Blue and Gray was the obvious choice. Rowdy was charged with grand theft and arson. Specifically, he was accused of stealing a car off the lot of Mod City Motors, driving it to the Beaver Creek Baptist Church, and setting it on fire so that he could be accepted into the White Knights of the Ku Klux Klan. Beaver Creek was a parish with a predominantly African American congregation. The Commonwealth claimed that Johnson was the one who poured the kerosene throughout the sanctuary and lit the match. The government had flipped the alleged getaway driver. He had turned state's evidence against Johnson and was testifying against him.

Though Johnson admitted to going to a couple of meetings, he insisted that it was only for the free beer and burgers at the home of Granville Pearl.

But Pearl had yet to be charged in the Beaver Creek arson. The Commonwealth needed a conviction in the Rowdy Johnson trial, so they had the leverage to force him to help them build a case against higher ups in the Klan, including Pearl. Despite not having been charged, Pearl was watching the case. He had a financial and potentially personal stake in the outcome. News coverage on the Johnson case was very bad for Pearl's business. Park attendance had dropped over twenty percent since the Johnson indictment had been returned.

Pearl's longtime lawyer was Harlan Parker. Parker had deflected criminal charges and lawsuits against him for years for all manner of malfeasance, negligence and perversion. But Parker couldn't represent Rowdy Johnson because he would later be conflicted out of representing Pearl if Johnson were to eventually testify against him. So, when Johnson said he wanted to hire Gray, Pearl was more than eager to pony up. For him, $10,000 wasn't a problem. He made more than that from a couple of days gate at his park. When Johnson put cash money on Dan Jack Gray's desk, Gray didn't ask or care where it came from. But he didn't doubt it that it came from Pearl.

The Honorable Mackenzie Beauregard Renfro presided over the case.

Although Savannah was sitting second chair in the Rowdy Johnson trial, she wasn't going to simply be a potted plant watching her father try the case. She had done that many times before, and it had planted a seed. Fifteen years later that seed had now grown into a lawyer that was about to be tested for the first time.

And Dan Jack believed the only way to learn how to be a trial lawyer was to do it and fail at it and fail at it again and again until you found your way. Gray had tried over 100 trials to a jury in his 20 plus-year legal career and understood that great trial lawyers weren't born but formed: by the many mistakes they made and learned from. But he wasn't going to just throw Savannah into the water without a life preserver. He was going to be right there by her side, watching her closely, gradually giving her increasing responsibilities with each succeeding case until she mastered every phase of being a trial lawyer.

Savannah stood up and turned to the 120-person jury panel.

Judge Mac Renfro asked Dan Jack to introduce her and his client only to go on and do it himself. "Now turning to the Defense. Mr. Gray, could you please introduce Ms. Savannah and the rest of your trial team and of course, your client? Hello, Savannah. So nice to see you in my courtroom."

Savannah just nodded to the judge and smiled, touched and only slightly embarrassed.

Renfro then turned his attention again to the jury panel while smiling back at Savannah. "Savannah is Mr. Gray's daughter and she's been coming to my courtroom to watch her dad since she was in grade school. During trial breaks we'd sneak down to the snack machine on the first floor and I'd get her a candy bar behind her father's back."

Many in the jury panel chuckled and smiled as they glanced over to Savannah while listening to Renfro's every word.

He continued. "This year she graduated from law school and passed the Bar exam. She's come back to Summerville to work alongside her father in his law office. I'm quite sure you'll be very impressed if you're lucky enough to be selected to serve on this jury. You may continue, Mr. Gray."

District Attorney Jim Lesousky turned three shades of red as Renfro fawned over Savannah, but what could he do about it? The moment he tried to go to the bench and object, Renfro would turn into Mount Vesuvius and Lesousky would be made to look like a petty old man in front of the jury panel – and the entire courtroom for that matter.

After the jury was selected and an hour break for lunch, it was time for opening statements. The government went first.

Lesousky has been at this for over three decades and could do it in his sleep. He walks to the podium which is now turned to face the jury. "Ladies and gentlemen, first I'd like to take this opportunity to thank you for your service as you sit on this case. Our justice system is the envy of the free world and it's only because of people like you, ordinary citizens making extraordinary sacrifices through your service here today. The opening statement is not evidence but just a preview of what the lawyers anticipate the evidence will be."

Lesousky always starts his openings by thanking the jury. While many lawyers do it, Dan Jack never does. It isn't that he doesn't appreciate their service or sacrifice. It is that jury service isn't voluntary, so everyone who is here must be, out of a sense of duty or obligation. Though it was gratitude that Lesousky always expressed genuinely, if not handled carefully, could come off as contrived.

"The evidence will come from this witness stand," Lesousky continued, pointing to the stand in question, "through the testimony of six witnesses, who will show that Rowdy Johnson was a recent recruit in the Summerville chapter of the Ku Klux Klan. Witnesses will place him among the brotherhood on Wednesday meetings cloaked in secrecy, where Johnson was indoctrinated in the Klan's gospel of white supremacy and racial hatred. Their agenda? To strike fear in the hearts of African Americans in Crawford County, to terrorize God-fearing, law-abiding citizens who have contributed to the betterment of this community for generations."

Lesousky is known to be a straight shooter in the courtroom, methodical and to the point, but spinning Wednesday night barbeques, drinking cheap beer and drunken brawls as some sort of ritualized agenda of hate was stretching it.

Truth is, the KKK in Crawford County is mostly comprised of a bunch of angry, degenerate Jimmy Bobs and Bobby Jims strung out on meth. Most are either unemployed or on social security disability for some feigned ailment and if anyone had managed to advance beyond junior high school, they are vastly more educated than most.

Although the picture the prosecutor tried to portray sounded impressive, Gray knows that ultimately it is going to be difficult to back up.

Lesousky continued. "So, in order to be accepted as a full member
of the Klan, Johnson had to prove he was worthy. And the evidence
will show he did so by burning down the Beaver Creek Baptist
Church. You will hear from Rufus Baker, who will tell you that on the
afternoon of June 3, 2009 he drove with the defendant to Coleridge
Hardware and bought three canisters of kerosene."

Everyone was silent as they listened, though the silence was for
different reasons: Judge Renfro out of propriety, the jury out of fascination, and Dan Jack and Savannah so that they knew what version
of events they were up against.

"The two would ultimately use a stolen Mustang to travel to
Beaver Creek, where Johnson entered the sanctuary, poured kerosene
throughout, then struck the match to set fire to God's house and
burned Beaver Creek Baptist Church to the ground." Lesousky walks
from behind the podium to directly in front of the jury. "And at the
end of this trial I will come back and ask you to return a verdict of
guilty to both counts in this case. Thank you."

Lesousky nods his head to the jury and turns to walk to sit next to
Detective Wilt and his paralegal at counsel table for the prosecution.

Judge Renfro dips his head down slightly, lowering the lenses of
his reading glasses below his eyeline, and turns his head to the
defense table. "You will now hear the opening statement from the
defense. Mrs. Blue, it's your courtroom."

Savannah had excelled in public speaking and drama classes and,
like her father, is quick on her feet, mandatory traits for anyone who
aspired to be a great trial lawyer. From the outset it is obvious she had
paid close attention to her father. She took to the courtroom immediately as she rose and returned the nod to Judge Renfro.

As she walked out into the middle of the courtroom in front of the
jury box, she looked directly at them without making eye contact, a
trick she had figured out that helped her not to lose track of her
thoughts. While even highly experienced lawyers might use notes or
talking points they glance at from behind a lectern, Savannah would

have none of it. She does her opening free style, without a safety net, notes or a podium. Standing directly in front of the jury without physical barriers could give her a subtle but important advantage making it easier for her to connect with the jury. Watching her father in trials over the years taught her about maximizing the advantages of room and body dynamics.

Some judges don't allow such freedom to move around and instead require lawyers to address the jury from behind a podium. But Renfro doesn't need such rules to maintain order in his courtroom. He does so by the force of his personality, a deep baritone voice and his larger than life stature. He gives lawyers the freedom to move about, understanding that some are more comfortable and thereby more effective for their clients. He also believes that it could add a certain drama and excitement to proceedings which could create more interest for the jury.

Savannah began. "May it please the court, Mr. Lesousky, ladies and gentlemen of the jury. The Commonwealth has told you what they expect the evidence to be. But at this point I want you to try to think of this trial as a picture that has yet to be painted, a blank canvas which will only be filled in by the witnesses and other evidence in this case. Then we will come back at the end of the proof and argue what that picture shows, what the evidence has or has not shown. You will then go back and deliberate, and it is then and only then that you should form a judgment and render a verdict."

Dan Jack had taught Savannah that opening statement rule one was to take away any of the momentum of the prosecution. Comparing a trial to a picture yet to be painted is a creative way to do it, and he thought that Savannah had explained it perfectly.

Lesousky looked across at Dan Jack and smiled, shaking his head back and forth. It is important for each side to try and put the other on the defensive from the outset, and even Lesousky couldn't help but be impressed.

Savannah saw this small exchange but didn't let it distract her. "The one thing that there will be no dispute about is that Rufus Baker was the only person who can be conclusively identified on video surveillance committing crimes here, and that he stands to get a significant sentence reduction in return for his testimony against Rowdy Johnson in this case. On the night of the fire, Rowdy Johnson was watching a movie with his girlfriend at the Compton Movie House."

Now, like her father, Savannah finished her opening with a fast ball of her own. "The government's case can be summed up in three categories. Facts that are not true. Facts that cannot be proven. And the third and most frequent you will hear, facts that are true that don't prove anything."

Just as Savannah had predicted, the Commonwealth's proof didn't hold up and Rowdy Johnson was found not guilty on both counts.

Granville Pearl exhaled a huge sigh of relief.

During the Beaver Creek case, Johnson had lost his job because he was spending six months in jail until he was found not guilty. When the trial was over, Pearl showed his appreciation to Rowdy for not ratting him out and hired him to do maintenance on his roller coasters.

But in Pearl's mind, Johnson still owes him one after he'd paid his legal fees. Now he is ready to cash in his chips to find out what happened to his lawyer.

Tuesday, 9:25 am, October 10, 2017

Pearl calls Rowdy Johnson into his office located at the park entrance on the second floor of a white, two-story cinderblock building. Patrons are checked into the park as they pay admission to an attendant stationed at a drive-through window on the first floor. It's fall break for Crawford County schools and the final month of the park season at the Junction. The punishing heat of Indian summer has given way to cooler temperatures of autumn in recent days, so Pearl has opened the window in his office is sitting with his feet resting up on his desk. Screams of kids riding rollercoasters rambling over wooden track echo in the distance.

Rowdy walks up to the door of Pearl's office and sticks his head in. "What's up, Mr. Pearl? Heard you needed to speak with me."

"Yeah. Come right on in, Rowdy. Have a seat. I need you to do a little undercover work for me. A little recon ranger."

The word "undercover" makes Rowdy uneasy. He's had his fill with law enforcement and isn't in any hurry to be involved with anything associated with it. "What you are talking about, Mr. Pearl? I can't be involved in nothing illegal. The police are stilled pissed that I walked on Beaver Creek."

"It's nothing like that, Rowdy. I just need you to go over and get a job working at Lonesome Pine, doing something where you can overhear the buzz going on out there. And not tell anyone that I put you up to it. I'm certain that Brock Braden had something to do with Harlan's disappearance. Probably used Kenny Martin to do it. You know, that no good, bill collector of Braden's. And I'm sure that somebody's talking about it over there or at least knows something."

Pearl knows Kenny Martin is a thug. He'd roughed up one of Pearl's employees who had gotten behind on payments with Braden for some contracting work. What Pearl doesn't know was that Rowdy and Martin used to run together in their wild and wooly days, and Rowdy decides it's probably best not to mention it.

"I need someone over there with an ear close to the ground to get some intel on that thug. All you have to do is do your job and listen. Nothing illegal, at all. I'll even pay you as if you worked here in addition to what they're paying you over there. And if you find out something good there might even be a bonus in it for you."

"Sounds like a plan, Mr. Pearl. Count me in."

Pearl is long past the point of being big-headed from all his money. He is now referring to himself in third person. "Good man! Now get on over there and find out some scoop! Nobody going to whack Granville Pearl's lawyer and just skate away like nothing."

7

THE MARTIN BROTHERS

W*ednesday 3:32 pm, October 11, 2017*
Harlan Parker's phone is processed for fingerprints. No complete prints are found, but there are several smudged prints lifted that are unidentifiable. They're sent off to the FBI crime lab in Quantico, Virginia to compare with 50 million sets in their database. It will take months before Wilt will know if there are any hits.

Patrol officers have gathered information that Parker keeps his BMW in a lot behind Compton Movie Theatre. Wilt and Andrews want to know if he retrieved it from there the evening of October 6th, the last day he was seen in Summerville, and if anyone else was with him.

They go over to the movie theatre and manage to get the security camera footage without a warrant. The employees are used to vandalism cases and think nothing of turning the footage over to the police. Wilt and Andrews return to the station and review the footage from the video surveillance camera mounted at the top of the Compton Movie House. The camera records activity in the parking lot.

There's very little activity at the lot for most of the evening of

October 6th except for two men wearing sunglasses near dusk while sitting in a red pickup about twenty feet from Parker's car.

When Andrews observes footage of a man getting out of the truck in a Bill Clinton mask and crouch behind a dumpster at the end of the alley, his curiosity is piqued. "Who wears sunglasses when the sun goes down?"

Wilt has no difficulty unraveling the mystery. "Someone who doesn't want to be identified in that lot on that evening."

Andrews laughs. "That's a disguise? You can't be serious! Who'd be dumb enough to do that!"

Wilt answers without hesitation. "The Martin brothers. That's Kenny Martin in the driver's seat and Wally sitting next to him. I sent Kenny to Eddyville State Penitentiary a few years back for grand theft auto. But the most interesting part here is that there's a strong Braden connection. He works out at Lonesome Pine."

"Then what's he doing hanging around a dumpster wearing a Halloween mask?"

"My guess is, again, he's using another disguise and waiting for someone to come down that alley. My gut tells me that person is Parker who has to walk through the alley after work to get to his vehicle. But Parker doesn't show, so at 8:03 pm the two leave the lot to go somewhere else. Maybe they've been tipped off to where Parker is at and are headed there to finish the job."

Andrews is excited and immediately ready to follow up and go squeeze a confession out of the Martins. "So we should go interview both of them!"

"Approaching Kenny at this point may be counterproductive. He's done hard time and isn't going to be impressed when we show up at the door. Anytime I've approached him for information he's told me to take a hike. Wally doesn't have a criminal record, at least that I'm aware of. We'll have a much better chance getting something out of him, but we need to develop more information before we approach him."

As they continue to watch the footage, the last notable event occurs about fifteen minutes after the Martins leave the lot. A woman with black hair tucked under a Fedora walks toward the BMW and glances side to side as if to see if there was anyone nearby. She is wearing large oval rimmed glasses and a men's overcoat that is several times too large. The video footage shows the woman holding out her fist. Then she opens the door of the BMW. Hidden in her hand must be a remote to open the car's electronic door lock. She gets in and drives away, out of frame. Initially, Wilt can't quite make out who she is, but it doesn't take him long to figure it out.

Wilt's thinking about something else. *What is Kenny Martin up to and why did Wally get involved? He's always steered clear of Kenny's antics before.*

Kenny Martin, also known as K-Mart, is a large, fit man at 6'3", 220 pounds, with a full head of thick, wavy dark brown hair. He possesses rugged features and a large dragon tattoo on his back. While he had also grown up in Summerville like Dan Jack, he's fifteen years younger and has achieved a very different sort of reputation. Since high school, he has spent his time drifting from job to job and had never held one for more than a few months. Then he did some time in the state pen for second degree assault with a deadly weapon and grand theft auto.

Wally Martin is Kenny's identical twin, and like his brother, has a nickname anyone could guess. While Kenny is outgoing, intense and at times reckless, Wally usually keeps to himself. Since reaching adulthood he has been as placid as a mountain stream and will only go so far with Kenny's mischief. He's never been accused of anything except looking like his more intense, irresponsible brother.

For the last few years Kenny had supervised one of Brock Braden's paving crews at Braden Construction. Kenny now works at Lonesome Pine, where he supervises course maintenance and the guys in the club barn who store, clean and repair golf clubs for members. Wally also works in maintenance at Lonesome Pine. He trims azaleas and mows greens and fairways.

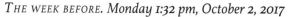

THE WEEK BEFORE. Monday 1:32 pm, October 2, 2017

When Kenny Martin returned from lunch, Lonesome Pine's resident club professional told him that Braden was looking for him. Martin immediately went to Brock's office. Brock looked like he hadn't slept. "Kenny, got another job for you, but it's not like the others. It involves something considerably more intense."

K-Mart just grinned as he sat in a leather chair in front of Brock's desk. "All your jobs are intense, Brock. Just ask any one of em. Who is it?"

Brock was in no joking mood. "I'll get to that in a moment. But before I tell you who it is, it's worth $100,000 to you if the job gets done right."

Martin's eyes opened wider. The other jobs he'd done for Braden were all $5000. That amount of money could only mean Braden wanted him to do one thing. "That's a pot of money, Brock."

Braden continued. "I'll even pay you ten thousand up front before you do it. But it's a job that must be handled quietly and quickly."

Then Brock pulled out a bank bag and counted out a hundred $100-bills. He stacked them in front of Martin on his desk. "You're going to have to make someone disappear. Someone well known in the community. At first, there'll be a lot of publicity and attention from law enforcement."

Kenny turned his head slightly. His curiosity was rising sharply.

"You might even be questioned by the police about it, though I doubt anyone would suspect you. But you need to have an alibi set up for whenever you do it."

"If no one's gonna suspect me, then why do I need an alibi, Brock?"

"It's always best in these types of things to have an explanation in advance. Being questioned is a possibility you must be prepared for. Can you do that and are you interested?"

Martin was starting to have reservations. He took a few moments to think about it. "Depends on who it is, I guess. Sounds like you want me to ...".

But before Martin could say it, Braden cut him off.

"Stop right there! If you have to ask a lot of questions about this maybe you aren't up to a job like this. I've got at least five other guys who would jump at this opportunity without asking questions."

Martin, seeing he was about to blow it, didn't hesitate this time. "Okay! Alright. I'll do it, if it's not someone real old or a kid."

A smirk ran across Brock's face.

"Of course, it's not a kid or an old person! It's Harlan Parker. And this is the last conversation we're going to have about it. I don't want to know how you do it or where you put him when it's done, but you must make sure it's someplace no one will ever find him. And not Lonesome!"

Brock never dispelled the rumor there were bodies on his golf course, thinking it would motivate his employees. And he knew Kenny believed it.

"How long do I have to do it, Brock?"

"I'll give you a couple of weeks. If it isn't done, you put the ten thousand back in my desk drawer." Kenny nodded as Brock continued.

"But if you do it, we're still not going to speak of it again. You're not giving me any signal or indication that it's done. I'll know it's done when everyone in town is asking where he is and what's happened to him."

Kenny was more interested in the money than talking about how he was going to whack Parker. "Then how long after it's done will I get paid the rest, and how, Brock?"

"I'll drop the money someplace where only you will find it. And don't ever dare come to me asking where the rest of the money is or else it all goes back in my bank account. Understood?"

"Got it, Brock!"

"All I want to know right now is if you're in, Kenny."

Martin glared straight ahead in Braden's direction as if looking right through him. Nothing else need be said. Martin stood up, grabbed the stack of $100 bills and walked out the door.

~

TUESDAY 5:45 PM, October 3, 2017

Dan Jack Gray finished his day's work at his law office and walked down the square to Deadwood Rose, home of the best wine selection and steaks in town, located at the corner of Deadwood Street and Rose Avenue.

On Tuesday, Deadwood was always packed with attorneys, judges, businessmen and hungry college kids. It was $5 burger night, when you could get the best burger in town for half the price. And October 3rd was no exception. Waiters and waitresses in black pants and white button-down shirts filled beer mugs and mixed drinks from behind the bar. The smell of cheeseburgers and onions wafted throughout as patrons sitting along a 30-foot bar located down the left side of the room gorged themselves on beer and fried chicken wings, burgers and sweet potato fries as they conversed and watched sports on two TVs, mounted above the bar at each end.

Also, among the crowd was Brock Braden, but he wasn't eating as much as drinking, and way too much, as usual. It was a problem he was well known for all over town. Dan Jack Gray and Brock Braden were just a few years apart and had even gone to the same grade school as kids, but their age gap was too great to hang out together. But Dan Jack's father, also a criminal lawyer, had gotten the teenaged Brock Braden out of at least a half dozen drunk driving (DUI) charges, that is, before Mothers Against Drunk Drivers (MADD) lobbied the state legislature to stiffen drunk driving laws. But as Braden grew into adulthood his drinking problems sloshed along with him, so Dan Jack inherited Brock Braden as a client after returning from the U.S. Attorney's Office. And he almost had the same level of success achieved by his father. But Braden never showed his appreciation, not in ways that he easily could have.

While Gray handled Braden's drunk driving cases and other criminal matters, even ensuring Braden avoided federal prison for bribing state transportation officials, the high-end legal work was always doled out to a bigger firm in town or even ones in Louisville. Though Blue and Gray would be more than proficient in corporate litigation, suing subcontractors, enforcing non-competes and enforcing and negotiating contracts, Braden Excavation & Paving never threw any work Dan Jack's way.

And though he never brought it up, it was something Dan Jack never forgot. As a result, Braden thought their connection was much stronger than it was.

When Dan Jack saw Braden visibly drunk and waving him over, he just nodded and walked by him to the other end of the bar and sat down. Not a man to be ignored, Braden jumped off his bar stool and stumbled over to Dan Jack taking the seat next to him. "What was that all about, Dan Jack? There's something I need to talk to you about."

He wasn't about to acknowledge the suggestion that he just blew Braden off, sailing right past the thought. "What's up, Brock? Is there a talent deficit at Cork and Cleavage tonight?" It was a reference to the strip club Braden frequented between his bad marriages and sometimes during them.

Braden laughed at the quip, far louder than the remark justified. "Cork and Cleavage! Ha! You don't know how close you are, Dan Jack." Then he slapped Dan Jack on the back as he looked down the bar to get the waiter's attention, pointing to his glass for another gin and tonic. "Let me buy you a drink, Dan Jack. He's done it to me again!"

Dan Jack Gray didn't drink but rarely, and never socially, and he only frequented Deadwood Rose because it was also a restaurant that prepared their food in-house, one of the few places left in town that wasn't a franchise that warmed up processed food full of things designed to extend its shelf life that also shortened yours. But he had a pretty good idea who Braden was referring to even before he mentioned who he was talking about. "Brock, you're going to need a ride home. You can't afford to be pulled over again. I can't get you out of another DUI."

"You're overreacting. I'm fine."

"Judge Renfro isn't a golfer and he doesn't like you anyway."

"I gave money to him last election."

"He thinks you're a rich, self-entitled prick."

Braden wasn't offended in the least with Dan Jack's remarks, one, mainly because he was too drunk to catch it; and even if he did it was the kind of thing, he heard all the time. Besides that, he was focused on something far more serious. "I'm going to kill him! Christa's filing for a divorce and filed an emergency protective order against me and got me kicked out of the house yesterday. And Harlan Parker is handling the whole thing while he's sleeping with her."

Not only was Parker now representing his current wife, he had represented two of Braden's three former wives in divorce cases against him. And now, with Christa's EPO, he'd had enough.

Dan Jack wasn't exactly surprised Braden's marriage had imploded. All his others had. Nor was he surprised that anyone wanted to kill Harlan Parker.

"Do you have any idea how many people in this town have said that they're going to kill Harlan Parker? If I had a dollar for every time someone's told me that I wouldn't have to work anymore. But I'm very sorry to hear about you and Christa, Brock."

Just for a moment, Braden turned sentimental. "I know she had the depth of an oil slick, but she was the love of my life, Dan Jack."

"Come on, Brock, I don't mean to sound insensitive, but she's what, your third, no, your fourth wife? Anyway, how are you so sure it's Parker?"

"I had a private investigator follow her for a couple of weeks. She's driving over to his condo every few days and pulling into the carport after he raises the garage door. An hour later the garage opens, and she leaves. Same pattern, every time. But it's the last time Parker's going to do this to me or anyone else."

"What are you talking about Brock?"

"Harlan Parker is about to disappear and he's going someplace no one will ever find him. I've got it all set up. I've already hired K-Mart to do the job."

Dan Jack was not impressed with idea and less impressed with the hire. "K-Mart? Really? Are you kidding me? You hired K-Mart to whack Harlan Parker?"

"Is there a problem with K-Mart?"

"K-Mart's so inept he couldn't commit the crime of solicitation if you gave him $100 and put him on a street corner next to a prostitute that looked like a supermodel!"

"Good subs are hard to find in that line of work, Dan Jack. Anyway, I've found him to be very reliable on certain things."

"And if nobody's going to suspect anything, then how are you going to keep K-Mart quiet? And, why are you telling me?"

"Because I've got to tell somebody, or I'll go crazy. God knows I'm already halfway there. Anyway, there's nobody else to tell. And I know you hate him almost as much as I do."

At least Dan Jack couldn't argue with the last point. He motioned to the waiter and told Braden to pay the tab while discretely grabbing Braden's whiskey glass and slipped it into his overcoat pocket. It was time to leave. "Just so you know, Brock, the idea is to tell your lawyer after you've committed the crime. Not when you're planning it. And not before you actually kill someone. Now, where are you staying at tonight?"

"A vacant townhome out at Lonesome."

"Okay. I'm driving you there. Tomorrow you're going to wake up and straighten out whatever it is you've started with K-Mart."

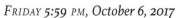

FRIDAY 5:59 PM, October 6, 2017

Kenny Martin and his brother Wally sat impatiently in a red Ford pickup in the parking lot behind the Old Compton Movie House.

They were waiting for Harlan Parker, who was known at the end of the workday to walk through a nearby alley on the square that ran between Sears and Roebuck and the Old Compton Movie House to retrieve his car. But what the Martin brothers hadn't figured out was Parker's Friday routine was different.

He usually began his weekends by walking from his office to Deadwood Rose for a couple of drinks to scout the premises for a willing companion for the evening. His metallic blue, seven series Beamer was still sitting in its designated parking space behind the town square so the Martins thought Harlan must be working late.

Kenny could barely contain his excitement as the two waited, parked about 25 feet behind Parker's car. "Tonight, it's on, Wally. The real chimichanga! When that big white buffalo saunters from his office into the far end of the alley we put on our masks and I move to behind the dumpster in the back of the movie house."

Kenny had driven twenty minutes to a costume shop in Cousin the day before and picked up two rubber, presidential pullover masks.

Wally's left eye twitched as he nodded affirmatively. He'd never done hard time in the penitentiary like brother Kenny, so he was more than a little nervous. But Kenny had promised him that he didn't have to hurt anybody, just to hold Parker's arms for a couple of minutes and help throw him in the truck. And Kenny would take Parker somewhere and do the rest alone. Still, he wanted to go over things one last time. "Okay, Kenny, but go over the part with the flashlights again, and real slow this time.

Kenny started to regret getting Wally involved, but he had no other options. Parker was a large man. He was going to need help hoisting Parker into the back of the truck. So, he took a deep breath. "Okay, Wally. I'll explain the flashlights for the third time."

Talking loudly and slowly as if he was a third grader reading a book out loud to his class, Kenny picked up two flashlights, one in each hand.

"I've jerry-rigged these two flashlights. One that I've screwed in a green Christmas tree light bulb and the other a red. I'll be standing behind the dumpster in my Bill Clinton mask while you stay in the truck and watch out for Parker. You've got a clear view of the alley from the truck. The moment you see Harlan Parker walk into the far side of the alley and no one else is around flash me the green light and it's a go and I know he's about to come out the near end of the alley."

Wally looked at the dashboard nodding his head as Kenny explained the plan. "And if I see anyone with Parker or another person shows up behind him after I've flashed the green light, I'll flash you the red light to call it off for the night."

"You got it."

Wally frowned. "Yeah. And I want to make sure you got it, Kenny. I'm not hitting Parker or nobody else. Just so we're double clear."

"That's right, brother. The moment his bald head reveals itself on this side, I'll tackle him to the ground, and you jump out in your Bill Clinton mask, grab his arms and hold him down while I cover his face with the wet rag. When he's knocked out, we throw his big haunches into the truck, got it?"

Wally didn't want to know anything else about it. All he knew is that he wasn't going to be there and was in line for $30,000 cash when it was over. The two had been to the parking lot twice in the past week scouting the area to figure out when foot traffic was least frequent.

And tonight, it was on! They were going to abduct Parker and render him unconscious by covering his face with a rag laced with chloroform. Then Kenny would take him to another location to kill him and dispose of the body. But Kenny didn't tell Braden that his brother was in on it. Braden wanted as few people in the loop as possible and Kenny thought he might find somebody else to do the job if he told him.

What the Martins didn't know was a video surveillance camera was mounted at the top of the Compton Movie House recording activity in the parking lot. Their every move was being captured just as it had been earlier that week. And their baseball caps and dark sunglasses weren't the best disguise considering they were sitting side by side in a big red truck, and almost everyone in the county knew the Martin brothers.

After Kenny and Wally waited a couple of hours and Parker didn't show, they called off the abduction for the night and left the lot.

〜

WEDNESDAY *10:38* AM, *October 11, 2017*

Kenny Martin was in his office at the club barn at Lonesome Pine as workers in the adjoining bag room clean, repair and store golf clubs for members. Word had spread throughout town was that Parker was missing and presumed dead, and K-Mart was deep in angry thoughts.

> *Somebody else has gotten to Harlan, and I've lost*
> *$90,000. The man said he was going to give me*
> *two weeks and went and hired someone else.*

Martin wanted to march right into Braden's office and give him a piece of his mind, but he knew the moment he did he'd be on the street. He figured Braden was his usual self, impatient and erratic. That he'd just lost it and couldn't wait any longer. *Should have known not to take him at his word.*

At that moment, a guy from course maintenance walked in the door. "Hey, K-Mart. Gotta mow the backside. Need keys to the tractor."

The club's last tractor had been recently stolen, so Martin had started keeping the keys to all the heavy equipment in his desk drawer. He retrieved the keys and gave them to the worker. "Thanks."

"No joyriding," K-Mart replied out of habit. It was a long-running joke. "Bring her back as soon as you're done." But he wasn't looking at the worker. There was something else in the drawer, a typed note.

Tree hole. Cherokee marker between the fourth and the fifth hole.

Native Americans used marker trees to guide them through the wilderness and many can be seen throughout the countryside, even today. Early in a tree's development, when its trunk is still soft and flexible enough to manipulate, it was bound and bent at two places in the shape of an L to point towards a certain direction. As it grows, the tree matures and hardens, keeping its L shape, thereby becoming a marker for others to follow.

When Lonesome Pine was built, the course architect found two marker trees on the property and decided to use them as natural guideposts for members. One was a large oak tree between the fourth green pointing in the direction of the fifth tee.

Martin was curious what the note meant so he drove a golf cart out there to find out. It was mid-October and a cold and blustery day, so very few golfers had braved the conditions to come play. When Martin reached the marker tree, he saw a black object barely sticking out of a tree hole located about eight or nine feet up the vertical section of the tree's L shaped trunk. It had been placed so high and in such a way that if you hadn't been directed to it, you'd never have noticed it.

K-Mart looked around first to make sure nobody was in sight. Then he climbs and stands upon the horizontal section of the trunk and reaches up to feel the object. It was cloth in texture and Martin was just tall enough to get his thumb and forefinger on it. He tugged but could only move it slightly. The girth of the object was wider than the size of the hole it had been pushed through to get it into the tree.

But he had a slightly better grip now, so he pulled harder, this time moving it enough to see it was a sack. The black sack now protruded out of the hole about six inches. *One more pull should do it.* He stood up on his toes, wrapped his left arm around the vertical section of the truck, and reached up with his right hand to grab the bag. With a third and mighty yank, several $100 bills fell out of the tree hole, were swept up by the wind, and flew onto the course.

Martin jumped off the tree trunk, chasing cash down the fourth fairway.

8

THE PARALEGAL

Wednesday 5:27 pm, October 11, 2017
Detective Wilt pays a visit to the office of Blue and Gray. He's impressed with how well the Victorian building has been restored. He would have never guessed that Dan Jack's law practice was struggling. Savannah tells the investigator that Parker was at the office with Dan Jack for a deposition until about a quarter to six before leaving the building with him. Dan Jack mentions his last interaction with him.

"After we finished our deposition, Harlan left at the same time as Savannah and April Lindsey, the court reporter. He didn't mention any plans he had for the evening, but as long as I can remember he's been known to frequent Deadwood on Friday evenings, sharing a drink or three with his friends."

"Do you happen to know the names of any of Mr. Parker's friends?" Wilt asks.

Dan Jack's expression remains placid. "No, I'm sorry, I don't. Harlan and I attended the same high school together, but we were never friends. He was a jock, and I wasn't." He shrugged and smiled.

Wilt nods. "Thank you for your time."

Savannah glances at her father and then gives Wilt a wry smile. "I think my father is too polite to mention that Mr. Parker had a more than professional interest in the court reporter."

"That doesn't mean anything," Dan Jack says. "Harlan has a more than polite interest in half the women on the planet. The other half he hasn't met yet."

"He had plans to spend the evening with her," Savannah contradicts. "I walked out with them, remember? I couldn't miss the way he was putting the moves on her."

Dan Jack gives in gracefully. "Then I stand corrected." He pulls out his wallet and hands Wilt a business card. "This is the court reporter we used on the case."

"If I had to make a blind guess, I'd say Mr. Parker took her to Deadwood Rose for dinner," Savannah puts in. "He asked her if she had plans for dinner as I separated from them." Wilt is impressed. "Thank you, Mrs. Blue."Dan Jack gives his daughter a proud half-grin.

Wilt then goes to Deadwood Rose to speak with its owner, Tony Scaloppini. Scaloppini can't specifically recall if Parker was there last Friday evening, October 6th as it's their busiest night. However, he does say Parker's frequented the bar to kick off the weekend. When asked who he might have left the bar with, Scaloppini laughs loudly. "Anything with two legs and no standards, Detective."

FRIDAY 5:37 PM, October 6, 2017

The conference room has ceilings twelve feet high finished with plates of pressed tin with designs popular in Victorian buildings. This one houses the law office of Blue and Gray, located on the town square in Summerville, Kentucky. Dark cherry red chairs line each side of the long thin conference table, each with a leather cushioned seat and back. At the back of the room is a credenza with a mini bar to entertain clients, complete with shot glasses and bottles of gin, vodka and of course, Kentucky bourbon.

Over the credenza is a 1920s photo of Sheriff Daniel Jackson Gray standing in front of the old courthouse, Dan Jack's namesake and grandfather. On the other walls are enlarged period photographs of the town square dating back to the early twentieth century. One is a model T parked next to a horse carriage on Main Street. Another is of the prohibition era, showing women in fancy white dresses on one side of the street holding signs saying, "God's Will" and "Save our youth from the scourge of alcohol" and men on the other, holding signs saying, "We want Beer!"

The court reporter handed her business card to the lawyers at the conclusion of the deposition complete with instructions on how the lawyers could make payment. The witness, the plaintiff and Gray's client, briefly talked with his lawyer agreeing to reach out the next week before walking out the door as the videographer packed up his camera and followed behind him out of the office. It was late Friday afternoon and everyone had left for the weekend, save the court reporter, Savannah, Dan Jack, and their adversary, Harlan Parker.

Gray was trying to settle a medical malpractice case filed against Parker's client. Dr. Randall Smith had botched a shoulder surgery on a 40-year-old man rendering his right arm permanently useless. But it was far from a done deal. Gray had been down this road before with Parker, who was well known for his ability to fix juries and get his way with the court.

Over the years Gray had wasted tens of thousands of dollars he'd fronted suing Parker's clients only to have his client's cases dismissed before even getting to trial. Or if he did make it to one, he got screwed over by some bogus ruling made by a judge who always seemed to have a personal connection with the person or party Gray was suing. Gray knew his chances of success, even with great facts, were significantly lower with Parker on the other side.

And Parker wasn't shy about reminding him. "You've got to be more realistic, Dan Jack. You remember what happened in the Langley case? Juries in this town just don't like it when people sue doctors or hospitals."

"Harlan, I'll admit that the juries that sit in your cases haven't liked them very much. My client's a self-employed electrician and can't earn jack anymore because of what Smith did to him. And the jury will like my client a lot more than yours when they find out about his other settlements."

"Those are confidential, Dan Jack. I doubt Judge Renfro will let you mention them."

"Oh, he'll let me, alright. But let's keep talking. My client is willing to come to the table, Harlan, that is, if you're willing to come up with some more money."

Parker walked out of the office alongside the court reporter just as Savannah was leaving to go home for the weekend. The two exchanged small talk as they walked down the stairs from the second floor and exited the building. Savannah's skin crawled walking beside him but was adept at concealing it, at least for a minute or two. As she broke off from the other two to go to her car, you'd never pick up on her dismay with the court reporter who seemed to actually enjoy Harlan Parker's flirting. Male attention from someone like Harlan Parker was no compliment.

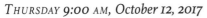

THURSDAY *9:00 AM, October 12, 2017*

Detective Wilt's first task of the day is to speak with Tori Stevens, Parker's paralegal. He offers to come to her office, which she accepts. Wilt introduces himself as he takes a chair in front of Steven's workstation, but before he can begin his routine questioning the receptionist contacts Stevens over speakerphone.

"Tori. It's Mr. Swanson, again. He's very upset this time. I really don't know what to tell him. Nothing has changed since yesterday. Can you please do something?"

Stevens gives Marshal Wilt a brief, apologetic smile. "Sure, patch him through."

"Oh, Tori, you're a lifesaver!"

"No problem. Really."

"Okay, here he is."

The phone beside Tori's hand rings. She picks it up. Wilt could hear a male voice on the other end but can't make out the words.

"Hello, Mr. Swanson," Stevens says calmly. "No. We still don't know any more than yesterday. I'm very sorry for your trouble but I'm still holding out hope that Mr. Parker will show up. Yes, I promise I'll call you the first thing I hear something."

Stevens hangs up the phone and lets out a big sigh. "I'm sorry, Detective. Things are coming apart at the seams around here. You can see how much everyone relies on Mr. Parker."

Wilt sees she's overwhelmed. "We can do this next week if you like, Ms. Stevens."

Stevens sits up and massages her eyelids with her thumb and index finger before sliding them to her nose. Then smiles at Wilt. "No. No. It's fine. I'm afraid things next week will only get worse."

Wilt nods in agreement. "Alright then. When was the last time you had contact with your boss?"

"Do you mean the last time I spoke with him or the last time I messaged him?"

"Both, Ms. Stevens. But let's start with the speaking part."

"Okay. It was Friday October 6th. Mr. Parker had a deposition over at the office of Blue and Gray. He left here just after 1:00 pm, and indicated he was walking over for the deposition."

"What about text messages? When was the last one you received from him?"

Stevens picks up her cell phone from the desk and scrolls through her text messages, going back to October 6th. "That would be 7:42 pm the same day. Mr. Parker wanted me to take his car back to his condo. He indicated that he had been drinking and had met an old friend and wouldn't need the vehicle that evening."

Wilt takes in Stevens' casual tone. "Is that something you typically do for Mr. Parker? Do you have a set of keys to his car?"

Stevens laughs and pauses for a moment to choose her words carefully. "Detective, have you ever been an assistant to an attorney who doesn't have a wife? I did everything for the man but tuck him in bed. I've driven his car home at least a dozen times over the years. I have an extra set of keys in my desk for that very purpose."

She takes the keys out of her desk and hands them over to Wilt. "Here they are in fact. And just like that night, I usually get the calls on Friday nights. Mr. Parker has lots of—friends on Friday nights, and he's always very careful not to drive if he's had a few drinks."

Wilt is relieved that she had answered the question truthfully. However, Stevens' appearance in the fuzzy footage raises more questions. "Do you typically wear a Fedora and a man's trench coat, Ms. Stevens?"

She smiles. "No, not typically, Detective, but this is a small town and the minute some wise guy sees me drive Harlan Parker's car the next thing you know he's my sugar daddy. Do you feel me, Detective? Yes, I was incognito, and his trench coat could have fit three of me inside it. The only thing to keep his hat on was all my hair tucked underneath it." She laughs and shakes her head.

Wilt thinks the answer makes a lot of sense, except for one thing. "Why doesn't Mr. Parker leave the car where it is and come get it in the morning?"

Stevens is ready for that one too. "Well, Detective. You already know the answer to that question. Would you leave your $80,000 BMW parked overnight behind Compton Movie House? Every teenager in town is there on Friday night. How many vandalism calls does your department make responding to complaints of broken windows or key scratches along luxury sedans behind that theater?"

Wilt nods in agreement but has one more question for Stevens. "When you parked the car in his car port did you go into his condo?"

Tori looks at him like he's a three headed monster.

Seeing that he has offended her, Wilt tries another approach. "I'm sorry, Ms. Stevens. That's not what I'm suggesting at all. What I'd like to know is if you put his phone back on his nightstand."

Stevens tilts her head and stares at Wilt for a moment as if to ask him to clarify the question, before answering. "No, and no, Detective, I've never been in Mr. Parker's residence. No offense, but he's a little old for me and a little—large. But I understand that you have a job to do here so I won't take your question to suggest I was sleeping with Mr. Parker."

"That was not my intent," Wilt reassures her.

Stevens continues, "Mr. Parker was far from perfect to work for to be sure, but we had a very productive and professional relationship. He paid me well and gave me opportunities other lawyers wouldn't have and he taught me a lot about the practice of law. He was my boss and my mentor professionally, not personally. This is all very difficult for all of us."

Wilt moves on to the line of questioning he feels is more important. "Do you know of anyone who threatened Mr. Parker? A client? Another lawyer?"

Stevens laughs again, but this time so loudly it could be heard all over the second floor. "Yes, and they would be too numerous for me to mention here, or to keep track of. Mr. Parker would have had to pay me a lot more money than he did to do that. But I will tell you that he loved it when opposing attorneys and people he sued threatened him. It was like affirmation that he was doing a great job."

Wilt frowns. "So, he didn't take those threats seriously?"

"You mean maybe he should have?" Stevens suggests. "I agree, the thought crossed my mind when Mr. Parker didn't answer his phone or text me. His typical response was to laugh them off, as I said. Why, even when Obadiah Adam threatened Mr. Parker in court with all that Blackacre nonsense, he didn't take it to heart."

"Blackacre nonsense?"

Obadiah Adam is a local celebrity of sorts, a critically acclaimed poet who Parker had lost a copyright lawsuit against just in the past month. After the verdict, Adam approached Parker and made a cryptic threat against him. Parker just ignored it like all the others. Stevens refrains from rolling her eyes, but she looks as if she would like to.

"Some pseudo-religious speech about Mr. Parker reaping his just rewards. I must admit, it sounded pretty weak to me. Besides, that was one of the rare cases in which Mr. Parker lost."

Wilt is more than skeptical.

"Even if Obadiah Adam did threaten Parker, I find it highly unlikely he would carry through with it. He'd be the last person in Summerville I would suspect."

"What can I say? You asked, Detective, but I agree, poets are high-strung types." She changes the topic. "You know that Mr. Parker also handles divorces, don't you? There were a few people who were very disappointed with the outcome of their cases. Some who threatened him. He took those more personally."

"Can you give me any names?"

Stevens pauses for a moment and softly taps her cheek. "Brock Braden is the one that stands out but that was several years back. Parker had represented a couple of his wives in divorce cases. Very ugly. The others just all seem to run together. Let me think about it and maybe we can do this again soon now that I know what you're looking for, Detective."

Wilt thinks Tori Stevens is believable. But he also thinks it's slightly suspicious that she didn't ask him if he knows any details about what happened to Parker. Most people working so closely with someone would have asked some questions. But again, Parker probably was a jerk to work for, too. So, he all but eliminates her as a suspect.

His last thought as he walks out of the office is that she answered the questions so smoothly that if she is lying, Tori Stevens is definitely a sociopath.

9

PERCY'S 7-IRON GOES MISSING

Thursday 10:30 am, October 12, 2017

The same morning that Wilt and Andrews interviewed Tori Stevens, Rowdy was in K-Mart's office at Lonesome Pine looking for a job. And as fortune would have it, there was a recent opening in the bag room, the place where members' golf clubs were kept. During last week's golf tournament, someone had stolen a golf club belonging to Lonesome's rising star, Percy Ridge. The security breach cost one staff member his job.

K-Mart explained to Rowdy what happened.

As the legend goes, Persimmon Danforth Ridge was born with a golf club in his hand, and it was a 7-iron. By the time he was twenty years old, he was already the best golfer ever produced by Crawford County. This wasn't all that surprising considering his father and grandfather played professionally. But that still didn't diminish Ridge's prodigious young career.

At the age of seventeen, he won the Junior U.S. Amateur Championship and then went on to be a two-time NCAA champion at the University of Georgia. At the age of twenty, he was low Amateur at Augusta where he was interviewed in Butler Cabin along with Tiger Woods and Phil Mickelson before a national viewing audience.

And like any other aspiring professional golfer, when Percy graduated from college, he played on the Web.com tour, which is where you must play in order to qualify for the PGA tour, where purses and endorsement deals with club manufacturers were ten times of the junior tour.

The first few years Percy had traveled all over the country, grinding it out, playing the grueling schedule trying to earn his card. And his father wasn't about to pay for plane flights or five-star hotels for young Percy. If he was going to make it, he was going to earn it himself, just like his father and grandfather. Percy drove his Volkswagen van hundreds of miles each week to the next event and stay in budget hotels trying rank in the top 25 at the end of the season to earn his card. The first five years he had never finished better than 31st, so far denying him his coveted tour card.

But this year it was going to be different. The golfing gods were smiling down upon Percy Ridge. Going into the final tournament of the season, he was ranked 19th. And, better still, the season's final event was none other than the Lonesome Pine Invitational, played on Ridge's home course, where he held the course record.

Sunday October 8, 2017

It was the second weekend of October, Sunday and the final round, and Percy had one hole to go, only needing a par 5 on Lonesome's last, the 588-yard dogleg to the right to finish in the top 25 and finally earn his card. But it would be no easy task, as the 18th had been the most difficult hole on the course that week with a stroke average of 5.23.

The reason was the player had to drive the ball 340 yards to a rising fairway to get past the course's signature 240-foot conifer and have a chance at the green in two shots. And there wasn't a golfer alive who could do it. The longest hitters in the world could manage no more than 300 yards off Lonesome's 18th tee.

The best way to attack the hole was to place your drive on the far-left side of the fairway, as far as possible while avoiding Abner's Revenge. Then, for the second shot, fade a long iron, bending it around the lonesome pine to set up a manageable mid-iron third shot into the hole's iconic island green.

And Percy had played the first two shots perfectly. He was now 183 yards from the pin, which just so happened to be the perfect distance for Percy's 7-iron. He led the Web.com tour in distance to the hole on shots 175 to 185 yards because he was the best on tour with a 7-iron. His family waited for him at the 18th green ready to celebrate Percy's breakthrough moment. A national television audience was watching as Jim Swan and Mickie Waldo called the action.

"Once again, it all comes down to Lonesome's last, Mick. Percy Ridge has navigated through Abner's Revenge and faded his second shot perfectly around the Lonesome Pine, and he now sits right in the middle of the fairway. All he has to do is hit his 7-iron like he's hit it all season long, and he's finally got that elusive PGA tour card. And his life will be changed forever."

Swan notices Percy's family in the crowd.

"Look, it's a family reunion at the 18th with Percy's father, Frank Ridge, and grandfather, John, waiting to congratulate their boy, that is, if he can just land it on Lonesome's island green and get out with a two putt."

Waldo recalls one of Frank Ridge's greatest tour victories.

"Yes, Jim. It must be very emotional for Frank right now. Who could forget his battle with Nicklaus to win the Refrigerator Open in Boise."

"Ah, yes! The Duel on the Tundra. Frank Ridge sent the Bear into hibernation that day, Mick. Hold on a minute. Things appear to be getting a little chippy between Percy and his caddie. What seems to be the issue, Dave?"

The broadcast team cut to Dave Charity, the roving reporter assigned to follow Percy and his caddie throughout the course.

"Percy's 7-iron seems to be missing from his bag, Jim. I'd relay the conversation to the viewing audience, but we'd be banned by the FCC. The palatable translation would be, 'You momma's lover, son of an Irish Setter. Where in the act of passion is my 7-iron? Did you even bother to count my fornicating clubs this morning?'"

Swan strikes a concerning tone back in the broadcast booth.

"Oh my! What's your read, Mick?"

"Well, it's tough, Jim. There's no room for error and the club he uses for this distance is no longer an option. For weekend golfers it's not a big deal. Just club up or down and scramble for your par. But to Percy, it's a huge deal. Professional golfers are creatures of habit and, with water surrounding the hole, 90 percent of the time they only have one swing for this situation. But there does appear to be a slight headwind. Maybe he can fly a soft 6-iron into the green. If not, I'm afraid it's another year sleeping at the Bed Bug Inn for Percy Ridge."

Just as Mickie Waldo had feared, Percy overshot the 18th green sending both his ball and PGA tour card into the water. After the tournament, infuriated that Lonesome Pine's staff could allow some stranger in the bag room, the Ridge family walked into Braden's office and withdrew their club membership.

After a one-day investigation that was more like the Spanish Inquisition, Brock Braden fired the bag room manager. K-mart concluded his story. "Personally, I think it was Christa who came in and pulled it. She had full access to the bag room and word around here was that Percy had been seeing her, in a manner of speaking. Rumor was that he'd just broken things off. My guess is that she just wanted to get back at him for dumping her. But keep a lid on it, Rowdy. Wouldn't want the boss man to catch wind of that."

"No problem, K-Mart. Won't hear a word from me. When do I start?"

～

THURSDAY 10:45 AM, October 12, 2017

Andrews returns to the office and reports in with Wilt after an interview with the court reporter, April Lindsey. She confirmed that she and Parker walked out of the office of Blue and Gray early the evening of October 6th and that he'd asked her to dinner which she politely declined. At which point she turned into the street to approach her vehicle wishing Parker a pleasant weekend. She also stated that Parker was taking a call on his cell and engaged in a conversation as he waved goodbye to her. Although Lindsey didn't hear anything to indicate who had called Parker, she said it prompted him to immediately turn around and head in the opposite direction.

Lindsey was the first witness interview Andrew had conducted on his own. Though it was routine, the trust Wilt had placed in him had its intended effect. Andrews began to express his opinion more freely.

"We need to check who's calling Parker at a quarter of six and we might find his Friday evening companion!"

Wilt nodded in agreement.

Wilt retrieves one of the other pieces of evidence they currently have, the call history from Harlan Parker's phone. "Here. A short call came in around the time Mr. Gray reports they were all going home. It's a one-minute call from Dan Jack Gray. It's nothing. They had been trying to reach a settlement out of court."

"Which leaves us with the Martin brothers," Andrews insists. "Probably hired by Brock Braden, just like Mrs. Braden said."

"If that's the case, we're going to need a lot more evidence," Wilt replies.

～

Thursday 5:00 pm, October 12, 2017

Parker hasn't been seen in seven days, and Barnes knows that he can't hide the ball much longer. He calls an office-wide meeting to express the importance of the firm getting its story together and showing a common front. It will be a challenge because Parker, Barnes and Jeffries aren't a real law firm in the traditional sense. The firm is simply a collection of ten lawyers who share space and make money referring business to each other.

The letterhead only gives the appearance of a mid-size law firm to attract affluent clients and businesses. But Parker's castoffs fed all of them far better than if they would have been somewhere else, even though they had to pay him a hefty percentage for referrals. When everyone is seated in the conference room, Barnes begins.

"I thought it best for all of us to get on the same page about Harlan. We need to buy time. At this point, we don't know if he's coming back, but we must be able to continue if he doesn't. The firm has several valuable clients that need our reassurance that he's coming back. If they think he's gone, they'll soon follow, and we're not long for the square."

There are twenty people in the room, but if anyone is worrying about Parker's welfare, no one is showing it. Questions that concerned coworkers usually ask are absent. And the reason isn't difficult to figure out. All but a couple of them have a story about Parker driving them to the brink, shorting them on referrals or demanding long hours from them to keep working for him and throwing them crumbs in return. But Barnes isn't calling the meeting for Parker's hand-me-down clients.

"If Harlan's not coming back, they'll find someone else anyway. That is, unless we're proactive. As second partner on the letterhead, it's incumbent upon me to serve as the face of the firm until Harlan returns. So, if any of our business clients contact any of you, I suggest you refer them to me, just to make sure we're not giving them different stories on why Harlan isn't here. In the meantime, I'll call each of them and assure them that things are well in hand. Remind them we're available for anything they need for the time being."

Though no one in the firm was personally close to Parker, the third partner, Mark Jeffries was closer to him than anyone else. Fifteen years Parker's junior, Jeffries was the guy Parker tabbed to sit second chair during Parker's trials. Though Jeffries rarely examined a witness, he was viewed by clients as the lawyer to call if Parker was tied up in another case. If anyone stood to benefit from Parker's permanent disappearance, it was him.

He had little regard for Barnes and had never seen him as anything but an overdressed counterfeit of a lawyer borrowing on Parker's professional reputation. He viewed the impromptu meeting as a power play masked as a sincere attempt to save the firm.

"Well, Ridley, we all know that none of them are actually firm clients. They're Harlan's clients. And what kind of advice are you going to give them? What sport coat to wear with that paisley tie?"

The small group exchanges glances and no one bothers to stifle their snide chuckles. Jeffries continues.

"Why are we even having this conversation, Ridley? Half of them have already contacted me this week and said that you've already called them. And just to let you know, they see right through you."

Barnes flashes a big smile. While other lawyers specialize in tax or criminal law, his specialty is social banter.

"Good one, Mark. And what are you going to do when they expect you to do something other than carry Harlan's briefcase?"

While lawyers in the firm are fighting over Parker's clients, his paralegal, Tori Stevens, just sits in silence.

Neither one of you could even draft a simple contract if your life depended on it. I know more about civil litigation than every lawyer in this room combined. If I had my law license right now, they wouldn't be calling either one of you water boys.

She's right. She'd spent the last four years cultivating relationships with every one of Parker's A-list clients and they all love her. It just so happens that she's spoken to every one of them this week, too, reassuring and subtly reminding them she'll have her law license very soon. Just in case Harlan doesn't come back.

10

ROWDY GOES UNDERCOVER

F*riday October 13, 2017*
Five days after Percy's near miss, the heartbreak continues to reverberate through Lonesome Pine. Ridge was Lonesome Pine's guy, and Braden could envision the course's prominence in the golfing world rising with his success. Braden had also heard the rumors about his wife and Percy. And he doesn't doubt it for a second. But, in his mind, that was a ship that already sailed, so he's past the point of trying to salvage his marriage. Deep in his heart, he knows that his one true passion is Lonesome Pine, and now he must do some serious damage control to save her.

Rowdy is sitting in the bag room in front of a wash bucket with a brush in his right hand and scrubbing a 4-iron in the left when Braden walks into the bag room. "Hey, Rowdy. Looking for K-Mart. Seen him this morning?"

"Yes sir, he closed the door to his office a few minutes ago, to take a phone call. Still in there."

Braden taps on the door and quickly steps in, closing it behind him. Rowdy follows right behind and stands a couple of feet from the door but gets only bits and pieces of the conversation.

"This can never get out. You understand that, don't you, Kenny?"

"How's it gonna get out, Brock? Who's going to talk? You and I are the only ones who know about it, and I'm not talking."

"If word ever got out that Christa came in here and compromised a player's bag, we're done. Finished. No more marquis events. No Mickie Waldo. No Jim Swan. We'll be no different than Summerville Country Club. Just another redneck-duffer, back-acre-pretender, cow pasture in the middle of nowhere."

Still struggling to hear what they are saying, Rowdy walks up and puts his ear up against the door. Reception is much improved. He can clearly hear Brock Braden's voice now.

"Nobody's ever gonna find out what happened here. Gonna stay buried at Lonesome Pine."

"You can count on me, Brock. What happens at Lonesome stays at Lonesome."

"Good! If we can just keep our heads about us and our mouths shut, we'll be alright. The last thing we need is for someone to have a reason to come out here and start digging around."

Rowdy's eyeballs get as big as silver dollars as he softly steps back and takes a seat at his wash bucket. Braden then opens the door, nods at Rowdy and walks out of the building. On his lunch break, Rowdy drives across town to tell Granville Pearl all about his scoop.

"I heard it as clear as I'm hearing you now, Mr. Pearl. Braden walks into K-Mart's office and closes the door. Then he told Kenny that if anybody ever figures out what happened out here, then it was over for them."

"What's over?"

"Their lives are gonna be over because they're going to the big house, the lockdown Riviera. That's what they said, now. Verbatim."

"Who said it, Rowdy?"

Rowdy takes a deep breath and slowly exhales.

"Brock Braden said that they killed Harlan Parker and buried him under the Lonesome Pine!"

"No way!"

"Yes, he did! He told K-Mart that if they keep their mouths shut, nobody will ever have a reason to come out and dig Harlan Parker up under that big tree. That it's the last place anyone would suspect he'd be buried. His exact words!"

Even though that's exactly what Pearl had sent Rowdy to Lonesome to find out, he never imagined Rowdy would hear something so quickly.

"You must be sure about this. We can't be wrong. Once we do this, there's no going back!"

"I'm as sure as the dimples on my baby's cheeks, Mr. Pearl!"

"I didn't know you had a baby, Rowdy."

"Wrong kind of baby, sir."

Friday 3:13 pm, October 13, 2017

That afternoon, Rowdy is in Wilt's office relaying what he'd heard at Lonesome Pine. In Wilt's mind, the information isn't enough to convict anyone, so an arrest is not yet an option. Everyone in town knows that Pearl and Braden aren't friends. And Granville seems a little too eager to put the cuffs on his former son-in-law. But it might enough for a search warrant.

The District Attorney and Wilt sit in Judge Renfro's chambers as he reads over the unsigned search warrant and Wilt's affidavit relaying the statements of two witnesses and detailing the Martin brother's antics near Parker's car.

Renfro is skeptical. "Has anyone been out there to even see if the ground's been disturbed around that tree?"

Wilt explains why that isn't so easy. "There's no way to walk out to the Lonesome Pine discretely, your honor. They have the tree under 24-hour video surveillance, complete with real time night vision video. The second we get anywhere near it, course security will alert Braden and Martin."

"Then just go play a round of golf out there and hit one under the tree."

"Don't currently have any officers, confidential informants or undercover operatives who are golfers, your honor, except the police chief, who refuses to do anything to put his free membership at risk."

"Oh, boy. Pathetic! Okay. I'll sign the warrant to allow you to search the entire property, the outside, that is. But if the ground isn't disturbed anywhere and especially around the Lonesome Pine, leave it be. That tree brings a lot of money into this community."

~

SATURDAY *8:15 AM, October 14, 2017*

The following morning, with backhoe and digging crew in tow, Wilt serves Braden and Kenny Martin with the search warrant. Other officers are dispatched throughout the course to look for overturned soil or patches of newly laid turf.

When Wilt tells him where they would start digging, you'd have thought Braden had gone into a seizure. "No! Not her. You can't disturb her root system. She'll never survive it! There's nothing out there but Lonesome!"

"Well, forgive me, Mr. Braden. I didn't know that Lonesome wore lipstick and rouge."

In a last gasp effort to save his beloved Lonesome, Braden kicks into a dead sprint down the 18th fairway, his arms driving back and forth with an upright posture as he runs past the backhoe headed for the Lonesome Pine.

Martin tries to explain his boss's bizarre behavior. "I know it looks crazy, Detective, but Lonesome is the longest and most stable relationship Brock's ever had. She's the one who never betrayed him."

Braden reaches Lonesome and drops down on his knees, just in front of the approaching, menacing machine. Acting as a human shield, he lies down spread eagle in front of the majestic white pine. Wilt motions to the operator to cut the engine and come down off the backhoe. Officers walking around the tree look to Wilt, turning their heads to indicate there was nothing to suggest anyone was buried nearby. Wilt then directs them to move on to the rest of the course.

Even if he doesn't find a body, he is still using the search warrant as an opportunity to get a statement from Braden.

"Mr. Braden. It doesn't have to be this way. I know how much the tree means to you, but we have a search warrant. You can save everyone a lot of time and trouble if you can just answer a few questions about your relationship with Harlan Parker."

Braden sits up and looks around to see the officers are walking away from the tree. Sensing that it is safe for now, he comes to his feet, brushing himself off.

"There is no relationship, detective. He's a lawyer." He hands Wilt a card. "Here. Sounds like you want to talk to mine. Dan Jack will be happy to set something up with you."

Wilt leaves Lonesome with nothing remarkable but at least he made Braden lawyer up, which probably means he's guilty of something far more serious than being a tree hugger.

Despite having swung at Braden and missed, Granville Pearl remains unwavering in his belief that he killed his lawyer, and he isn't shy about his disapproval of Wilt's decision not to dig around the Lonesome Pine for Parker's body. Pearl calls his buddy, Chief of Police Hank Justice to complain and try to get Wilt removed from the investigation. But he gets nowhere.

"Cool your jets, Granville. If anyone's going to nail the killer, it's Wilt. You're too emotionally wrapped up in this. You need to take a step back and let us handle it. Whether you want to admit it or not, there are hundreds of people in this town who wanted to see Parker in the ground! Renfro thinks Wilt is Elliot Ness reincarnated, and I'm not about to risk my job by removing my top investigator. Why in God's name would you want to remove Wilt? You're the only two guys in town who give a damn about what happened to Harlan Parker!"

11

THE WOMAN IN THE EL CAMINO

Monday 12:34 pm, October 16, 2017

Detective Wilt is at his desk going over paperwork as Andrews quickly taps on his door and walks into the office. He's carrying his laptop. Andrews has just finished his latest assignment, reviewing footage from a streetlight cam in Bluegrass Commons, Summerville's master planned community and the home of Ridley Barnes. He walks around the desk where Wilt is seated and places his laptop on the desk. Wilt moves over slightly to give his assistant more space.

"What ya got, Andrews?"

"I've been watching footage of the coming and goings in and out of Mr. Barnes' residence the evening of October 6th, and I think I've found something, a couple of things actually." Wilt rubs his hands together eagerly anticipating what his assistant has come across. "Okay, Let's have a look see."

Andrews punches several keys on the laptop as Wilt bends forward to see the video. Andrews continues. "I've watched this for several hours, and there's no visible activity around Barnes' residence from 5:30 Friday afternoon until just after 11:00, when this happens."

Wilt leans forward looking at the screen. A silver El Camino, early

1970s model, approaches the rear of Barnes's townhome as the door
to the carport opens. Wilt takes off his glasses, wipes them on his
shirt while keeping his eyes focused on the computer. He puts them
back on and pulls his chair closer to the screen. There's an object
several feet long that's lying in the open truck bed. Wilt leans in
closer still trying to make it out.

"What's that in the trunk?"

Andrews thinks he has the answer.

"A canvass bag with a zipper down the middle. Looks like a
Christmas tree storage bag or duffle bag. I've seen bags like that at
camping stores that contain tents?"

Wilt, who did two tours of duty in Vietnam, shakes his head in the
negative while keeping his eyes on the screen.

"I haven't been camping in about 30 years, but that doesn't look
like a tent to me. Looks more like a body bag. Did you run the plate?"

"The light pole cam doesn't get a clear shot of the license plate. I'll
have to freeze some shots of the rear of the vehicle and blow them up
to get a closer look. But keep watching for a few more seconds."

As the El Camino enters the townhome, the carport light turns on
revealing a woman in the passenger seat. Wilt stands.

"Christa Braden!"

Andrews nods his head in agreement. "Hold on. There's more."

He fast forwards the video twenty minutes. At 11:38 pm, the
carport door opens again, and another car backs out, a black Volvo
full size sedan. Andrews continues.

"The El Camino stays in the carport till a little after seven the next
morning when it pulls out of the carport, without the bag."

Wilt retakes his seat.

"Alright Andrews, what are you thinking?"

"The first question that comes to mind; is that bag still at Barnes'
residence? If it's just a tent of duffle bag, the answer should be, yes.
My second question is, why is Mrs. Braden at Barnes' residence the
same evening Parker disappears? Andrews turns his eyes away from
the laptop and toward Wilt. Did Barnes say that he and Ms. Braden
were—friends?"

"I never asked him. Nor did he volunteer it. But if Barnes is the driver, he's got some backtracking to do. He said he was in Louisville having drinks with a stranger at a steakhouse that evening."

Andrews picks up and closes his laptop tucking under his arm.

"I'd hardly call Mrs. Braden a stranger. But I also have a hard time believing that she would be involved in the disappearance of her divorce lawyer. She wants him around, at least until the divorce is over."

"Ordinarily I'd agree with you, but Parker's not going to be much help to Mrs. Braden, at least in any divorce settlement. It's not the first time I've investigated Braden. I handled the complaints from two of his other ex-wives. Braden has an air-tight prenup. Neither one of them got anything for their marital trouble with him. I doubt he's handled his marital affairs any differently with Christa Braden."

Andrews's eyes twinkle as the possibilities race through his mind.

"But Barnes stands to benefit considerably if Parker is out of the way, and if she's hooked up with Barnes—We should re-interview him!"

Wilt again nods in agreement, then picks up a notepad and writes something before handing it to Andrews.

"Agreed, but not before we get a blowup of that license plate for the El Camino and the Volvo, and here's the name of the place Barnes says he had dinner at the evening of October 6th. Contact the Louisville PD and get a hold of the light pole footage on Bardstown Road nearest to Jack Fry's steakhouse. Let's see if Mr. Barnes really was where he says he was."

12

CONSORTING WITH THE ENEMY

Within a couple of weeks after Parker's disappearance, Tori Stevens is preparing herself for the prospect of looking for another job. She knows that if she had the stuff to work for Harlan Parker, she could work for anyone. And she also knows she would have little trouble finding a job. In fact, two lawyers in town had contacted her with offers within days of Parker's disappearance. And why wouldn't they? Stevens presents exceptionally well, exhibiting all the qualities that any successful attorney would want from someone supporting them.

Her skill set is top tier. She could handle anything any lawyer could do and, in most cases far better. The only exception is she couldn't appear in court, but that is only because she doesn't have a law license yet. She is a crack legal researcher and writer and can handle any legal issue thrown at her no matter how complex. Stevens goes from knowing little to nothing about a topic to mastering it within a short time. Her work ethic is unsurpassed. She is used to handling multiple projects at once and frequently working long hours, even weekends, to get the job done. These traits made her seem totally devoted to Parker.

And she is fantastic with Parker's clients: keeping them up to speed on the status of their case, reassuring them, listening to them in long conversations and always making Parker look good.

> *I understand completely and I can promise you*
> *that Mr. Parker is giving your case top priority.*

Stevens is charming and knows just how to turn a phrase to say the perfect thing at precisely the right moment, coming off as sincere, thoughtful and kind. She has a gift for making others feel like they're special.

> *What's happened to you is so unfair. I don't know*
> *if I could have survived something like that.*
> *I know the future is uncertain, but it will reveal itself*
> *in a way you can accept and find peace. Stay*
> *strong and know that Harlan and I are with you.*

But she says those kinds of things even when she doesn't think someone is all that special, which is basically almost everyone she talks to, but no one would have ever picked up on it.

Tori Stevens is the poster child for proving that the only thing a strict upbringing does is raise a good liar.

For much of her childhood, Stevens never lived in the same place for more than a year or two, that is, until high school, when her father was hired to train Saddlebreds in the rolling hills of Shelby County, Kentucky. Alex and Janet Stevens raised their children in the belief that the Old Testament instills a strong work ethic and morals, a doctrine in which using the rod on your children was considered an act of love when they strayed from God's teachings.

The Stevens' oldest child was a frequent recipient of corporal punishment. The less freedom she was allotted, the more deceptive she became and the more severe the consequences. By her early teens she figured out the only way she was going to get what she wanted was by playing earnest and sincere, promising her parents she would walk the straight and narrow. And when her parents caught her straying, it just helped her refine the appearance of remorse and contrition, raising it to an art form and sometimes avoiding the rod altogether.

Although she graduated near the top of her 300-member high school class, Stevens didn't go to college. Her parents never went, and they didn't instill any expectations beyond finding a job after high school to begin fending for herself.

So, after graduation she went to work for a couple of law firms in nearby Louisville, first as a receptionist, then to support attorneys at the law firm of Cooper, Ryan and Lantham. Her immense abilities and strong work ethic quickly caught the eye of Greg Lantham, who plucked her away from a mid-level associate and made Stevens his own assistant. And while working for Lantham, Stevens had secretly sought out and obtained a job with Harlan Parker, and while her boss was litigating a case against him, no less.

April of 2012

Harlan Parker had represented the estate of Ron Thacker, a a 58 year-old pediatrician and former colon cancer patient at Archellian Healthcare. The complaint alleged that Archellian's treatment of Thacker was below the standard of care expected from an oncologist in the treatment of cancer. Allegedly, Thacker's colon cancer was detected at an early stage and should have been treatable. However, the oncologist administered a chemotherapy drug designed to treat a specific type of lung cancer which was widely recognized to be ineffective against colon cancer. As a result, Thacker's cancer metastasized causing his death. During litigation, Parker was frequently at Cooper, Ryan and Lantham (CRL), taking depositions of Archellian employees.

The litigation between the Parker and Lantham had been toxic, with each side doing their best to gain the advantage. No subversive or unscrupulous tactic was beneath either lawyer. And while Parker had grown accustomed to getting his way practicing against lawyers he routinely overmatched in central Kentucky, Archellian's corporate headquarters were in Louisville, so the lawsuit had to be filed in federal court there, where the competition is considerably tougher.

Add in that the judge presiding over the case, Wilson Branch, was a close law school friend of Lantham's law partner, John Cooper. While friendships between judges and lawyers are common in the legal community and rarely impact the outcome of a case, there's more than a grain of truth in the old lawyer axiom:

Good lawyers know the law; great lawyers know the judge.

It was a rare time where the deck was stacked against Parker.

In the early stages of the case, Parker would show up to take depositions, sitting opposite Lantham and his entourage, which included an associate and Tori Stevens. She'd bring meticulously organized file boxes full of pre-numbered, colored exhibits. At certain points in the deposition, Lantham only had to glance in Stevens' direction and she would hand an exhibit to the associate, who would quickly review it and pass it to Lantham, with the efficiency of a gold medal 4 x 100 relay team passing a baton at the Olympic games. In litigation such organization, particularly during a trial, is what separates the men from the boys. It's the gold standard that few lawyers attain and it's possible only with the best of the best supporting them.

Lantham was shutting Parker down at every turn: winning rulings from the court, denying Parker's motions to compel discovery, and preparing Archellian employees so well that Parker could establish next to nothing to prove his claim. Time was running out.

∾

MAY 1, 2013

It was a Monday morning after a Friday deposition at CRL when Parker received the unexpected email.

I hope you had a safe and pleasant
trip back to Summerville, Mr. Parker.
Tori Stevens

Parker sat at his desk looking at the message for a couple of minutes. He tried to come up with an explanation for how the message could be interpreted as something related to the case. But none came to mind.

Ms. Stevens was twenty years younger, and beautiful at that, and she was saying hello? A more risk-averse lawyer would simply not respond to a personal message from the assistant of the attorney they were litigating a case against. Most lawyers would respond with a quick thank you, just out of courtesy, and go no further. A few lawyers would inquire about the purpose of her email and quickly end the matter. And there's always some prude who would immediately contact her boss and tell them what just happened, resulting in a reprimand or termination of the assistant.

But Stevens had seen enough of herself in Harlan Parker to know he would do none of those things. And her instincts proved to be correct. Parker quickly evaluated the risk versus the reward. In his egocentric mind there was only one explanation for the email. And not being one to pass on such an opportunity, he responded immediately.

It was a very nice trip back to Summerville,
thank you, Ms. Stevens. I'd love to treat you
to lunch sometime and discuss it in more detail.

With five minutes, Tori Stevens got the response she'd expected and wasted no time accepting the invitation.

It would be entirely my pleasure, Mr. Parker.

Two days later, Stevens and Parker were standing next a hostess waiting to be seated at the Lovely Bean, a quaint café and coffee bar located in the building adjoining Parker's law firm. Stevens called in sick to make the 45-minute trip to Summerville.

After being led through the dining area and seated at a booth tucked in the back of the room, Stevens immediately got to the heart of the matter.

"Mr. Parker, I'm twenty-three years old and plan to be a lawyer one day. And I'm going to need the kind of flexibility and support that I'm not going to get at CRL. I've watched you closely in the case you have with your law firm, and I absolutely believe that we would be a perfect fit."

Though it wasn't what Parker expected, he had seen firsthand the work she did for Lantham and was still very interested.

"Well, I take it as a compliment you would be interested in working here, Ms. Stevens. What is it about our law practice that leads you to believe we would work well together?"

"Mr. Parker, you are clearly a highly skilled lawyer. Something that's obvious to anyone who knows anything about what lawyers do. But there have been times in my interaction with your staff when it has lacked a certain discipline and organization that I can provide. I saw the same thing in Mr. Lantham. In several respects, he was just like you. Someone who was already highly successful, who asked all the right questions and presented extremely well but was held back at times from presenting the best version of his own lawyer so to speak."

Though she frequently uses false modesty to get what she wants, this clearly wasn't the place for it. It was time for the Tori Stevens promotion campaign to kick into overdrive.

"I came in and completely reorganized his files, significantly upgraded his motion practice and gave his profile a polish and panache that took his litigation game to a new level. And I absolutely know I can do the same for you, if given the opportunity."

Parker couldn't help but be impressed with her confidence, and he had to admit to himself that Lantham's pretrial litigation game was as impressive as any he'd seen, but he wasn't looking to hire anyone. "I appreciate the perspective of someone with your background and obvious ability, Ms. Stevens. Please do tell me more."

Tori continued, "I'm talking about the perception people have of you, Mr. Parker. How you come across to the court and other lawyers in your pleadings. How you keep client relationships strong when you're in trial and they need to hear from you now. Relationships that will suffer if not given the proper attention. I'll make each one of your clients feel like they're your number one priority. It's something I take pride in. All these things and much more, and your practice would receive a considerable upgrade if I supported you, Mr. Parker."

This was the slippery slope Stevens had to negotiate if she was going to score a job offer from Harlan Parker. Convincing a narcissist there were flaws in his law practice significant enough to make substantial changes without offending him. It required the perfect blend of criticism, charm and nerve. She was keenly aware that Parker had never envisioned his professional image as being anything but the best of the best, including his staff.

"I have an assistant and two paralegals to keep track of everything I do now, Ms. Stevens. How are you going to come in and do the work of three people and do it better?"

Stevens wasn't fazed in the least. She'd prepared for the question the moment she decided she wanted to work for Parker.

"Don't take offense to what I'm about to say, Mr. Parker, but I've seen the work product your support staff has provided for you, and that's precisely why I took the chance to reach out to you. You wouldn't need anyone else but me to receive a significant upgrade in quality and professionalism."

As pleasant as the conversation had been to this point for Parker, his survival instincts began to creep in. Did Lantham send Stevens to set him up? Sending an attractive staff member to seduce, entrap and blackmail opposing counsel into a very favorable settlement was a card Parker had played more than once, and his reputation as a ladies' man with few boundaries wasn't lost on him, either. Parker thought it would be exactly the tactic he'd choose if he were Lantham.

"I don't doubt your abilities, Ms. Stevens, but even if everything you're saying is true, there's still the not so minor ethical dilemma of hiring you in the middle of a lawsuit I'm litigating against your firm.

If Mr. Lantham even knew we were speaking it would be a very unpleasant matter for both of us."

"How is anyone else going to know we met? Who's going to tell them? No one here even knows Lantham. Support people come and go like weather. It's, 'Hello, goodbye, next man up, and six months later it's, 'I need you to do it like what's her name. The day after I leave, nobody's going to care about where I've gone. I can easily make this work without anyone ever knowing."

Her response satisfied Parker, but he knew he had a lot more to lose if someone ever found out.

"Now, Ms. Stevens. When someone leaves there's always a missing file, a loose end, some detail they'll seek you out for. It's just too risky."

Both knew where the conversation was going. It was the unspoken reason Harlan Parker would want to hire her in the middle of litigation.

She had hoped she wouldn't have to mention it aloud to a lawyer as crooked as Harlan Parker. That it'd just be understood. For Parker, it was the only thing that could justify the risk, but he needed to hear her say it before he offered her the job. All the other reasons weren't enough. Stevens knew it, too.

"I can give you the Archellian case, Mr. Parker. I have access to records you've asked for in discovery that Lantham told you don't exist. And I know the names of the employees who altered records to cover up medical staff mistakes, including someone in medical records that Archellian moved out of state to keep you from ever finding. I know how to give you leverage to force them to cooperate with you. And finally, Mr. Parker, if you win anything close to the five million-dollar judgment you've been seeking, you stand personally to make well over a million. You don't impress me as a lawyer who would accept a contingency case for anything less than 49 percent."

13

THE GAME CHANGER

The following morning Tori was back at work at CRL's office, a three story, late 19th century Renaissance Revival residence modernized for commercial use in Old Louisville. She walked up one level from her workstation on an open flight of steps leading to Lantham's office to break the news. It was dubbed by associates as 'The bridge' in reference to where a captain is stationed to guide his vessel. The glass encased workspace overlooked the heart of the law office, an open atrium which housed the paralegal/secretarial station in its center and associates' offices lining the opposite wall.

In addition to being the most in-your-face manifestation of Lantham's professional assent, the bridge was one of the perks of holding the position of managing partner for a top tier law firm. It was also the envy of every lawyer who worked in the firm or had reason to be at the office. But as perfect as it was, nothing perfect lasts forever, and Lantham's days perched at the top were numbered.

He was sitting at his desk just ending a phone call with a client when Stevens approached. She tapped softly on the open door to his office before walking in.

"Greg, do you have a minute? There's something I need to speak to you about." Lantham nods at Tori and wraps up his phone call.

"Yes. Thanks. Goodbye. You, too." Lantham placed the phone down on the cradle and turned to face her. "Sure, Tori, what is it?"

"I've been offered a position with another firm that I've decided to accept."

Lantham, completely stunned, immediately stood up. He hadn't seen this coming.

"What? No. Please tell me you're joking! If it's more money you want, I'm sure we can work something out-"

Stevens cut him off before he tried offering her a huge raise that she would have to turn down.

"No. No. It's not that you haven't paid me very well. I've decided to go to college and then law school."

"Well, that's great! We could pay for your college and then your law school. I'm sure I can talk the other partners into doing something substantial."

Seeing that this wasn't going to be easy, Tori just stares at Lantham for a few seconds before letting out a big sigh.

"I've been accepted to Bellarmine for the summer semester. I've already cleped out of three full semesters of college and can get my bachelors in just over two years. It would mean that I can't work full-time here. The firm I'm going with is going to allow me to work twenty to twenty-five hours a week for a couple of years. Something I know you don't have the luxury to do."

Lantham immediately went into desperation mode. "We'd work through it! You'd be hired here as an associate immediately upon graduation and on the fast track to partnership. You're very well regarded here! Please reconsider, Tori!"

"That's not realistic, Greg. That's at least five years away, and we don't know who's going to be here making the decisions then. I know you mean every word of it, but I can't plan my life on something like that. I was hoping this would be something you'd be excited about for me."

There was a long silence. Lantham had only one arrow left.

"What about us, Tori? I thought this had developed into much more than a work relationship."

"Greg." Tori turns her head sightly, flashes a look of bemusement and walks around the desk close enough to touch Lantham. "You're married. We had our time. It was amazing. But life's about change and growing from that change. I know it's hard. It's just as difficult for me. Really. But what you're saying isn't realistic and you know it. This is what's best for my future and your family. That's another reason why I'm making a change now."

"Would it be inappropriate for me to ask who it is you're going to?"

"I'd rather not say at this point, Greg, if I ever tell you. Please don't be one of those guys that tries to follow along and diminish what we had. I'm asking you to respect my decision and let me go."

Seeing there was nothing he could do to change her mind, Lantham conceded. "I wasn't prepared for this, Tori. I'm not sure I could ever be. I'm not speaking professionally. But if this is what you want, then it's what I want for you. I wish you nothing but the best. Know I'm always a phone call away."

Stevens was now in her wheelhouse, where contriving sentimentality was child's play. Right on cue, she pulled a tissue out of the pocket in her blouse and began to dab her eyes, appearing to stop the rush of tears that were about to burst from them.

"I've learned so much from you, more than anyone, Greg. Know that I'll always appreciate everything you've done for me. And you never know what the future holds. It will reveal itself, in time."

Lantham stepped closer to Tori to give her a warm embrace.

The impact of Stevens' departure from Lantham to Parker was immediate and dramatic for both lawyers. At the next deposition it was Lantham who showed up thirty minutes late, out of sorts, unshaven and disorganized. This new version of Lantham, unkempt and scrambling as if her were a solo practitioner without any support whatsoever, would continue throughout the rest of the case and into the trial.

Parker used the information Stevens provided to win a $2.1

million jury verdict in the Thacker case and then quickly negotiate a healthy $1.8 million settlement to avoid a long and uncertain appeal. Archellian responded by dropping CRL. Lantham had repeatedly assured the client throughout the case that Thacker's lawsuit was under control; that it would certainly be dismissed or result in a defense verdict and billing them near $300,000 to defend the case in the process. With his promises not coming to pass, Lantham was sent packing within a couple of months for losing the firm's biggest client and over $500,000 a year in client billings.

∽

July 23, 2015

When Stevens went to work for Parker, it was a professional match made in lawyer heaven or hell, depending on which side you were on. She would soon prove herself to be a valuable addition in ways other than Archellian, such as in the trial of *Langley vs. Cross Medical Center*. The Plaintiff, Linda Langley, represented by Blue and Gray, sued her former employer for violation of her rights under the Age Discrimination Act. Cross was represented by Parker. Seated behind Parker throughout the trial was Tori Stevens.

Langley was a coder in her early 40s and had worked in the billing department for over twenty years when she had to take medical leave due to breast cancer surgery and chemotherapy, but she was discharged by Cross just before returning to work.

The hospital claimed that Langley wasn't discriminated against but simply a casualty of hospital downsizing, claiming the department she worked in had been consolidated with another, thereby eliminating her position. The hospital also alleged they offered another job in the hospital at comparable pay, which she declined to take. Langley said that the job was not comparable because it required her to work the graveyard shift every other week, was an hourly position as opposed to the salaried job she had held, and that her position was not eliminated but given to Jane Downs, a woman twenty years younger than Langley, saving the hospital $20,000 a year.

The most important piece of evidence in the case was a memo from Barb Swift, Cross's Chief Financial Officer where she directed the head of the billing department to transfer Downs into Langley's position while she was on leave. Just before Langley was scheduled to return to work, the departments were consolidated but it was Downs who continued to work in coding. Langley was informed her position had been eliminated. Gray had introduced the memo, marked as plaintiff's exhibit 6, through Swift, and like all other exhibits, was placed at the table next to the court reporter where it remained throughout the trial. As is the usual practice in any criminal or civil case, at the end of the proof, the judge directed each counsel to check and make sure all exhibits were accounted for before sending them back with the jury. It was a close facts case, but Blue and Gray felt exhibit 6 would get them over the finish line first.

While the court read the jury instructions on the law and how to consider the evidence, Savannah and Dan Jack went through all 27 exhibits, including exhibit 6, confirming that each one was accounted for and ready to go back to the jury. After the jury deliberated for two days the bailiff informed the judge that the jury had reached a verdict. Everyone in the courtroom stood as the jury filed back into the room.

Once the jury was in place, Wilson Branch went through his ritual. "Has the jury reached a verdict in this case?"

The foreman nodded affirmatively and handed the completed verdict form to the bailiff who walked up and handed it to jury. The parties, lawyers, and their clients stood, anxiously awaiting.

Judge Branch read, "In the case *Linda Langley vs. Cross Medical Center*, we find the jury in favor of the defendant."

Gray immediately walked over to Harlan Parker and shook hands, obviously disappointed and somewhat surprised. He then turned to Mrs. Langley. "I thought we had it, Linda. I don't know what the jury was thinking. I'm very sorry."

But Langley could not have been more appreciative. "No, Dan

Jack. You and Savannah did an amazing job. Yes, I'm very disappointed, but certainly not with you guys. Just having someone stand up for me and tell them what they did was wrong meant so much. More than you'll ever know."

For Dan Jack this one hurt more than most. Gray had taken the Langley's case on contingency and fronted $15,000 to fund the case, in addition to spending over 500 hours the previous two years getting the case to trial. If the jury had found for Langley, the firm stood to make between $200,000 and $25,000 from its share of a plaintiff's verdict and statutory attorney's fees, which Cross would have paid. The defense verdict meant Gray would eat the $15,000, and all the time they'd put in the case was for nothing. It was one thing for Dan Jack to lose; such is the life of a plaintiff's lawyer handling cases on a contingency.

But he wasn't just working for himself anymore. After Dan Jack and Savannah packed up their files and walked back to the office trying to persuade her to consider other options.

"Savannah, this isn't what I wanted for you. You have so many options that won't always be there. Mr. Oldfather is very impressed with your abilities. He's told me as much, several times. You'd make twice as much for him as you do here; business clients, health insurance, no jailhouse pre-trials."

"Dad, don't you even recall the one thing you told me all the times we drove past all those billboards with lawyers striking poses with their phone number? Or when we'd go to traffic court and see the same lawyers carrying around stacks of citations just to hold their clients' hands and plead them guilty without ever trying a case?"

Just because you make a lot of money and have a law license doesn't mean you're a lawyer, Savannah!

Savannah walks up to her father and stares at him so intensely he almost feels smoke coming off his eyebrows.

"If you were just trying to impress your teenage daughter with little witticisms, then shame on you because I believed every word of it! If I wanted to write letters to clients explaining their bill and then billing them for it why would I be working with you? I didn't come here to make a lot of money and look like a lawyer. I came back here to be a lawyer. We're not businessmen dressed like lawyers, Dad. We're trial lawyers! We lace 'em up, leave it all out on the floor and deal with it. Blue and Gray won't be defined by a verdict. Now get some sleep. We try the Morton case in six weeks."

That was the last time Dan Jack ever brought up the 'work somewhere else' thing to Savannah.

While Harlan Parker and Stevens were obviously pleased with the verdict, they were careful not to show it in front of Judge Branch, who was known to frown on courtroom touchdown dances and victory laps. They quickly walked across the street back to their office. By the time they returned, word of the verdict had already arrived. The two made a beeline to Parker's office as coworkers gave them atta boys and high fives for another win. Stevens entered first.

Parker closed the door behind them. He wanted to make sure nothing was left to chance. "Do you still have it?"

"But, of course." Stevens reached into her file folder and pulled out plaintiff's exhibit 6.

The jury had never seen it during deliberations. She gone to the table next to the court reporter just as Dan Jack and Savannah's backs were turned and pulled it. Because cameras and video recording are prohibited in federal court, and because Gray's client couldn't justify the expense of an uncertain appeal, it was unlikely anyone would ever figure it out.

Parker smirked. "Excellent, Tori. As usual, you can expect a very nice performance bonus." He glanced at the damning piece of paper and his eyes narrowed. "Now get rid of it."

Stevens walked over and fed the document into a shredder located just outside Parker's office. She turned back and smiled at him. "Thank you, Mr. Parker." What Parker didn't know was that Stevens was already paying herself bonuses from his business and personal accounts. Occasionally he told her to transfer money between accounts but never thought to check if she had. Why would he? Parker was so busy swindling everyone else he never suspected someone was doing it to him.

But it wasn't like she didn't earn it.

The piece of paper formally known as plaintiff's exhibit 6 slowly wriggled into the teeth of the machine.

THREE WEEKS before Harlan Parker's disappearance.

September 13, 2017

Even when it first opened 50 years ago, Scottish Acairs was a middling apartment complex in the heart of St. Mathews, a middle-class neighborhood in the Louisville suburbs. In the following decades, it was a good option for college students and young married couples who needed someplace to call home until they could afford something better, or for seniors living off their social security checks who could afford little else.

The property didn't age well, having been transferred from one real estate flipper to the next who rarely put money into it, other than paying for an occasional coat of paint or replacing what originally was mid-grade indoor carpet with economy indoor/outdoor carpet then, finally, mold, mildew and water-resistant outdoor matting; the latter being more of a product description than what actual carpet conditions were at the complex.

In the past twenty years, the building was converted to commercial use, though its residential neighborhood hadn't been zoned for it. Among its tenants are a tanning salon, an oriental relaxation parlor, a hookah lounge, tattoo shop and the Lantham Law Firm; a firm of one, that is.

There is no secretary, paralegal, or other attorneys you would expect to find in a real law firm. The receptionist is contracted offsite. Lantham uses an answering service based in Long Island, New York with specific instructions to answer the phone, Lantham Law Firm. The first few days, he called his number several times to make sure all the women at the call center correctly pronounced his name and the

name of the office. To Lantham, it's important to create the perception that there's a receptionist answering the phone at his law firm.
The New York dialect is charming to most people, and they rarely
pick up that it's just an answering service. Image is more important
than ever to Lantham, though it doesn't matter at all to the typical
client he's come to represent.

In instances where Lantham receives a call from a potential business client or well-heeled criminal defendant that would pay many
times over what he's typically paid now, he meets them at a coffee
shop or for lunch at a posh restaurant for the initial consultation,
saying that the office is being renovated or that he's in the process of
moving to another location. Those clients rarely call Greg Lantham
anymore.

To others for which first impressions do matter, the illusion that
Lantham's office is a law firm begins to evaporate the moment they
drive up and see the building's worn, dilapidated exterior. If they
don't immediately turn around and drive the other direction, they
proceed cautiously to park in the rear lot. They exit their vehicle and
negotiate around grass growing out of the cracks in the asphalt so
high and abundant, visitors to the complex will check themselves for
tics and bug bites upon returning home.

As they approach the back entrance, a black letter board with a
down arrow and the words 'Law Office Suite 102' directs them to an
outdoor stairwell which takes them to a floor below ground level.
Lantham found for it half price at the nearby hardware store. There is
no office directory, as tenant turnover is so frequent it would almost
require a full-time employee to maintain. It's the first evidence that
there's a law office in the building. Something that's an open question
until that moment. For some, it provides reassurance they haven't
inadvertently wandered off track to the wrong building; for others, it's
confirmation they've picked the wrong lawyer. At the bottom of the
stairwell, next to the rear entrance, there's another sign that says,
'Beware of Dog.' But no one takes it seriously, doubting any dog
would go to the trouble to guard the place.

By September of 2017, Lantham's halcyon days riding the wave of corporate clients were long gone. He was now scratching out a meager existence, relatively speaking, representing meth heads and wife beaters who he had to put on modest payment plans that they rarely followed through with past the first installment.

As depressing as it was, he was grateful for any business at all. There were more days than he would ever admit where no one walked through the door or called. Closing up shop and going home early wasn't an option. His wife would quickly realize that his fledgling practice was even worse than he was telling her. As long as he was at his office, at least he could say he was working on something.

So, he just sat there, hours on end, with nothing to do but think about how his life had plunged into street lawyer abyss. He replayed the Achillean Healthcare case over and over in his mind searching for a scenario where things would have turned out differently. But every time he put himself through the torment, he came to the same conclusion; his personal and professional trajectory turned sharply downward the moment Tori moved on, over four years ago.

But where did she go?

What was her life like now?

Did she ever feel the slightest regret about leaving him?

How would she respond to him if they had a chance encounter?

He clearly remembered the instructions she left about letting her go and not ever trying to contact her, and for four years he had respected her wishes. And where had it gotten him? What was the worst that could happened if he approached her now? She would tell him the exact thing she told him when she left. He decided he had nothing to lose now finding out now where she was and how her life had changed. If he located her, it didn't mean he was going to just walk up and say hello, at least not initially. If she appeared happy from a distance, then he could always turn around and never look back.

But what if she'd been struggling as much as he had? She might be thrilled to see him and embrace the chance to reconnect. The first place he'd search would be at Brandeis, the University of Louisville

Law School. Tori should be in her second or third year of law school by now, he surmised.

THURSDAY, *September 14, 2017*

The following morning, he drives over to campus and parks in the oval directly in front of the front entrance to the school and waited. At 11 am, as dozens of students leave classes going to their cars, he sees her, as beautiful as ever, walking to hers. It wasn't the kind you'd expect your typical law school student to drive, but a late model, Mercedes.

Lantham hadn't been so far removed from the high life to forget that such a ride went for no less than $50,000. *She must have married a doctor*, is his first thought. As she drives around the circle past him and out into to highway, the temptation to follow is just too great. He has nothing else to do, anyway.

Fifteen minutes later, he's still shadowing her as she crosses the county line headed south. An hour later, a feeling of nausea comes over him as she puts on her turn signal approaching the Summerville exit. When she arrives downtown and parks two blocks away from Summerville Square, he throws up in his car, which would have been concerning if the upholstery didn't smell like stale food to begin with.

He hadn't been back to Summerville since taking depositions at that law office, but he remembers exactly where it is, and even if he hadn't, it wouldn't be a problem because she is walking straight for it. By the time she opened the front door of the building, the mystery of why she was so insistent for him never to follow her was solved, and the quandary of the luxury sedan unraveled as well.

It all fit together so perfectly. He thought if he only had an assault rifle, Summerville would be on the national news that evening as the scene of America's most recent mass shooting. He would have followed Tori into the law office and killed her the moment she entered the lobby, then walked casually to Parker's office shooting everyone he saw along the way before finally doing Parker in.

But he didn't own a gun or even have access to one, so he roamed the town square and waited for her. It was a good thing, he feels. It will give him time to cool down and think about how he was going to handle it. He didn't want to rush in and shoot everyone only to then be picked off by some SWAT marksman, anyway.

Four hours later, Summerville Square is teaming with members of the Garden Party. It's a third political party styling itself as a centrist alternative to the Republican and Democratic parties which gardeners claim are out of touch with most Americans. In less than ten years, it has gone from a fledgling third party laughing stock to legitimate contender for state wide and federal office. Gardeners await the arrival of their candidate, John Nathan McNamara, Mayor of Summerville and founder of the Garden Party, to announce his candidacy for the U.S. Senate.

McNamara says the only requirements to be a member are to wear a sundress or Bermuda shorts to party gatherings and to imbibe Kentucky bourbon in moderation. At the heart of Summerville Square is a green space approximately and acre in size where a makeshift stage has been assembled for the occasion. A banner spanning its width hangs overhead, which reads:

WELCOME TO THE GARDEN PARTY. AMERICA IS YOUR GARDEN!

Upbeat elevator music blasts through loudspeakers as gardeners chant for their candidate to come out on stage.

Run Mac run!
Run Mac run!
Time to weed the garden!
Run Mac run!

There's an unpleasant surprise waiting for Tori Stevens as she walks out of her office to go home for the day, Greg Lantham leaning up against the driver side door of her Mercedes. He's calmed down considerably and feeling kind of cheeky.

"Very nice car you have here, Tori. Harlan must be paying you a lot better than I did. You should have told me."

"Greg, what are—it's so nice to see you again."

Lantham was the last person she expected to run into, but she gathers herself quickly and goes into her first gear, kiss up, sweetheart mode.

"How are Debbie and the kids? I've thought of you so often over the last couple of years, Greg. How's everyone at CRL?"

"I wouldn't know, Tori. They cut me loose after I lost the Archellian trial. But you wouldn't have known that because you left midway through that case. And now we both know why you didn't tell anyone where you were going."

The cheers in Summerville Square grow louder as McNamara walks on stage, but to Stevens and Lantham, they might as well be a thousand miles away.

"It was—some firm in Elizabethtown, if I remember, wasn't it?"

Tori's' tone immediately switches from lighthearted to scorched earth. "Well, you finally figured it out, and far faster than I gave you credit for, Greg. Is it my fault you can't support yourself after getting kicked off the corporate gravy train?"

In his four years supervising her, Lantham had never seen this version of Tori Stevens, or anything close. It's as if the fangs and claws are growing out of her mouth and hands right in front of him.

And she isn't done driving it in.

"You've got to be kidding. You followed me down here from Louisville? So, what's little Greggie going to do about it? Drive down to Summerville and make Tori cry? I've gotta a better idea. Why don't you get a life instead of snooping around like some pervo-creeper! You think you're still talking to that teenager that jumped every time you clapped those smallish hands of yours?"

Lantham's face turns beet red. His jaw twitches from the tension in his facial muscles as the hair on the back of his neck stands up. But he's prepared a comeback.

"Next summer, I'm sure the Bar's ethical fitness review committee won't hesitate to give you their stamp of approval and allow you to be sworn in as a lawyer after my narrative detailing how you went to work for a lawyer your boss was litigating against. Looks like Tori's going to be the most overqualified paralegal in Kentucky, the one with a law degree and who even passed the Bar, but just never could quite get that law license. Such a shame. She came so close. She had it all. She would have had an amazing legal career, that is, if she wasn't an ethical Chernobyl. But no need to worry, Tori. You can still prepare trial binders and rot in the file room the rest of your life!"

Tori decides it's time to end it.

"Well, I see you've finally upgraded your research skills, Greg. I remember so much about our time together. All the flowers you bought for me, the bottles of bubbly you had delivered to our room at all those five-star hotels. San Francisco, Chicago, New York. It's a shame Debbie missed out on all the fun. But, then again, three always was a crowd for you, wasn't it! How's Debbie doing? I'd absolutely love to catch up with her." Tori pulled her phone out of her purse. "Let's see. Still have her number, in fact."

Lantham doesn't react, other than staring at her for a several seconds, trying to think of a comeback. The only thing he had left since his steady unsensational professional decline was his marriage, and Stevens somehow instinctively knew it. As furious as he was, a calm suddenly comes over him. This isn't the place to get payback, at least not the kind that had the indelible impact he wanted, he thought.

No, there's a better way to do this.

He turns and walks away.

14

THE JOYS OF LANDSCAPING

T *hursday 1:15 am, October 19, 2017*

Wilt and Andrews are on a stakeout sitting in an unmarked police car a couple of hundred feet from Ridley Barnes' townhouse in Bluegrass Commons. The resolution on the blown-up photo of the El Camino plate isn't clear enough to see the license plate number, so Andrews has binoculars in hand, ready to get it as the El Camino enters or leaves the carport.

Wilt is the first to see the vehicle as it turns into the alley heading to the carport of Barnes' residence.

"There it is, Andrews! Give me a read out."

Andrews looks through the binoculars as the door to the carport opens. Wilt has a laptop containing federal, state and local criminal databases and license plate registration data and he's ready to input the plate number.

"Kentucky plate. RTN 327."

It comes back to Ridley Barnes' 29-year-old son, Colin. The photo in the police database confirms it's Colin that's just entered the home. He has a modest rap sheet, a 2010 conviction for public intoxication and 2011 convictions for possession of marijuana and paraphernalia in nearby Bowling Green, during his abbreviated college days at Western Kentucky University.

It's time for an impromptu interview.

Andrews and Wilt pull around to the front of the townhome, approach the front of the residence and ring the bell. Within a few seconds, Colin opens the door. He's got a three-day old beard, a deep dark tan, shoulder length sandy blonde hair and tattoos of black flames jetting out on each bicep which look like they've spent a lot of time at the gym. Just like the rest of him. Andrews takes the lead.

"Good afternoon, Mr. Barnes. Wes Andrews of Summerville PD. This is my partner, Detective Marshal Wilt. We'd like a few minutes of your time, if you're available."

As the detectives intended, Colin is caught completely off guard. "Well, what you want to talk about? I haven't been doing anything but weed for at least five years, and that's t-totally copacetic in Crawford, man!"

Andrews doesn't want to spook Barnes to the point of getting shut down before he asked a question, so he initially avoids mentioning Harlan Parker.

"No. Nothing like that, Mr. Barnes. We're here to ask you some questions about Christa Braden. We understand the two of you are friends. May we come in? Shouldn't take more than a few minutes."

Colin stands at the door without expression for a few seconds, then shrugs his shoulders with a bemused expression on his face. "Sure dude. If that's all you need, come on in."

Andrews and Wilt look at each other curiously as they follow Colin into the kitchen and take a seat at the dinner table. Colin pulls his chair up to the table still uneasy about the purpose of the meeting. He looks directly at Andrews.

"You're not seeing Christa or nothing like that, are you, bro? Cause, if you are, she definitely didn't tune me in to that scenario!"

"No, I'm not seeing Mrs. Braden. How did you meet her?"

Colin scratches his chin, thinking about his answer. "Well, it's a little personal, man. Why do you need to know about me a Christa?" Andrews looks over at Wilt and returns his eyes to Barnes. "It could be very helpful to her, Mr. Barnes. That's all we're at liberty to say right now." Although it wasn't true, Wilt is impressed his assistant is beginning to understand that sometimes the police must engage in a little deception to develop information. He nods to reassure Colin that Andrews' little lie is true.

Colin suddenly looks concerned. "Is Christa alright? No one has done anything to her, have they? I know her old man put his hands on her a couple of weeks ago?"

Andrews tries to reassure him. "Christa's perfectly fine. How did the two of you meet?"

Colin exhales slowly.

"Okay, had me a little torqued up there for a second. Well, Okay then. Here goes. I work for Summerville Landscaping. One of my jobs is to transport mulch to our customers. I use my El Camino. The first time I delivered to Christa was a couple of years ago. She just loved the way I spread out her mulch, man. Never seen anyone love my mulching as much as Christa. After my first delivery, she just kept ordering it. Got to the point where there was no place else to put it. Didn't matter. We actually ran out of Cypress Bark, then ran through the stash of wood chips and finally had to go with pea gravel. The orders kept coming, almost every week there for a while. Then her old man got wind of it and stopped paying for it. So that was the end of that."

Though Andrews wasn't picking up on what Colin was trying to say, the translation was no problem for Wilt.

"Okay, Mr. Barnes. There was obviously an interest between the two of you other than landscaping. Why did you have to keep bringing her mulch to see her?"

Colin smiles and shrugs his shoulders again. "What can I say? I had to justify my trips to her house to get to see her. She didn't have a problem buying it and I sure didn't have a problem delivering it. You don't choose passion, man. Passion chooses you!"

Colin starts to chuckle as he looks down and shakes his head. "Back at the store the guys called me a mulching legend!" He then catches himself and continues.

"Christa's a very nice lady and we enjoy each other's company now and again. She calls me occasionally, usually when she has a bad break up with one of her boyfriends. She wants to go camping. We've done it three times now, in fact. She's very outdoorsy."

Wilt shakes his head with a look of disgust on his face. "How can Mrs. Braden have boyfriends if she's married? And if you're not a boyfriend, then what are you, Mr. Barnes?"

"Christa's the kind of woman who expects to and has both. Nobody said life was fair, dude. As for me, I'm just her campground rebound. That's what she calls me, anyway. But don't feel sorry for me. It's no consolation prize, if you get my drift!" Wilt cracks a forced smile and continues. "When was the last time the two of you went rebounding, Mr. Barnes?"

"A couple of weeks ago. She was planning to run off with some golfer and he broke things off with her. She was really upset when she called me. Of course, I wasn't about to say no. I mean, have you ever seen Christa's snow-day, school-closing segments?" Andrews pipes in. "Yes, I certainly have, Mr. Barnes."

Colin looks at Andrews as if their mutual interest in Christa is a bonding experience. "Then you understand that missing school was only the second-best thing about snow days in these parts, man!" Andrews nods enthusiastically. Seeing that his partner has completely lost his focus, Wilt continues the questioning.

"Where did the two of you go, Mr. Barnes?"

"We spent Thursday night up at Red River Gorge. Got back late Friday night. That's the last time I've seen her."

"Do you know anything about Harlan Parker's disappearance, Mr. Barnes?"

"Just that my dad's real worked up over it, worried they're going to have to shut down the law office."

Colin then took the detectives to the garage and showed them his camping gear, which included the long canvass bag in the bed of his El Camino on October 6th. Investigators would also confirm Barnes' travel to Red River Gorge the evening of October 5th and day of October 6th through gas purchases made on his credit card. The plate on the Volvo came back to Christa and neighbors would confirm that Ridley Barnes was indeed at home doing yard work Saturday and Sunday.

FRIDAY 10:38 AM, October 20, 2017

Wilt is in the office Summerville Chief of Police, Hank Justice briefing him on the Parker investigation when his cell rings and he answers. It's Tori Stevens.

"Detective. I've thought of something that may be important, but I'd feel more comfortable discussing it in person. It would be more discrete if you came to me and made it seem like more routine questioning. Would you do that for me?"

"Absolutely," Wilt agrees. He and Andrews are at Tori's office in fifteen minutes. Stevens pauses for a few moments, tapping the side of her check, looking down, then back at Wilt before continuing. "It's a bit uncomfortable to talk about."

"I understand, Ms. Stevens. I get that a lot in my line of work. I'm not here to make you uncomfortable. Any information at all at this point is helpful."

"But I could be wrong."

"Let's not worry about that," Wilt says, turning on the gentle charm very few people see. But he demonstrates to Andrews that it's important for a detective to have the ability to have more than one gear when interviewing a witness.

"Well, before I came to work for Harlan, I worked for another lawyer at a law firm in Louisville, Cooper, Ryan and Lantham."

Andrews is impressed. "I'm aware of them. Pretty big outfit."

"Yes, I left them to work with Harlan about four years ago. It got to be personally unpleasant. My boss, a lawyer I worked for there, Greg Lantham was acting inappropriately toward me. At first it was an isolated remark, a comment on how nice I looked that day, something a woman would appreciate hearing, at first anyway. Then came the texts. Pretty explicit ones. I still have them."

Wilt frowns at the seriousness of this revelation. "Did you come to work here because you were sexually harassed, Ms. Stevens?"

"Yes, but that's only part of it. Mr. Lantham was also litigating a case against Harlan when I left. I was suffocating, not knowing how to handle the situation. I knew I wouldn't get anywhere going to the other partners. They were all in the same club, if you know what I mean. Harlan had an opening and I needed a lifeline. But I didn't say where I was going. I told them I was going to law school."

Wilt is soothing. "Okay. That's probably not the first time something like that's happened in your line of work." Personal opinion of her aside, she has his full attention. He wants Tori Stevens to keep talking.

"I'm sure. But Mr. Lantham lost the case. It was a fairly substantial client, and as a result the firm lost the client. The firm let Mr. Lantham go. Apparently, he's struggled quite a bit since the termination. I didn't know anything about it until about a month ago."

"Has Mr. Lantham threatened Mr. Parker?"

"More than once. He feels that Harlan hiring me was the reason his career tanked. A few weeks ago, he actually waited at my car for several hours, to confront me when I left work. Told me that payback was coming. That I would have to find a new employer soon. He may have been just venting. But that threat is the most recent, so it stands out more than the rest."

"Thank you for telling us," Andrews says with sincerity. Wilt makes a mental note to himself to talk to Andrews on how and when to project sincerity to maximize opportunities in an interview setting. Under the right circumstances, it's a valuable investigative tool.

Friday 1:30 pm, October 20, 2017

As word of Parker's disappearance travels between the Bar and judiciary throughout the state, it eventually finds its way to Donald Norton, chief legal reporter for the Courier Journal, Kentucky's only statewide newspaper. To Norton, Parker's disappearance is both significant news and a bad break professionally. He'd covered several of Parker's trials in state or federal court and had been a frequent beneficiary of confidential tidbits via Parker that other lawyers would be hesitant or refuse to talk about. Tips are critical for any investigative reporter who wants anyone to read their stories. In return, Norton would give Parker publicity whenever possible, putting his photo on the front page when he handled a high-profile case and quoting him at every opportunity.

Norton had covered hundreds of cases, but Archellian distinguished itself in his mind because of the trial within the trial that was Lantham vs. Parker. He jokingly dubbed it as the *Thriller in Louvilla* because of the epic clash between the two lawyers. It was the only trial he could remember where U.S. District Judge Wilson Branch lost control of his courtroom, and the antics of counsel and their personality conflict became more compelling than the case.

The week after the disappearance of Harlan Parker, Norton overhears a couple of lawyers talking about it in the county courthouse. He begins compiling a list of suspects and Greg Lantham is at the top. Like everyone else in Louisville, Norton is aware of Lantham's dramatic reversal of fortune just after the Archellian trial, recalling the scuttlebutt at the time was that the former was caused by the latter. He immediately drops all his other stories and hit the beat to unearth the mystery. Job one is paying an unannounced visit to the Lantham Law Firm.

As Norton enters Suite 102, he can hear yelling coming from Lantham's office. "It was $1,500 cash, Ricky. Not a $1,000 check. I already cut you a break charging you $500 less up front, but you had to bring me old man cash to get the deal! A deal is a deal, and when I cut somebody a break on a fee, I better get paid. There's not enough money in your account to wipe my big white butt with this!"

"That sounds like a threat, Lantham."

"You obviously don't understand the dynamic going on here, boy. You were caught with three grams of meth with a Ruger under your seat. The conceal and carry permit doesn't mean jack to that prosecutor if I'm not your lawyer. Then it's seven years at the Big Edward!"

"Who you calling a boy? Say it again and I'm gonna punk you up, chump! I'm not going to no state pen! I have a permit for that gun!"

"I'm out. Get out of my office. Now! I do enough pro bono work representing bums like you! Out!"

The client busts out Lantham's door and storms past Norton. Lantham follows him into the lobby and just catches the front door of the suite to keep it from slamming against the wall before sticking his head out into the hallway yelling as the client leaves the building. "Don't forget to write me from the Big Edward!"

Lantham turns to see Norton. "What's going on, Nort? Did you ever hear of calling a guy in advance?"

"Sorry, Greg. Your office is quite—rustic. Your clients must feel very at home. here."

Lantham didn't find Norton's humor amusing but responded in kind.

"It's important to decorate to your client base, Nort! Let me guess. You were in the neighborhood for some hookah and a table shower and decided to stop in and say hello."

"Ha. Good one, Greg! Actually, I've included you in with a select few attorneys in the state on a series piece I've been working on, focusing on those who represent clients at both ends of the spectrum. Not only the high-end corporate stuff but those with little means who oftentimes find themselves on the short end of the justice system. It's going to be called, *From the Boardroom to the Cellblock, Elite lawyers with the Common Touch*. I thought you'd be perfect for it given your background. That is, with your approval of course."

Norton knew the only way he could get Lantham to discuss Harlan Parker was to schmooze him with the idea of some flattering publicity. And Lantham jumped at the false opportunity.

"Then I'm your guy, Nort! I'm a man of the people now. I've got some time this afternoon if you'd like?"

The two retreated to Lantham's office where Lantham waxed on about how he had lost sight, albeit however briefly, of what was really important only to rediscover the virtue of service to others. After several minutes it was time for Nort to transition to the true purpose of his visit.

"You know, Harlan Parker could be another lawyer that could be included in this piece if his motivation wasn't completely different from yours, that is." Did you hear that he's been missing?"

Lantham stares at Norton curiously for a few moments, turning his head and squinting his eyes. "Parker's connections really don't confide in me so much anymore, but I don't guess you've heard that." He smiles sarcastically.

Not to be deterred, Norton tries again. "Have you heard anything about what happened?"

"I'm sure nothing you haven't already heard, Nort. You're the investigative reporter. Tell me something good!"

"Well, since you're down there quite a bit I thought you'd heard something."

"Where did you hear that from?"

"You know I can't reveal my sources, Greg. Sorry."

"Didn't realize I was so important that my being in Summerville is the kind of information that would prompt you to protect a source, Nort."

"The failure to recognize sarcasm could be a sign of early onset, Greg. You should get yourself tested."

"Give it up, Nort! Who told you?"

"I've got an old college buddy that sells real estate in Crawford County. Says you've been down there looking to buy a home."

Lantham again pauses for several seconds.

Norton continues. "You know I keep my ears to the ground and pick up all kinds of things, Greg. Is it true? Are you moving to Summerville?"

"Well..." Lantham coughs. "Yes. So what? I've been planning on moving the family there for well over a year now. What's not to like? Such a charming little town. Has a killer golf course, great restaurants, an amusement park for the boys, and the wife is actually a graduate of Summerville College. She's been pushing me to do it for years, and you can get twice the house there for the same money."

"And there's also a sudden demand for a lawyer who practices criminal defense and commercial litigation."

"Ha. You ought to perform on late night TV, Nort. The truth is that move is a wash professionally. In fact, I'm probably going to lose money moving down there. But I'm sure you wouldn't reveal a confidential source." Lantham smiles. "Anyway, how are you so sure Parker's not still alive? They haven't found a body. For all we know he could have taken a friend to Europe for a few weeks or become a preacher."

"You seem pretty upbeat about the deal. Harlan being gone, I mean."

"Why should I be getting all teary eyed, Nort? I had one case with the guy. Harlan Parker's no different than any other lawyer I've gone up against. You play hard, shake hands and move on. Haven't had contact with that guy or anyone else in that firm for almost four years."

"Well, if you hear anything interesting, let me know."

"It's a two-way street, Nort."

15

CLIENTS WITHOUT LAWYERS

A couple of weeks after Parker's missing person case opens, PB&J's rivals are making door calls to court lucrative prospects suddenly back in play like girl scouts peddling samoas and chocolate thin mint cookies. Other firms come from out of town for meet and greets and power lunches. In the practice of law, when a lawyer with substantial business clients suddenly dies or is even presumed dead, good things usually do not come to who those who wait for a phone call. Those sitting at the top rung are not sitting at all, but instead exhibiting good form on the outside while secretly knifing their rivals to garner the cream of the crop.

Criminal cases which would likely have landed with Parker and quickly doled out to his minions for a kickback find their way to Dan Jack Gray and a half dozen other criminal lawyers in town. As for Parker's business clients, the vandals arrive at the gate almost immediately. Those that aren't snatched up by Oldfather and Young are being actively solicited by firms in Louisville and Lexington. But most clients who'd paid Parker a healthy retainer in advance didn't have enough money to hire another lawyer.

For generations, Summerville Square has been the local epicenter for celebrating America's greatest victories and witness to its greatest struggles. It was a place that represented the living embodiment of the First Amendment, where the oppressed and powerless marched and spoke truth to power. In the 1940s, thousands of residents filled the center of town on V-E Day to celebrate the Allied victory over Hitler's Germany in Europe, and they did the same on V-J Day for the victory over Japan.

In the 1950s coal miners marched on strike, protesting their paltry pay and abhorrent working conditions. In 1960, students of Summerville College came in droves to see John F. Kennedy and to returned later the same decade to protest the Vietnam war.

In 1970, parents of African American parents gathered on the square to protest the school board's refusal to integrate Summerville's public schools despite the Supreme Court having ordered it two decades before in *Brown v. Board of Education*. But they were met with an angry white mob armed with bricks, baseball bats and tire irons in a scene that turned violent. But bringing bricks to the altercation proved to be a bad idea for the white mob, who bore the worst of it by far, as their intended targets turned out to be far better throwers. It had never occurred to them that the bricks could be picked up and thrown back at them. The Governor would eventually call up the National Guard to restore order.

∿

November 2017

Within a few weeks after Parker's disappearance, it's assumed all over the Crawford County he's dead, and Summerville Square teeming again with another epic protest. But this time the marchers aren't railing against the government, greedy coal barons or racial injustice. They are clients who'd paid Harlan Parker huge retainer fee. Now they are out of money and don't have a lawyer to finish the job.

And there are scores of them.

And they want their money back.

Parker was not only the most popular criminal lawyer in town, he

was also Summerville's most prolific divorce lawyer. He only represented women who were looking to take what wealth was left of their
well-heeled, no good, cheating husbands. There are over two dozen
active divorce cases pending in family court with Harlan Parker listed
as legal counsel. In every case, he had been paid retainers from
$5,000 to $20,000. The same is true of Parker's 32 active criminal
clients, except the retainer could be as much as $250,000, which was
what Parker charged for complex white-collar criminal cases. The
amount of money which had been paid to Parker by clients with
active cases that had yet to be earned exceeded $1.2 million.

And PB&J can't come close to paying them back.

And they didn't even try.

When criminal lawyers are paid a retainer, there's typically an
agreement saying that it's non-refundable, that is, unless the lawyer
terminates the relationship. And if a lawyer dies in the middle of a
case, the client could at least file a claim against the lawyer's estate.
But no one could prove that Parker was dead.

So, Ridley Barnes and Jeffries's response to Parker's clients was
they were out of luck, claiming that the engagement letters were only
with Parker and not the firm. Then the clients went to the Kentucky
Bar Association but got the same answer. They wrote the judges in
their cases begging them to help. In criminal cases, the court offers
the services of a public defender, not an acceptable alternative to
clients with expectations of ones who had paid the kind of money to
Parker. And with clients languishing in civil cases, courts had nothing
to offer them. So, they called PB&J nonstop. But for a law firm,
screening phone calls was business as usual. PB&J developed a
system to immediately patch numbers of Parker's clients to voicemail
for a message that would never be listened to.

It didn't take long for clients to figure out PB&J was ignoring
them, so some took matters into their own hands and went to the law
firm demanding their money back. Terry Horn, union rep for electri-
cians 123, is the self-appointed spokesperson for the band of brothers.
"I've got this, guys. I've negotiated collective bargaining agreements
with management and lawyers, and I know the lay of the land."

The others agree to follow Horn's lead as they ride up the elevator to PB&J's lobby. They think showing up in numbers and calmly appealing to the firm's sense of fairness might work. Twenty of them exit the elevator into the second-floor lobby and approach the receptionist, asking for Ridley Barnes. The junior partner strolls down the hallway, in no hurry to walk into the hornet's nest. The temperature in the room begins to rise as the hoard watches Barnes stop to talk to another lawyer for a couple of minutes and then again with a paralegal.

Several minutes later he finally reaches the lobby. Wearing a tweed sport coat and pastel bow tie, Barnes directs the group into a nearby conference room. "I believe I know the purpose of your coming here and rest assured that we're prepared to finish the job for each one of you."

Translation: You aren't getting your money back.

Horn is a working-class stiff who'd never worn a tie or button-down shirt in his life. Images begin to flash through his mind of Barnes at the checkout counter of the Preppy Peacock, the clothing store down the street where he'd seen lawyers buy their fancy courtroom clothes. In Horn's daymare, Barnes is spending his retainer on lime-colored jackets and sissy pink ties with blue ducks on them.

And the thought screams within him: *There ain't no such thing as a blue duck!*

At which point whatever cool, deft, savvy negotiating acumen Horn possesses immediately liquefies into a molten rage. "We want our damn money back, Ridley Barnes, and we're going to get it back the easy way or a very unpleasant way. That is, for you guys!"

Standing behind Horn was Stan Kramer, who takes the conversation to the next level. Stan paid Parker $10,000 to defend him on a federal moonshine charge. "Dang straight, you sorry slime ball! Pay us back now, or I'm gonna pull those man diapers over yo bald haid where you've tacked on what looks like it was ripped off coon's butt. Then I'm gonna slam you to the ground and roll you down the square like a barrel of Kentucky firewater!"

It is now clear to Barnes that blowing off Parker's clients wasn't the best strategy. "Now gentlemen, I completely get it. I really do. That's why I'm extending to each of you the opportunity to have someone else in the office handle your matter, with no additional charge. It will be a win-win for all concerned!"

But Clyde Carter, under indictment on child porn charges, isn't impressed. "I've seen every one of you guys in court and none of you could try your way out of a speeding ticket. Harlan was the only stud among the lot, and he's gone, gone, gone and you've got our money!"

Barnes continues in vain to explain. "I'm sorry, but that just isn't how things work around here. Harlan pocketed all his fees and the rest of us are on our own except for what he referred to us. He owes us money too, his share of the rent and paying support staff and a lot of other things. If we don't panic and stick together, we can get through this!"

Jess Jones had paid Parker his last penny to represent him on an assault charge from a bar fight, and he has no sympathy for Barnes. "Oh, I get it now. So that's why you say on the front of your building that you're Parker, Barnes and Jeffries, giving us the impression that you're all together as one big law firm, but when it comes down to

nut cutting time, you're nothing but a bunch of street lawyers sharing secretaries and splitting rent. Well, there's another name for that and it's called fraud!"

Earl Wathen is out $25,000 and still facing federal gun charges and didn't like the idea of paying that much money only to end up with a public defender. "Pity the lawyer who ignores the plea of a desperate man, Ridley Barnes. We will be trifled with no longer. Just because I'm not supposed to carry heat doesn't mean I don't. Country boy will survive!"

In the end, PB&J's purse strings would not be pulled because there were none.

But still, the answer isn't good enough for George Handlon. He isn't just going to take it and crawl away. He has another idea. He goes the courthouse and gets a printout of Parker's active cases and then proceeds to track down every one of Parker's clients. Herb organizes. He goes online to social media and discovers he's not the only one.

Women who paid retainers who are now stuck in divorce court without a lawyer had formed a website called, *Aspiring Divorcées in Waiting* which posts online discussions attempting to problem solve and provide emotional support. Handlon joins forces with them and they take things to another level.

They begin to host meetings and encounter groups at George's house where Parker's clients would share stories of getting screwed out of their money, some tens of thousands of dollars and more. Some had mortgaged their homes to pay Parker's fee, all but being assured they would not only get it back but back several times over. Some cashed out their retirement accounts to pay Parker's fees. Some used their children's college funds, Christmas fund or law mowing savings, but all for naught. They are stuck in the middle of litigation without a lawyer and without the means to hire another one. They form lifelong bonds of friendship and support to help them get through the ordeal. But George Handlon isn't there for friendship. His mission is to shut PB&J down and erase them from the central Kentucky legal map.

The plight of Parker's clients would not be in vain but prove to be the inspiration for what would grow to a national movement, Clients Without Lawyers. Sort of like Doctors without Borders but not in a good way. Clients Without Lawyers would lobby the Kentucky Bar Association and the Kentucky State Legislature to create a fund to aid clients who still had a case but no longer a lawyer, paid for through fines and penalties of lawyers suspended for not serving their clients in all the usual ways. In a very short time, each state would form its own chapter.

And membership numbers explode when the New Jersey chapter expands membership to include people in litigation who have crummy lawyers, inept or lazy ones who never returned phone calls or conferred with them before resolving their claims. Why just limit the group to clients whose lawyers were physically missing when millions of people were just as bad off with the lawyers still around but missing in action? Louisville was the first city to host CWL's national convention where a client bill of rights was estab-

lished, outlining the sacred tenants of the attorney-client relationship.

- Article One: An attorney shall always return their client's
  phone calls.
- Article two: An attorney does not ask for a continuance
  without consulting their client and getting written
  approval.
- Article Three: An attorney shall not covet their client's
  escrow money.
- Article Four: An attorney shall always refund unused
  retainers within 30 days of conclusion of attorney-client
  relationship.
- Article Five: A lawyer shall not charge a contingency fee in
  excess of twenty percent of recovery.

Law Schools begin teaching law students how to deal with the
angry client who enlisted CWL to go after them. A separate cause of
action developed in the US Court of Appeals for the Ninth Circuit
called, negligent infliction of emotional distress by an attorney.
Cottage industries develop not only for mental health counseling for
despondent clients but also for weary attorneys caught in their
crosshairs. CWL membership would eventually grow to over twenty
thousand and would serve as the impetus of reform in America's legal
system, finally holding arrogant and unresponsive lawyers account-
able to their clients.

And it all started with the disappearance of Harlan Parker.

By the second week of November, Handlon organizes a picket line
on Summerville Square that exceeds 500 people, including Parker's
forlorn clients and family of those clients but mostly people who just
don't like lawyers. The rhythmic chants of angry clients holding signs
and marching around the square take over the business district.

> PB&J. What you have to say
> You took all our money

And just walked away
Doing clients dirty
Ain't very purdy
So now you gotta,
Now ya gotta,
Gotta go away!

But still, it does nothing to force PB&J's hand. The rest the firm's net worth combined can't compete with the kind of money Harlan Parker made. Unable to quell the storm, the law firm begins laying off staff as business continues to fall off.

16

BEACHCOMBER COVERUP

November 1, 2017

Seeing the Martin brothers on video surveillance behind Compton Movie House on October 6th was suspicious enough to make them suspects, and they're all Wilt has left. Chief Justice forbade any further investigation into Lonesome Pine out of fear of losing his complimentary membership. But there's nothing stopping Wilt from investigating Kenny and Wally Martin. So, Wilt seeks out Wally Martin for an interview. The brothers now live at Beachcomber Trailer and RV Park at the edge of town. Although there are no beaches for several hundred miles, Beachcomber's owner chose a name intended to capture the mood of summer, beaches and fun. They are in Summerville, after all.

The neighborhood is marketed as a moderately upscale, trendy, mobile home park, primarily consisting of retirees and self-sufficient empty nesters. The park wouldn't accept just any run-down trailer but had stringent building standards. Its units must withstand category three force winds, which tornados in Kentucky can produce in spring and fall. There is even a neighborhood association, a monthly newsletter, elected officers, minutes of meetings and they even have an annual art fair that was really just a yard sale. But art fair sounds more sophisticated.

Wally and Kenny had just moved into separate units in the past couple of weeks and were warmly embraced by park residents. And Wally's trailer is much nicer than Wilt expected, a 2010 model manufactured by Rebel Roar Prefabricated. Each model is named after a Confederate general. Wally had chosen Rebel's 2nd most popular line, the Ole Blue Lights model, named after Stonewall Jackson. Brother Kenny lives in Traveler, part of Rebel's RV line, the most popular model, which was named in honor of the horse ridden by General Robert E. Lee.

Wally opens the door.

Wilt flashes his badge. Wally's left eye begins to twitch. "Are you Wallace Martin?"

Wally nods his head affirmative.

"My name is Marshal Wilt, Homicide Detective for the Summerville Police Department. Do you have a few minutes? I'd like to ask you a few questions. Shouldn't take long." Wally had never given an interview to a cop. He thinks that if he says no it would sound suspicious. "Well, all right. I guess. Come on in and make yourself comfortable."

Martin's abode is much nicer than the detective expected on the inside, too. Cherrywood paneling lines the interior. A large screen TV is mounted on the wall. Shiny new appliances adorn the kitchen. Wilt wants to start the interview off in a positive tone. "Now this is one nice doublewide, Mr. Martin."

"Well, thanks, but it's a prefabricated, modular home. Manufactured to withstand zone three force winds. Meaning that it was control tested in a wind tunnel to withstand a cat four hurricane. No twister round here is gonna take this baby down!" Wally pats on the wall. Wally has a right to be a little sensitive about his new home. He'd spent most of his childhood and adult years drifting from one run-down trailer park to the next.

Wilt's first thought is how a guy mowing a golf course could afford such a nice home, even if it is a trailer. But he doesn't want to ask that question just yet. It might spook Martin into ending the interview before he gets anything useful. "Mr. Martin, I'm here to talk about Harlan Parker. Do you know Mr. Parker personally or do you know who he is?"

"Yeah, I know who Mr. Parker is, but I don't know him. I've never been arrested or had reason to hire a lawyer."

"Well, did you know that Mr. Parker has been missing for about a month now?"

"You'd have to be dumb as a Yokohama hen walking over a fox hole not to have figured that one out, Mr. Wilt. Everyone in town has been talking about it."

"My question to you is if you have any idea where he's at?"

Wally's left eye begins to twitch again. "No, sir. I have no idea. Why would you be asking me that question?"

"Well, the week he disappeared there's this video of you and your brother sitting in a Ford pickup near Mr. Parker's vehicle. And you were wearing a baseball hat and sunglasses at dusk."

"Is there something wrong with sitting in a truck, detective?" But Wally isn't the hardened criminal Kenny is. Even back talking this much seems to exhaust all his remaining nerve. "But if you really want to know, I'll tell you."

Wilt maintains a calm demeanor. He doesn't actually expect that the Martin brothers could get away with murder for an entire month without him noticing. Even if Wally does tell him the truth it won't be about anything important. "Yes, I want to know, Mr. Martin. That's why I'm here."

"Well..." Several explanations race through Martin's mind. And then it comes to him. Something that makes him look vulnerable and sympathetic.

"Well, my eyes were red and puffy. You see. I'd been crying all week. My dog, Bo, had just got hit by a Betty Bake Double Cream Cake truck. Just clipped him as it tuned to avoid him. I can still see it all so vividly. Bo, hunkering down, bracing for impact. Betty Bake Cakes flying around like alien spaceships invading Beachcomber."

Wally sounds as if he's on the verge of tears as he talked about Bo, his lower lip quivering.

"I can hear him yipping and hollering in pain right now, Betty Cream all over him." His voice drops to a whisper. "So much suffering." He swallows hard. "I had to put him down, just like Ole Yeller." Wally pinched the bridge of his nose to stop the tears from flowing. Wilt isn't buying it but plays along. "I'm very sorry, Mr. Martin. What kind of dog was he?"

"He was a—Cockweiler. A Cocker Spaniel Rottweiler mix. Cute as the dickens, but he'd bite your hand off if he don't know ya. Bo was very protective."

"Where did you bury him?"

"Oh, I didn't...I wouldn't put Bo in the ground. He was fosterpedic. He didn't like to be in small spaces. I had him cremated."

Wilt politely tries to correct him. "I believe you mean, claustrophobic."

Wally doesn't like to be corrected, even when he's lying through his teeth. His tone switches from emotional to surly. "No, sir. I know of what I speak. Fosterpedic is the word they use when the dogs have it."

Wilt, not to be thrown off course, continues. "Okay, fosterpedic then. And where was Bo cremated, Mr. Martin?"

"Mr. Wilt, you're asking a lot of personal questions."

"Just want to exclude you as a suspect in Mr. Parker's disappearance, Mr. Martin. Now where did you have him cremated?"

"Am I a suspect, Mr. Wilt?"

"Everybody in Summerville's a suspect, Mr. Martin. Where was Bo cremated? And is there a receipt?"

"Over in Cousin. Cousin Critter Cremation. They fired that baby up to over 1400 degrees, just burned em up. When it was over Bo was nothing but a pile of breadcrumbs. Straight cash. No receipts. No Questions. And they assure confidentiality. Gave me a tube with Bo poured in it. I took him over near the chicken house where we used to chase the chickens around in the yard and just sprinkled him around like Kentucky fescue. Bo just loved chasing those chickens. It's where we spent our best days."

"Well, your brother, Kenny, must have been attached to Bo too, because he was wearing the same thing you had on, a baseball hat and sunglasses at dusk."

Wally needs a little time to think about the answer to that one. "Excuse me Mr. Wilt, I've got to relieve myself. I'll be right back."

A couple of minutes later, Wally comes out of the bathroom with his answer.

"Well, Kenny was just trying to make me feel like he was going through it with me. You know, like when a brother shaves his head to look like his brother that's gone bald prematurely to make him feel like he's not alone in it. I know it sounds funny, but we're the only family we got."

"Then I guess that's why your brother was running around the parking lot with a President Clinton mask on, Mr. Martin?"

"It was Halloween, sir."

"No. It was over three weeks before Halloween, Mr. Martin. Where was he trick or treating several weeks before Halloween?"

"He was getting ready, sir! He really loves Halloween a lot. Everyone that knows Kenny knows that much about him." Wally is starting to run out of answers. He thinks it's time for him to be somewhere else. "Now it's been nice to meet you, Mr. Wilt, but I've got someplace I need to get. So, thank you for the company."

Wilt thanks him for his time and as he walked out the door. "What did you pay for this nice prefabricated home, Mr. Martin?"

"Let's just say I got a bargain, Mr. Wilt. I don't discuss my personal finances. Thank you for your interest, though. Goodbye, sir."

Wilt leaves Beachcomber with more questions than answers, so Wally Martin is now officially a suspect. As he walks away, he knows that he'll have to check out the Cousin Critter Cremation story, seriously doubting it would hold up. And Wilt could say one thing with certainty. Wally Martin is too dumb to be the sociopath who texted Ridley Barnes asking Barnes to go to Cousin in order to cover a nonexistent court case. Wally was one of the worst liars he had ever interviewed.

Wally calls Kenny as he looks out the window watching Wilt drive away. "Hey, it's Wally. There was a Detective Wilt that was just out here talking to me. He has a video of us behind Compton near Parker's car. And he was asking some questions about my lightly used prefabricated modular home and us wearing sunglasses past sundown."

Kenny is rattled. "What did you tell him? Didn't have to tell him nothing. I told you somebody else did it. If you don't talk to him, he's got nothing."

"Don't bust a gasket, Kenny. I've thrown him off the trail. Here's what I said. Now listen up, so we can keep this straight." Kenny listens, but all he can think about it how he wishes he'd left the money hidden in the tree.

17

THE LAWYER MAKEOVER

Andrews drives to Cousin to visit the crematorium to check out Wally's story. He finds that the animal funeral home was running a promotion during the period Wally says he visited, which resulted in four times the usual number of visitors. It was on a walk-in, cash basis, and no one kept any records on how many people used the service or how many pets were cremated. There is only a ledger of dollar amounts. Any of the transactions could be for Wallace Martin, or none of them. Andrews returns to Summerville and reports his findings to Wilt.

By Thanksgiving it is all over for PB&J but turning off the utilities and disposing of office furniture. For the lawyers Parker left behind, continuing to practice law in the same space without him isn't an option. It is the most expensive in town and Parker had carried half the monthly rent. Now their rainmaker is gone, as are the once steady stream of cases he fed them with.

When all the picking was done, the lawyers at PB&J had little to show for their time there. Only Barnes and Jeffries, who went their separate ways, managed to hold onto a manufacturing plant and a couple of car dealerships. The other lawyers played tug of war over what scraps remained, like hyenas fighting over a zebra carcass rotting in the Savannah.

With each passing week, lawyers leave for more affordable options without taking the furniture they used while working with Parker, but not because they had other furnishings waiting. As a condition of working at his law firm, Parker had insisted that each attorney and member of the support staff use his furniture and pay a yearly fee for doing so. This was not only to make sure everyone was using pieces that were up to Parker's professional standards, but to give the appearance of one law firm. It was also another way he made money off those who worked there, like some bizarre, white-collar coal town where Parker was the baron gouging his workers at every opportunity. But at least it was top tier stuff.

By mid-December, everyone has moved on and Ridley Barnes has negotiated a lease buyout with the landlord, which meant the premises are to be vacated by month's end. Tori Stevens is appointed conservator to manage Parker's property until the body is found or a death determination is made to begin to probate his estate. She had finished law school a semester early and is busy studying for the Bar exam, but it is also her responsibility to figure out what to do with all of Harlan's furniture, enough to adorn a half a dozen law offices. So, she decides to have a fire sale at the now defunct law firm. It is a great opportunity for someone to beautifully appoint their new space and with all the trappings of success without ever having achieved it.

~

FRIDAY DECEMBER 15, 2017

When Lantham closes his law office in St. Matthews, he gives away his drab cast-offs to the first client who shows up and agrees to haul it away. They are an embarrassment to him compared to what he'd grown accustomed to, and he isn't about to take the junk with him to Summerville. Collectively, they aren't even worth the rent he'd have to pay for a truck to take it there.

But the demand for legal work created by the void Parker left behind is Lantham's golden opportunity to start over, in a new town with a rebranded law practice that exuded competence and significance. The appearance of success breeds success he thinks, as he arrives in Summerville and begins the search for office space. He picks up the latest edition of the Summerville Songbird to check out commercial rental property when he sees something too good to be true, listed on an advertisement which took up an entire page of the Bird's classifieds.

FIRE SALE: Tomorrow from 8 am to 9 pm at the former offices of Parker, Barnes and Jeffries. All must go by December 22nd. Traditional law office furniture of the highest quality. Excellent condition. Queen Anne, Victorian and Renaissance period furnishings hewn in oak, deep cherry and mahogany. Bookshelves, secretarial desks and workstations, credenzas, attorney desks, leather chairs, sofas, coffee tables and other lobby furniture, conference tables and chairs, oil paintings, classic framed prints, plus other assorted office appointments and much more. For more information, call Tori Stevens at 568-988-5544.

SATURDAY 7:45 AM, December 16, 2017
Lantham walks through Summerville Square only to see bargain hunters already hovering in front of the building, each jockeying to be the first in the door to get the best deals. Lantham quickly takes up his position. But he isn't there simply to buy high-end office furnishings. He could do that in any number of places.

He is there for Harlan's things. To make Harlan's things his things, and more to the point, so he could be Harlan like. He can't be Harlan Parker. Who can? But at least he can have Harlan's stuff and put on airs of his success. Lantham had admired his décor and sense of style from the first time he sat in Harlan's office, so each piece was already committed to memory. The stunning antique, two-way Versailles office desk and matching chair, the French Henri II credenza hewn in dark walnut, the antique wine and bar cabinet which had sat to the right of Harlan's desk, his bespoken grandfather clock with a circular face and twist on top which stood back left as you entered his workspace. And, grandest of all, the vintage mahogany bookshelves with sliding ladder which spanned the entire left side of the room. And today, all of Harlan's most coveted pieces would be his own.

The day he figured out Tori had left to be with Harlan, it had been time for some serious introspection. Harlan obviously had something he didn't, and Lantham was determined to figure out what that was. He spent weeks looking inward, a brutally honest self-analysis that was oft times emotionally precarious, treading into the darkest edges of his being. Lantham finally concluded the only thing separating him from his rival was Harlan's exquisite furniture.

With Parker now out of the way, Lantham would simply step in and take his place, emotionally that is. Then Tori would come back to him. And even if she was really coming back to Harlan and not him, he'd take it.

He was halfway to Harlan already, being an unscrupulous jerk and throwing out almost as much shade. He'd gained 50 pounds since being a street lawyer. He no longer had time to work out regularly or follow a healthy diet which now is comprised mostly of foods high in preservatives, sugar, pork and beef fat. And his hairline had receded to the point where it looked better cut off anyway, at least on the top.

He was tired of living a lie, trying to cover his gaping bald spot every morning, constantly primping throughout the day. So, he went with the Harlan look, or what's been described in centuries past as a Friar Tuck and more recently as a horseshoe haircut. Store bought hair coloring products couldn't replicate the magic of Harlan's mad side tresses, so Lantham went to a salon to get as close to it as possible and dyed his locks with what the stylist called a translucent frost. But he kept his thick eyebrows their natural black color, giving him a sort of Andy Warhol vibe.

Lantham discovered being a chrome domer with side curls was

not only low maintenance but quite liberating. If the look worked for
Martin Van Buren, 8th President of the United States, it was good
enough for him. And the best part about it? At least as far as his physical appearance, he kind of looks like Harlan with dark eyebrows.
Getting the furniture is the final piece of the puzzle. It is time to close
the deal.

Ten minutes later Stevens unlocks the front door and returns to
her makeshift sales desk as the eager hoard of furniture buyers flows
in. Lantham walks directly in front of her, nodding to say hello, not
speaking. Because his physical appearance has changed so drasti-
cally, Tori twists her head slightly downward and squints and shifts
her eyes throughout his rounded physique, covering her slightly
open mouth with her fist the moment she sees him. She recognizes
glimpses of someone in her distant past, just not remotely sure who
or where it was. It's as if she's looking at a ghost, just not Harlan's.
"Can I help you, sir?"

He knows the moment he says a word the mystery would be gone.
He isn't going to make it so easy for her, waiting several more
moments before revealing himself.

"It's Okay, Tori. What you're feeling is sexual tension. It's
completely normal. It's a healthy thing in fact. I read it in a men's
health magazine."

"Oh my...Greg? Is that you? What have you done to yoursel—
hair? It's very frosty. Going for that sage, learned counsel look now,
Greg?"

She catches herself before she rips into him. There are too many
witnesses.

"It's quite—interesting. An eye catcher for sure. Really. It's a
period look, isn't it? Kind of has a Constitutional Convention feel to it.
Are you playing Benjamin Franklin? No. I think his hair was a bit
stringier. George Washington! Yes. That's it!" She pauses as the fact of
his presence sinks in.

"What are you doing here, Greg?"

"I've recently moved to Summerville to open my law office. I need
office furniture, everything. Harlan has—had excellent taste, didn't

he? I saw your ad in the paper and it's the perfect opportunity to knock it out all at once. I'm here for one stop shopping, Tori. I'd like to buy all his things. His desk, bookcase, wine cabinet, his artwork. Not everything here." Lantham looks about the room. "We're talking just what's in Harlan's office."

Hypnotized by his opaque glow, Tori barely hears a word he's saying. "What! Since when did you move to Summerville?" She thinks.

"Oh, I know. You're in the witness protection program or something? What's Debbie think about all of this? Must be quite an adjustment living under an assumed name? You probably shouldn't use your actual name, even with me. Don't you think?"

"Nothing like that, Tori. Debbie filed for a divorce, but it's Okay. It was mutual. I've moved to Summerville just recently for a fresh start. How much for Harlan's furniture and things? All of it."

Knowing Debbie's out of the picture, Tori immediately realizes she has no leverage to run Greg off, at least not for the moment. She isn't a lawyer quite yet, still having to pass the Bar and clear the ethical fitness review board, the one Lantham had previously threatened to report her to just a few months before. She has no choice to but to be cordial, even kind to him. "I'm very sorry to hear that, Greg."

"It's Okay, Tori. It's for the best. How much for Harlan's furniture?"

To get him out the door and away from her, Tori agrees to sell Lantham everything in Harlan's office for $10,000, which is far lower than what she could have certainly netted for it.

Though she doesn't immediately fall heads over heels for him, Lantham tells himself that she still has feelings for him because of the great deal she gave him. And she doesn't even threaten him this time. He decides to take things slow with her. In his mind, it's only a matter of time before they are together again.

Tori has other ideas. As soon as the fire sale is over, she is going straight to Detective Wilt to update him on Lantham's new appearance and his new office filled with Harlan's personal affects. On one level, it's beyond bizarre Lantham would have anything that belonged to Harlan, considering how much they hated each other. But from another perspective she thinks it's brilliant. It's almost like he is planning to take Harlan's place. Stevens believes that Lantham had given her exactly what she needs to convince Wilt he's responsible for Harlan's murder.

18

TORI WEARS A WIRE

Monday 9:00 am, December 18, 2017

Two days after the furniture sell-off, Tori is at the police station with Wilt, updating him on Lantham's recent office move and platinum makeover. "First, he makes a veiled threat just two weeks before Harlan disappears, and now he's opening a law office less than two months after Harlan's gone, adorned with Harlan's furniture, no less. And most bizarre of all, he's trying to look like Harlan, but fortunately for him, it's a very poor likeness."

But Wilt, always the skeptic, is less impressed. "The guy's 44. It's the age they go a little crazy, but just for a little while. Do you know how many times I've been involved with a middle age man who suddenly alters his appearance, quits his job and moves in with a 24-year-old. She soon meets a man her age and files an EPO to kick him out. Then to compensate, he contacts a teenage girl online that's really an undercover cop. Then he turns 45, goes back home and the world is right again."

Tori isn't conceding anything. "Well, think I'm crazy if you want, detective, but it sounds like a motive to get rid of Harlan to me!"

"Sure, Ms. Stevens. But if I know anything working over at the courthouse, it's that there are a lot of starving lawyers out there. If his wife just filed for a divorce, it's far more likely he just wants someplace to start over. Sounds like a smart move to me. I've checked this guy out closely. He has nothing in his background to suggest he's capable of murder. Sounds far more like he's flipped out a little."

Then Wilt has an idea. "How close are you to this guy? Enough to set up a meeting?"

"He offered me a job at his new law office. I kept things open. Didn't want to offend him, so I told him I would think about it. He went ahead and purchased office furniture for me anyway. It wouldn't be out of the norm for me to call him and set something up to discuss the offer, I suppose."

"If you think you can get him to speak in confidence with you it may be an opportunity to find out if he is in fact the killer, but you'd have to wear a wire. There's a little role playing going on that you'd have to sell."

"It's not my nature to be less than genuine in my personal and professional relationships, detective, but if you tell me what to say, I'll do my best for you. I don't know if Greg did it or not. I just want justice to be served for Harlan, that's all."

Wilt comes up with the script for Tori to follow. She would contact Lantham and ask for a mid-afternoon meeting at the Lovely Bean Café to discuss the job offer. The lunch crowd will have thinned out by then, but there should still be enough background noise for others to not overhear the conversation yet clear enough for the surveillance tech in the sound truck to listen to and record the conversation.

Tori then calls Lantham who agreed to meet her at 3:00 that afternoon. A few hours later, a female officer places a recording device under Tori's blouse. Then a surveillance tech does a sound check. Wilt goes over the plan. "If you're trying to get someone in casual conversation to admit committing murder, the secret is to control the conversation without coming off as controlling. Do you think you're up to something like that?"

"I think so, Mr. Wilt. I'm so nervous. I've never been very good at acting."

"I'm sure you'll do fine. We're going to do this at the Bean, so if something goes wrong, he'll be less likely to do something that would draw attention. This recording device is very sensitive; picks up almost everything. If you move around during the conversation, we won't be able to hear anything except what sounds like the wind blowing. So, try to stay still without being rigid while you're talking to him. We're listening to everything in real time, right outside across the street in an unmarked surveillance truck. Are we good, Ms. Stevens?"

"Got it!"

~

MONDAY 2:50 PM, *December 18, 2017*

Tori arrives early and finds a booth far enough away from other patrons so that Lantham would be comfortable talking. Within ten minutes the receptionist walks Lantham over to the cubby hole she'd selected. He's glowing with joy.

"I'm so glad that you called, Tori. I was worried that you wouldn't even consider working with me again, especially after our blowup a few months ago."

"I should be the one worried, Greg, after everything that's happened."

"That's all in the past, Tori. All that matters now is the future."

"You don't know how many times I've thought about you over the last couple of years. Going to work for Harlan was the worst mistake of my life, on every level. But there was no way for me to undo it. Harlan would have tried to destroy me. I didn't know what to do. I'm so sorry, Greg."

Lantham reaches across the table and grabs her hands, gently fondling them.

"I know. I felt the same. There were so many times I started to call you, Tori, only to stop myself. It was the hardest thing I've ever done!"

Wilt sits in the truck amazed at how good she is. She didn't need his advice. She's a natural.

"I was lured into a nightmare by someone I wasn't equipped to deal with. And now with Harlan disappearing, as horrible as it sounds, I'm almost relieved it happened. If I ever found out who did it, I'd never say a word because whoever did it literally saved my life. I'm forever in his debt."

Lantham just sits there looking into Tori's eyes, then looks down at the table. He takes a deep breath, then exhales slowly before looking up at her again.

"There's something I need to tell you, Tori."

"What is it, Greg? Are you Okay?"

There is another pause. "I did it for you, Tori. I did it for us."

Wilt nearly falls back on his chair listening in, not believing how soon she got a confession out of him. But he needs more.

"Oh, Gregory!"

"He's never going to hurt you again, ever. I made sure of it. Know that he suffered a death I wouldn't wish on anyone else but him."

Tori wipes a nonexistent tear from her eye. "You have no idea how this changes things for us, Greg. It makes me feel like I'm safe again, with you near."

"That means everything to me."

"What happened? But only if you want to share it with me. It could be a way of telling me you've let everything go, so we can move forward. How did you do it?"

Lantham looks about the room, reluctant to go further.

"Tell me, Greg! Now!" Tori catches herself. "But only if you're comfortable with sharing something so secret with me."

Lantham looks at her curiously, but only for a split second before providing detail.

"Well... after we argued in the parking lot a few months back Harlan confronted me as I was walking to my car. He'd been watching us from a distance. He told me that I would soon regret ever seeking you out. I then realized what he was capable of. I didn't know what he might do to you because I found out you went to work for him. I wasn't about to wait around to find out. So, a couple of weeks later, on a Tuesday evening, I took matters into my own hands. It was all planned meticulously. It's done, Tori. That's all that matters."

"But how did you kill him, Greg? I need to know."

"Let's just say I took care of it, Tori."

Tori turns her head slightly, looking at him skeptically. "Did you shoot him? Did you slit his throat? Did you tie him up and dump him in the river? How Greg? How was it done?"

"Why does it matter, now? He's as dead as the bear that lines my winter coat."

"Because I need confirmation that he's really gone! I thought that you of all people could appreciate that. I won't sleep until I know the details. I'll just continue to wonder if he's just around the next corner."

Wilt listens in awe as she adapts to Lantham's every diversion.

> This woman may be even better at role playing than Harlan!

"Let's do this another way. What did you do with the body?"

"I dumped him in someone else's coffin that died within a week of Harlan. A pretty tight fit with two of em packed in there, and a little more digging than I would have preferred."

"Where, Greg?"

"Within a day's drive from here. I'll say that much, but no more."

Though Lantham didn't give her every detail she wanted, Tori thinks it's more than enough to convince Wilt that he's the killer. Pressing any further might tip him off that her interest is something more than seeking reassurance.

Lantham turns the conversation to work. "Now let's talk about the job offer. I can start you out at seventy thousand, and if things go the way I think, more with an eye towards a 50/50 split."

"Let me think about it, Greg. It's all I can do to study for the Bar right now. I've got three other offers to think about as well that are very competitive. I need to consider all of this rationally and not just with my heart. Please give me room to make the right choice. I'm exhausted from all of this, and I need to get back to Bar prep. I'll be in touch."

Tori heads to the ladies' room and waits for Lantham to leave the restaurant before walking across the street to join Wilt in the truck. Wilt isn't convinced by Lantham's confession, not by a long shot.

"I'm impressed Ms. Stevens. You did an incredible job, but he'd say anything to have a chance to be with you. That comes through loud and clear. He provides no verifiable details to prove he's the killer."

She is aghast that Wilt isn't ready to arrest him.

"He admitted to killing him detective! And he even told me how he got rid of Harlan's body. What else could you need?"

"If I had a dollar for every time a guy lied about killing somebody to impress a woman I sure wouldn't be working here anymore, Ms. Stevens! There are hundreds of cemeteries and family plots within a day's drive, maybe thousands. And he couldn't have done it on a Tuesday. Parker was killed between Friday evening and Monday morning the first weekend of October. And another problem; Parker was well over 300 pounds. Lantham couldn't carry someone half that size by himself."

Despite how effective Stevens was getting her former boss to talk, the voracity with which she urged Wilt to make an arrest raises some question in Wilt's mind about her motivation. He'd never seen anyone cooperate so willingly as an informant who wasn't doing so to avoid prison themselves. She seems just a little too eager for Lantham to be charged.

Wilt decides not to interview Lantham, thinking it better for him not to know he was a suspect, for the time being. Doing so would also expose Stevens as a cooperating witness, which he also wanted to avoid so early in the investigation. He asks Stevens to keep things cordial with Lantham, at least for now, to keep open the opportunity to use her again as an undercover asset.

Tori has no choice but to take the offer graciously, wait, and look for another opportunity to implicate Lantham.

19

GUM POND ROAD

ednesday April 4, 2018

W The Lovely Bean, locally referred to as the Bean, is the best café not only on the square but in all central Kentucky. Its hot brown is better than where the dish was created, Louisville's iconic Brown Hotel. Its bourbon balls had been featured *in Elite Chocolatier, Sweeter Living and Coco Ecstasy* magazines. Foodie TV did an entire show in its southern fare series showcasing the Bean's tender and moist not-your-grandma's cornbread and its legendary Derby pie.

And its iconic southern fried chicken, too special to have the name of just one state associated with it, was prepared in a skillet the man in the white suit with a black string tie couldn't carry across the street. Each day the Bean also offers original, fresh, off-menu selections that are displayed and handwritten in colored chalk on a portable chalkboard which stood just outside the café, giving passersby a glimpse of the culinary treasures that awaited within.

The Bean had many loyal customers, Hanley Oldfather being among them. At 79 years, Oldfather is the patriarch of the Summerville Bar, having practiced there for almost 60 years. And in a third of that time, he had managed to build the largest firm in town.

But unlike Harlan Parker, Oldfather had done it by working long hours, promptly returning phone calls to his clients, and treating staff and lawyers both inside and outside his firm, with respect. He is so highly regarded among his colleagues, even lawyers just a few years his junior refer to him as, Mr. Oldfather.

Hanley Oldfather is what's referred to as the highest compliment one attorney can give another.

A lawyer's lawyer.

And like most everyone else in town, Oldfather never cared much for the antics of Harlan Parker, and he wasn't surprised in the least that someone had more than likely rubbed him out. Oldfather knew Harlan Parker all too well, having given him his first job out of law school over twenty years before. But the hire lasted all of nine months, ending after multiple infractions, including Parker trying to steal business clients from one of Oldfather's junior partners, in addition to complaints by several women describing lewd and lascivious behavior in varied degrees of perversion, anyone of which should have landed him in the county jail if Oldfather hadn't used his good name to keep the District Attorney from bringing charges.

Among the recipients of Parker's unwelcome overtures were two of the firm's staff, a client, an attorney outside the firm he was litigating a case against for which the firm had to pay a six-figure settlement. Oldfather counted the hire as his biggest professional mistake but was too much of a gentleman to ever say so. Not that he ever had to.

Each Wednesday, Oldfather meets several of his contemporaries for lunch at the Bean where he can still exchange pleasantries with younger attorneys in town and partake in recent courthouse scuttlebutt. But with the youngest attendee now in his late 70s, the august group had dwindled from six to four in recent years. Though none of them actively practiced anymore, Oldfather still goes to the office every day to read the paper, close the door and nap and give sage advice to the new associates, which is always appreciated.

It was six months since Parker's disappearance, and on the early side of lunchtime when Oldfather walked down to the Bean to be the first to check out the specials posted on its sidewalk menu and snatch up the best table in the house from which he and his fellow septuagenarians could have lunch and return the glory days, if only for an hour, while overlooking beautiful Summerville square.

Four blocks away, Wilt is still waiting on the crime lab to return its forensic analysis of Parker's phone. All other existing leads had either hit a dead end or were getting colder by the day. Wilt is now within a year of mandatory retirement. Even if he had five years remaining, it isn't enough time for him to pass onto his understudy the whole of essential advice that wasn't taught at the academy. Tricks of the trade that could only be gleaned from tracking the steps of a killer, then losing the trail and finding it again, unwritten gems he and he alone knew, the wealth of subtlety and nuance that was the sum of Marshal P. Wilt's 30 years as a homicide detective.

Wilt is kicked back in his office with feet up on his desk as apprentice detective Wesley Andrews sits alert, attentive to every word Wilt uttered. But his confidence is growing. He has begun voicing what his training and instincts told him. Wilt is much more comfortable this way. Having a give and take, back and forth is what he expects from having a partner. Wilt begins, "You've heard of the tactic of good cop, bad cop. Two detectives work in tandem, one threatening and intimidating a suspect into the welcoming and reassuring arms of the other. But it's not as simple as TV makes it seem. People aren't dumb sheep to be herded by a few barks."

"So how does it really work?" Andrews asks. "Are there any books I can study about it?"

"There's no flow chart, no instruction manual that could be used every time. It's fluid, dynamic. Its direction and likelihood of success depends discerning several variables, including the emotional condition of the subject, the leverage that can be brought to bear upon him and the subject's personal or family relationships, and most importantly, their importance to him."

Andrews nods and takes copious notes.

Then the call comes from Julia Sweet, the owner and culinary queen of The Bean. She was distraught. Mr. Oldfather had just pointed out that some miscreant had vandalized her curbside menu board, erasing the Bean's Thursday selections.

"Detective Wilt, our offering of grilled amberjack served with a bourbon demi-glaze accompanied with a spring mix with artichoke hearts topped with Maytag blue cheese dressing has been erased! And it's been replaced with some macabre verse with a distinctive Edgar Allen Poe bent."

"Is that so? I'm sorry. This must be very concerning for you, Ms. Sweet." Wilt rolls his eyes as he speaks to her over the phone. He's trying to sound interested and concerned, but he thinks it's just another fraternity pledge at Summerville College, going through initiation. Ms. Sweet is known to have a flair for the melodramatic.

"Concerning? This is vandalism! No one wants to read a poem about a dead lawyer when they're trying to decide what to eat for lunch!"

Wilt takes his feet off his desk, immediately morphing into detective mode. "Dead lawyer?"

"Yes! Of all the awful things, the poem's about a dead lawyer buried somewhere."

"Ms. Sweet, I need you to immediately photograph the message with your phone and bring the chalkboard inside someplace where no one has access to it. And please don't mention this to anyone else or say that you've spoken to law enforcement. We're on the way over."

Within five minutes Sweet was in front of her café with Wilt and Andrews explaining she doesn't need to attract any more attention than necessary. She proceeds to lead them through the main dining area, by and around a maze of tables filled with young professionals and college kids.

The three then turn into a long narrow hallway which leads down to a room with freezers marked with all manner of beef, poultry, fish and shelfs stocked full of canned culinary wonders. As Wilt approaches the back corner of the room toward the menu board, he began to quietly mouth the verse written in chalk, colored in a blood red.

A liar sleeps eternal
Inside a steel cold keep
A Lincoln and a lawyer
One-hundred-nine feet deep

Among forsaken pieces
Upon its limestone floor
A crypt with tinted windows
And space where once a door

Gaze upon the fortunes
Of one who found great wealth
By serving ends of justice
That only served himself

Just follow Bubba's junk
Where they roll tide roll
Down to the murky murky
Just off Gum Pond Road

Wilt's first impression is predictable. "Clearly the poetic ramblings of a sociopath!" Wilt also sees the poem as a treasure trove of clues that can lead them to Parker's body and thinks it's a good opportunity to engage Detective Andrews.

"What do you think, Andrews?"

The junior detective stands there for a moment, rubbing his chin.

"Well—I think it's obvious that a poet named Bubba murdered Harlan Parker—and the body is located somewhere in the shade under some gum trees in Florida. No, Georgia."

Wilt exhales as he looks over at Sweet. He is embarrassed for Andrews' sake.

"You never played sports as a kid, did you, son? And you never watched sports on TV? Never heard of Paul Bear Bryant, I guess?"

With a confused look on his face, Andrews wonders if the question was some kind of a surprise test of his investigative abilities.

"No sir. Gaming, science fiction novels, and classic cars. Wasn't into sports too much. But I had a couple of swimsuit issue pinups in my room before my mother threw them in the trash."

Wilt's instincts are confirmed. "Sounds about right."

But when Sweet hears the name Harlan Parker, she immediately realizes the significance. Her menu board is as a key piece of evidence in a murder investigation. Other than preparing delectable dishes, one of her favorite things is deciphering riddles and clues. She thinks herself quite good at interpreting them to solve a mystery. Seeing that the young detective was struggling, she attempts to help him out a bit, and it is a chance to play investigator, however briefly.

"Detective Andrews, I think you're definitely onto something here, but I believe it highly unlikely that the author of this poem would identify himself by name. Bubba is a place, a culture, a way of doing things, not a person. Now you must ask where someone named Bubba would reside?"

Wilt interjects, "Bubba is in Alabama, where they yell, roll tide roll for the University of Alabama Crimson Tide football team. And sometimes Bubba dumps things off a Gum Pond Road, like in a lake or pond. Someplace that's deep. Probably not a pond."

Not about to be upstaged by a chef, Andrews fires back.

"Well, lakes aren't that deep, but oceans are. And Georgia has a shoreline more than a hundred miles long. It has high and low tides that roll in, too. And it's a well-accepted fact that there's more Bubbas in Georgia than any other state. So, Harlan Parker's somewhere in Georgia, in a pond, close to the ocean that's near a thatch of gum trees."

Sweet, now brimming with confidence, feels like the lead detective in a homicide investigation, and continues with her thoughts.

"Well, wherever Parker is, he's on a limestone floor. Where do you have a lake with a flat rocky bottom? Of course! An old rock quarry that's now a lake! Harlan Parker is inside a Lincoln Continental without a door at the bottom of a rock quarry off Gum Pond Road! And there you have it, detectives! I won't send you a bill until after you've gotten the conviction!"

Now clearly threatened by Sweet's investigative acumen, Andrews counters with a profile of the killer.

"Bubba is confident which is why he doesn't care if we know his name. For him this is all a game. Part of the thrill of the chase. And Bubba owns a junkyard or a scrapyard where he has lots of old rusted farm equipment that's visible from the road, Gum Pond Road. And like all Bubbas, he pronounces China with an R, 'Chiner'. And he's so confident he's leading us straight to junk in his junkyard."

Sweet, now feeling it, counters Andrews with her own profile of the killer.

"The killer doesn't flaunt his junk, Detective. He sinks it. And I doubt he owns a junkyard. And I wouldn't exclude the possibility that the killer is a woman. Whoever it is, they are clearly highly educated. Probably a college degree in literary studies, creative writing or poetry. Perhaps a masters of even a doctorate, judging from this quality of work. Check with Orchid and Oak, the literary club at Crawford House, where poets and writers hang out. The killer probably frequents the place or recites their poetry there. Wellington Worth, its curator, may even recognize the killer's writing style if you show him this."

She waves a hand at the poem on her chalkboard.

"The author also appears not to like lawyers very much. And yes, he's confident, sending us on a little scavenger hunt to find the body. He doesn't have much money. Is jealous of Harlan Parker's money. Someone who thinks of Harlan Parker as a self-serving sort. Someone who Parker enriched himself from, now bitter. A client, maybe someone he sued."

Wilt nods, wonderstruck by Sweet's insights, then looks down and scrolls to the map app on his phone. He types in Gum Pond Road.

"There appear to be three Gum Pond Roads, all in Northern Alabama, and all within a hundred miles." Wilt then looks at Andrews. "None in Georgia!"

Wilt can't contain his high regard for Sweet's keen investigative instincts.

"Very impressive, Ms. Sweet. I may have to deputize you if you keep this up." He smiles at her. "Except the last part about thinking Parker a scoundrel wouldn't exclude anyone in Summerville. But I think you're spot on!"

He then directs Andrews to put on his evidence gloves and retrieve the chalk board before departing.

"Thank you, Ms. Sweet. You've been very helpful. If you have any more thoughts on the investigation, I'd be very interested in hearing them."

Wilt hands her a card with his contact information. Walking out of the Bean, Wilt contemplates the next step.

"Andrews, get your wetsuit and oxygen tank. Next, we locate the Gum Pond Road with a nearby rock quarry and start diving."

20

ON THE BEAT IN BITTY

ay 10, 2018
Command Central, District One, the brain center of law enforcement for the southern half of Bethune County, Alabama is, by design, intended to lull the unsuspecting criminal element into a false sense of confidence. *That's when we've got you*, says Constable, Rodger K. Small, in an interview with the Lynnville Bee, Bethune County's bimonthly newspaper.

According to Small, Command Center One's facilities and furnishings are intentionally understated for that very reason: a 30 by 20-foot lobby with adjoining restroom, one office with a desk, and three chairs. No windows. No computer, fax or telephone. Now someone who didn't know better might think that the modest surroundings were because the county had so few people and there wasn't enough tax revenue to fund even one pen and notepad.

But Small would quickly correct them. He'd point to his perfect conviction rate, the no escapes on his watch, and no murders or other violent crime on his five years on the beat. His name might be Small, but there's nothing diminutive about the surveillance or crisis response capabilities of his department of one. Just before his last election, he told the Bee that the locals were in good hands. And his remarks proved to be convincing, as he went on to win reelection by 35 votes.

Nothing goes on in this part of the county that I don't know about. I'm the gatekeeper, the first and last line of defense between the worst of the worst and the fine citizens of southern Bethune County.

So, when Detective Wilt told the constable that there was likely a dead body in a rock quarry in his district, he scoffed at the idea.

"Detective, I certainly wouldn't want to impede the efforts of a fellow brother in arms, but I'm quite certain that you'd be chasing a rabbit down an empty hole over here. The command center is located on Gum Pond Road. That means the would-be killer likely would have driven right by my office to get to Quarry Lake, if what you're saying is correct. And Command Central One doesn't sleep on the job, sir. I'm afraid that you'd be wasting your time even driving here."

Undeterred, Wilt, Andrews and newly deputized Julia Sweet travel down to Bitty, Alabama to meet with the constable. Small indeed confirms that Quarry Lake is over 100 feet deep, and that dumpers occasionally got rid of old farm equipment and other abandoned junk there, but the constable assures them he had shut that kind of thing down a few years back by coordinating with the land owner to put surveillance cameras at the entrance and overlooking the lake. "If anyone had tried something suspicious over the first weekend of October, last year, I would have been the first to know about it. I can assure you, detective. Nothing's happened at Quarry Lake in over a decade, and never while on my watch!"

But he went on to explain the quarry's dark past.

About eighteen years before, two men from out of state came to the area as part of a plan to kill a pawn shop owner who lived in nearby Bitty, Alabama. They were brought there by a third man, the ringleader of the group, who lived near the rock quarry. He had told them that the store owner, a 70-year-old man, was thought to keep large amounts of cash in his home, where he lived with his wife.

The day before the murder, the killers went to the pawn shop acting like they were interested in buying some musical instruments, but they were sizing up their future victim. The following evening, after the owner and his wife had just returned from church services, the two men forced their way into the home, killing the man and thinking they had killed the woman. They bound the two in duct tape and threw them in the back of a van. The ringleader had directed the men to dispose of the bodies and the van where no one would ever find them, at the bottom of Quarry Lake. But when the killers got there, they made a critical mistake that would send them to the gas chamber.

Instead of driving the van into the water, they put it in neutral and tried to push it in. And once the front wheels of the van crossed over the limestone edge, the undercarriage of the van dropped and hung up on the rocky bottom. The two men tried frantically to push it in, but the van would move no farther. So, they went to a nearby farm to steal a tractor to use to push the van into the lake, but the farmer who owned the tractor heard a ruckus coming from his barn. So, he fired off his shotgun and called the sheriff. The killers fled the scene, leaving the van on the edge of the lake.

The next morning, the sheriff found the van, with its front wheels still hanging over the water. After a wrecker pulled it back from the ledge, a faint groan was heard coming from the back of the van. It was the pawn shop owner's wife, still alive, who had been beaten, her hands, legs, and face bound with duct tape. Laying on top of her was the bloody and battered body of her husband. She would be the prosecution's star witness and identify the killers. In his closing statement, the prosecutor told the jury that the killers would have gotten away with it if they had just driven the van into the quarry.

Wilt has heard enough. Now he is convinced that Parker is at the bottom of Quarry Lake. He persuades Small to give him the number of the quarry's owner, Ralph Hacker. They call ahead and arrange an interview. Small insists upon being present. After a brief introduction and reassuring small talk, Wilt gets to the point. "Do you keep the footage from your surveillance cameras, Mr. Hacker?"

"My surveillance cameras?"

"Yes, Mr. Hacker the cameras. I want to know if your cameras recorded illegal dumping activity early last October."

"They probably did, but we'll never know it. My cameras were stolen the first week of October last year. Stolen or broken, or both."

"Did you report the theft?" Wilt asks.

"Yes, I did."

Out of the corner of his eye Wilt sees Small's sudden apprehension. "This didn't concern you?"

"Every few years some wise guy tree climber steals my cameras." Somewhat uncomfortably, Hacker adds, "I meant to get around to putting more up. I just haven't done it yet. I'm a busy man, Detective."

Small, now clearly embarrassed, and sensing that there might be something to Wilt's story, tries to spin the situation his way. "Looks like it's time to call in the dive team, and the Bee will be interested in covering the search." He glances at Wilt and Andrews. "I'm afraid I need to pull rank and take the reins of this investigation, Detective. This is my jurisdiction. Thanks for the intel. I'll let you know if anything turns up. Have a safe trip back to Kentucky."

Hacker is very familiar with Smart's false bravado and is less than impressed with it. But he is more than willing to cooperate with Wilt. "Dive team, Rodger? Really?" He addresses Wilt. "He's talking about the snorkeling club at Lynnville High School. I allow them to use the quarry for their classes every spring."

Small looked at Hacker with a perplexed expression. "Well, Ralph, we've got to tighten our belt and watch the budget right now. These are lean times that call for creative solutions to our law enforcement needs."

But Hacker continues to push back. "You're going to need a professional on this, Rodger! An adult in the room! How far down do you think snorkelers will get? Ten feet? And I'm sure their parents will be thrilled at us for asking their children to look for a dead body down there! In a murder investigation at that! You're in the outer realm on this one, Rodger!" Hacker looks at Wilt and Sweet. "He's a part-time constable without a squad car who isn't even allowed to carry a firearm. This is what happens when you get someone with a

John Wayne complex who serves subpoenas and lawsuits. He's run for sheriff three times and he's o-fer. When you finish third in a two-horse race for sheriff in Bethune County, the consolation prize is constable."

Hacker looks back to Small. "You need to stand down and keep your powder dry, Rodger! Let the A-team handle this. And did you ever consider they may not want news coverage of whatever they find down there? If the killer sees you're on to him, he might fly the coup. Or you could have some nut job coming forward to claim responsibility for it because of what he read in the Bee. It could compromise their whole investigation."

The air races out of Small's britches like an untied balloon at the county fair.

Hacker doesn't care. "This is serious stuff, Rodger. It's going to take more than certification to handle pesticides to manage something like this!"

Small's real job is working as an extermination tech at Gum Pond Pest Control. But now seeing that he has embarrassed Small, Hacker tries to soften things a bit, to allow the constable to save face. "I'll make you a deal, Rodger. I'll let you come on my
property and stand in the background and I won't even call the sheriff to steal your thunder. You can take all the credit you want when Mr. Wilt and Ms. Sweet get what they need and give you the green light. But, until then, you let the trained investigators handle this!"

Hacker's olive leaf is just enough to get Small to embrace his ultimatum. "Loud and clear, Ralph! If that's the way it's going to be. Then, in the interests of reciprocity and cooperation between law enforcement agencies, we'll play by your rules. But if there's a body down there, I'm the one calling the coroner."

21

RETURN TO QUARRY LAKE

M*ay 21, 2018*
The Alabama Emergency Response Scuba Unit out of Birmingham is who you call in to investigate a crime scene that's 100 feet under water. A forensic search and recovery team comprised of police officers who are also scuba divers trained to detect and preserve evidence under water, they are prepared for any contingency. The clue leading Wilt, Andrews and Sweet to Gum Pond Road could well have just been a joke by some random prankster reading about Parker's disappearance in the newspaper. But, if the cryptic poem is legit, it could also be a killer sending investigators on a scavenger hunt, or something far worse.

The dive team also includes two officers from the bomb unit from Jefferson County Sheriff's Office in Birmingham. Four divers would descend 60 to 80 feet and scan the quarry bottom, while four others remain on the surface ready to dive in the event of an emergency. One diver would video the divers' descent to the bottom and provide a live video feed which would be transmitted to a large TV monitor up above so Wilt, Andrews, Sweet and local police will see what the divers are seeing.

Most of the topography around the quarry is uneven, jagged or hilly, making it all but impossible for a car to reach the water. But there are three possible paths leading to the lake that are passable enough where a vehicle could generate enough speed to clear the edge of the quarry and reach it. The head of the dive team, Captain Clint Wallace, concluded that if there was anything down there, it would be just off one of those three paths, straight down, 100 feet and change.

Wilt, Andrews and Sweet have microphones allowing them to communicate with Wallace. About ten minutes into the descent, the quarry's limestone bottom comes into view. It looks like an underwater war zone, a long-forgotten water world. The littered junk includes two John Deere tractors, a refrigerator, a piece of caterpillar heavy equipment, and a rusted out, black 1965 Ford pickup truck. And swimming in and out of all of it are enough blue gill, bass, catfish and crappie to feed a small town.

As they watch from above, Andrews is the first to see what they'd come looking for. He excitedly transmits to the dive team.

"There it is. Right there to the left of that tractor. The one with the missing door. Looks like a Lincoln Town car, early 80s model. Exactly like the poem said."

Wilt nods his head in agreement. "Andrews, I think you've found it." One diver then approaches the Lincoln holding a long silver pole called a flux gate magnetometer, which is an underwater metal detector. He scans the inside of the Lincoln, checking the polyester seats and plastic side panels for metal debris. Wallace has a video cam strapped to a selfie stick attached to his back that provides a 360-degree view of the underwater world, including the quarry floor beneath him.

As the Captain circles around the car and approaches the door opening of the vehicle, an object sitting on the quarry floor catches Wilt's eye. "What's that object next to the car? Looks like some kind of a hatchet." The diver picks it up and examines it.

"No. Somebody must have played a round down here and shanked a 7 iron, then took it out on the quarry. It's a broken golf club, snapped and dangling about six inches above the hosel."

As Captain Wallace examines it closely, he reads out initials carved into the club's grip, PDR. Wallace reports his other observations.

"The shaft has a small sticker on it with the most adorable little bitty pine tree you ever saw. But it's all alone. Kind of tugs on the heart."

Wilt and Sweet immediately look at each other realizing the objects' significance. Wilt nods to her and she radios the diver.

"That's not junk, officer. It's evidence. Please bring that up with you."

A mobile overhead crane is brought in to lift the car up to the surface with the assistance of ship salvage airbags, strapped on each side of the cabin.

When the door-less sedan is pulled from the quarry, a welding torch is used to open the trunk, and as suspected, a body bag is inside. A member of the forensic team cuts it open, revealing a badly decomposed body in a three-piece suit. It's Parker, which dental records would later confirm. The right side of his face and skull are crushed. A medical examiner later concludes that Parker died from blunt force trauma, inflicted by the golf club.

That opinion and the location of the body confirmed Wilt's instincts that Lantham isn't the killer as there's no way to establish he had access to the bag room at Lonesome Pine the week of October 2nd. Nor is there any other evidence to tie him to the murder weapon.

But for Wilt, excluding Lantham raises momentary suspicion about Tori Stevens. *So why is she so anxious to implicate him?* Wilt pushes the thought away for now.

Rodger Small walks up to Wilt and Andrews and extends his hand. "Please accept my sincere apologies, Detective, and well done!" Wilt nods in the direction of Sweet, who's now walking around the vehicle with notepad in hand trying to make out the VIN number plates located on the lower corner of the windshield and other parts of the Lincoln.

"I'm afraid you're giving credit to the wrong investigator, Mr. Small, but thank you." Sweet rejoins her partners.

"The author of this heinous crime is no Bubba, gentlemen. Whoever did this had the investigative acumen to know where every VIN on this vehicle is located. They're all defaced. It's almost like we're dealing with someone with a background in law enforcement."

Andrews nods in agreement and chimes in.

"Or someone experienced in stealing vehicles, like Kenny Martin." Wilt is now beaming with pride.

"As you can see, Mr. Small. I've got quite a team here."

Though they wouldn't be able to trace the car back to its owner, Wilt and his assistants travel back to Kentucky with a body, the murder weapon and a narrowing list of suspects.

22

THE RELOCATION

Tuesday 7:30 am, May 22, 2018
Brock Braden stands on his front porch in disbelief as he glares at the morning headlines of the *Summerville Songbird.*

Harlan Parker Found Dead in Rock Quarry in Alabama

Braden's surprise quickly fades to something more concerning when he reads that investigators were led to the Alabama rock quarry by clues in a poem written on a menu chalkboard outside the Lovely Bean and that the murder weapon was a 7 Iron from Lonesome Pine. He turns around and walks back into his study, flopping in a leather chair to consider the possibilities. None of them are good.

Alabama.

Door-less car.

7 Iron from Lonesome Pine.

Poetry.

K-Mart.

Poetry?

K-Mart writes poetry?

Braden begins to feel his heart pounding in his chest as his breathing becomes heavier. Beads of sweat appears on his forehead. There is only one reason Kenny would lead the police to the body and a murder weapon that came from Lonesome Pine.

K-Mart's trying to set me up!

His first instinct is to run down to the bag barn and confront him, but then thinks the better of it.

That's what fools do. They rush in and say something stupid.

What if the detective had already gotten to Kenny and wired him up and is just waiting for him to run down there and say something incriminating? What if the newspaper is in on it too, and the article is just part of an elaborate setup to get him to admit he paid Martin to kill Parker? Braden's paranoia increases with each scenario as they went from plausible to highly unlikely to completely irrational.

What if he just says nothing? Does nothing? Just went about business as if nothing unusual had happened. What were the chances Martin would break under pressure and admit to anything? Not with his background. That was unlikely, he thinks. Martin had spent time in prison and isn't going to be unnerved when some investigator shows up on his doorstep. But still, Brock wonders if he can really afford to take that chance.

Then the phone rang. It was Dan Jack. "See the headlines in the Bird this morning? We need to talk. Be in my office in thirty minutes."

An hour later, Braden is sitting in the conference room at Blue and Gray telling Dan Jack about how he left cash for K-Mart in a marker tree near the fourth hole the week after Parker showed up missing.

"You wasted your money, Brock."

Braden nods his head in agreement. "You got that right. Obviously, I should have gotten someone else to do it."

"No, Brock. What I'm telling you is that Kenny Martin didn't do it. You could have just as well gone to Vegas and blown all that money because you would have seen the same headline today."

"I gave K-Mart a $10,000 down payment to kill Parker and he

comes up missing within a week. And now he's dead. You're saying that's just a coincidence?"

"Do you really think Kenny would have led authorities to the body knowing he would have to pay back all that money to you or lose his job and probably end up back in prison?"

Braden just sits there, looking into space, thinking about it. "Probably not, I guess."

"And how does a guy write poetry like that who dropped out of school in the ninth grade when he can barely read? There's no way! You're talking about someone here a lot more complex than K-Mart."

What Dan Jack said makes perfect sense, but he is overlooking something just as important. Braden points it out. "Does it really matter if Kenny didn't do it if the detective figures out, I paid him money the week it happened?"

"And why would he tell them that, Brock?"

"How do you know he wouldn't? I need to keep him under control."

"I don't advise clients how to keep third persons with knowledge quiet, Brock. If that's what you want, you need a mob lawyer. Good luck finding one in Summerville."

Criminal lawyers usually inform clients that there's no law that requires them to answer questions from the police, so the best response is to tell authorities, *I'll be happy to talk, but my lawyer wants to be present when I do.* But that isn't what Braden is asking. Giving a client advice on what to tell a potential witness to say to the police in a murder investigation, especially where his client was a target of the investigation, is another matter entirely. It is an easy question for Dan Jack to answer.

"Don't tell him anything, Brock! Don't talk to him about it at all. Keep it professional. Go on as if nothing happened. If you tell him to keep his mouth shut, then it will end up being used against you as evidence of consciousness of guilt. And don't bring up the money at all. Let it go. Its walking around money to you anyway."

Braden thanks him for the advice and returns to Lonesome Pine. Though he usually took his lawyer's advice, he isn't going to this time.

It isn't going to help him much if the detective gets to Martin and turns him. For Braden, it isn't a question of what to do about it, but how it's to be done. He pulls out his phone and hits a number on speed dial.

"Hey, it's Brock. Got a relocation I need some help with. If you can get here by this afternoon, there'll be an extra five in it for you."

A couple of hours later, Kenny Martin is out on the 14th hole with the groundskeeping crew when he gets a text from Braden directing him to the vehicle maintenance barn at the far end of the course. Earlier that morning he'd heard the news about Parker from the guys in the clubhouse. There is little room to guess what Braden wants to talk about.

As he enters the barn a man is waiting, seated in the middle of the room on a work stool. Morning light tunnels through a half wagon-wheel window at the top of the barn arch, beaming onto the maintenance shed floor in front of him. Patterns of dust drift in the celestial dance of light between him and the man, making it difficult for Martin to make out who he was. He has no trouble hearing him.

"A poet among us."

"Who are you? Where's Brock?"

"He's nearby. He's listening to us."

"Are you a cop or something?"

Looking up and around, Martin directs his words to Braden. "Look, Brock. I didn't write that poem. Somebody else did it. Not me. Who? I have no idea. I'll pay the money back, if that's why this guy is here. You don't have to lean on me. It will take a while but I'm good for it."

The man just sits there, responding to Martin as if he was talking to him.

"He doesn't care about the money now. He just wants to forget about all about it. To make it all disappear. But you know all about making things go away, don't you, Kenny?"

If the man in the barn is supposed to intimidate Martin, it only agitates him. He looks up again, speaking louder now.

"Who's this guy talking like he knows me? Do I know you, buddy?

Brock, do you really think it's a good idea to be threatening the guy holding your stay out of jail card? Okay then. If that's the way you want it!"

Not getting a response, Kenny then turns to leave, but the door is locked. The man steps off the stool and walks slowly in his direction. Kenny looks back at him and frantically tries to open the door. Chains begin to rifle out of several ports of two overhead cranes, dropping to the ground and pulling back up and dropping again. The sound of metal hitting metal continues to reverberate throughout the barn, drowning out everything else.

23

POETIC JUSTICE?

After a poem led authorities to Parker's body, an image of the killer begins to come into focus: a poet with a very dark sense of humor and motive to kill Harlan Parker. The most obvious person matching that description was a person no one in town had imagined.

Obadiah Adam is Summerville's version of Elvis, its Luciano Pavarotti. But instead of music, Obadiah's gift is poetry. After graduating with honors from Summerville College's creative writing program in 2012, Obadiah moved to New York City where his work would eventually garner critical acclaim, make him a wealthy man and catapult him to the top of the literary world. And it all started in Crawford County.

The son of a tobacco farmer, Obadiah grew up working in the fields twelve-hour days during the summer and two during the school year to help his parents feed their ten children. The notion that he would have the time and luxury of reading, much less writing poetry, would be considered by his father the height of selfishness and disrespect for his family.

He was raised like most other boys in the country, with his father teaching him how to handle a gun and wield a hunting knife. Like his brothers, he was expected to continue the family tradition by working the tobacco fields. But he had other ideas. Obadiah's true love was poetry, and he never stopped writing, if only in his mind, expressing his feelings and thoughts, dreaming of the day his creations would be read and adored by all. But for the first 17 years of his life, Obadiah was only a closet poet, with coat hangers, mothballs and wool coats his only audience.

Then something unexpected happened. His old man, Earl Adam, died peacefully in his sleep during an afternoon nap when Obadiah was a senior at Crawford County High. Earl's wife and nine of his children were beside themselves with grief. And Obadiah would miss his father as well, just not quite as much. The dark, overbearing shadow that had smothered his creative light for seventeen years would blanket it no more. With his father now firmly in the ground, Obadiah could now push beyond the orbit of family's expectations that would have sentenced him to life in a tobacco barn.

The day after Obadiah graduated from Crawford County High School, he enlisted in the Navy and applied for its SEAL program. Six months later, after making it through the preliminary stages of the program, he was at the Naval Amphibious Base in Coronado, California enrolled in the Basic Underwater Demolition/ SEAL School where he was put through an arduous program testing his physical and mental strength.

He was schooled on water and land warfare, basic weapons training, rappelling, deep ocean diving, marksmanship and small unit tactics, including close quarter and unarmed combat in addition to training on survival, evasion, resistance and escaping the enemy. And Obadiah was prepared physically and mentally for his SEAL training having worked ten-hour days, six days a week for weeks on end in the hot and humid Ohio River Valley tobacco fields. His marksmanship skills with a high-powered rifle and ability to make decisions under pressure in extreme conditions set him apart from his peers. While he thrived, most of his classmates withered. Of the 56 recruits who started the program, only 10 graduated.

His career in special ops took him to Africa, Indonesia, South

America and countries in the former Soviet bloc where he would apply his training to subvert Taliban and Al Qaeda forces and rescue hostages.

But by the age of 29, after serving his country a dozen years in special ops missions all over the world, Obadiah had wrought enough death and destruction. As honorable and heroic was his service, his true purpose was to create through his art, to enhance, enlighten and bring a small measure of joy and peace to others.

He returned to civilian life and enrolled at Summerville College to pursue his passion. He would chart a path that would take him on a meteoric rise to literary grandeur and glory. He was the first Adam to receive a college education where he would thrive in Summerville's creative writing program. He would become the first student ever to win two of Crawford House's most prestigious poetry honors in the same year: The Raven Award, for work in the dark romanticism genre of Edgar Allan Poe; and its Golden Daffodil, for exemplary versification in the spirit of William Wadsworth, reflecting the spiritual connection of man's relationship with nature. In the spring of 2012, Obadiah graduated from Summerville College and moved to New York City.

Although he moved to New York City after graduation, he occasionally returns to Crawford House for poetry night and it's always a big deal. His cult-like following plan their calendars around his appearances and sit on the front row, hanging on every word.

24

TREACHERY AT ORCHID AND OAK

M*arch 2015*

Orchid and Oak has been the center of Summerville's literary scene since before the Civil War. Located in the old Crawford mansion, sonnets and soliloquies have seeped into the cracks of its brick and mortar walls and remained for generations. Summerville College's English Department associated with Crawford House in 1870 and transformed it into a haven for creative writing and a repository for the works of renowned Kentucky writers. And at the end of every spring semester, the school's creative writing workshop honors the student with the most outstanding compilation of creative writing with the Orchid and Oak award. The student's work is then bound and immortalized by being placed on Crawford's shelves along with the the like of Wendell Berry, Jessie Stuart, and Harry Caudill. The award also includes a lifetime membership in The Orchid and Oak Society, Crawford's literary club, which is by invitation only and reserved for the accomplished writer and poetry aficionado.

But Crawford's core philosophy isn't pompous, high-minded or exclusive. It holds that creative writing and poetry are things to be appreciated and encouraged throughout the community. Every

Thursday evening it hosts poetry night, where anyone could read or recite their own creations.

In warmer months, poets perform outside in Berry Amphitheater, built behind Crawford House in the early 20th century and named for Wendell Berry at the dawn of the 21st. Venue seating is partially below ground level and faces a stage which runs to the brick rear wall of the mansion. Carved in woodwork mounted above the stage is Crawford House's creed:

For all with a verse in their heart
and light in their soul.

As each poet takes their turn on stage, Wellington Worth, Crawford's curator, gives a brief introduction. He would share a fun fact with the audience about the poet to lighten the mood and to control the pace of the program. The whole thing typically lasted from 90 minutes to a couple of hours that included the offerings of ten to twelve poets.

The format is basic. The artist would say the name of the poem they were sharing and the inspiration behind it. And there were no limitations on content if it was the reader's creation. You could only perform your original work once, a rule established to encourage writers to write, which was, after all, the whole idea. Worth strongly believes that best way for the sublime to reveal itself was to completely free the creative license within the artist, and to never, ever limit or censure their presentation. In the program's 45-year history, no one had ever been cut off or removed from stage while reciting their poetry, a fact that Worth took immense pride in.

It was a beautiful spring evening at Berry Amphitheater, which was full with college students and poetry lovers throughout the community, almost all of whom were waiting for Obadiah. There were always a few regulars, some who had been writing and reading at poetry night for years, even decades. And there were always one or two newcomers. Wellington Worth always started and ended the program with his strongest writers to grab the attention of the audience from the beginning and keep it until the very end, and this night he would begin and end the program with Obadiah.

"Welcome friends of Crawford House for a very special edition of poetry night. Most of you already know our first artist. Obadiah Adam has lived in New York City for about three years now, and we anticipate big things for him there, of course, but we are always excited to see him back at Crawford, as his work never disappoints. His most recent compilation, like the work of other writers reading to you this evening, is available in Frost Foyer for purchase after the program. I've had a chance to get a sneak peek at some of it and I must warn you that it will absolutely change you. It's some of his very best work yet. So, without further ado, I give to you, Obadiah Adam!"

Obadiah walked onto stage to the wild applause and frenzied adoration you'd expect to hear for a rock star, except he looked the furthest thing from it. He was a broad, muscular man of higher than average stature, with a neck which only seemed the width of a fire hydrant. His soft, kind face was adorned with dark bushy eyebrows and a tightly cropped, full black beard, with piercing blue eyes which hid behind round spectacles resting on the end of his nose.

His signature look was intentionally understated, a flannel shirt in the winter or a T-shirt in warmer months with blue jeans that were held up by suspenders. His romantic work in particular captured the venery and agony of tragic love like no other writer Crawford House had ever produced, stirring the hearts and passions of his local following.

Obadiah lifted his hands just slightly to bring the fading applause to quiet.

"So nice to be back with all my dear friends at Orchid and Oak. As I bus tables in Manhattan contemplating where my next meal will come from, I often think of the ones I've shared with many who are here tonight."

Laughter filled the amphitheater.

"My first reading is a recent creation called *Her Silhouette*, and I hope you enjoy it."

I walked up to my window
As close as I could get
Reached out my hand to touch the face
That was her silhouette

She stood there still without a word
From my first love I never heard
Then night would come and she would go
But where she went I did not know

Sometimes it seemed that weeks would pass
Before I saw her face at last
I asked, I begged her not to leave
Seemed not to care my heart would bleed

And then, in time, I came to learn
Was not by light that she returned
But just a shadow carved in bright
Was with the dark she shared the light

If tears were cried, she never wept
A promise made was never kept
And when death came to-my-soul to get
The shadow was her silhouette

As Obadiah read to the audience, Silas Brown was alone, backstage in the C.S. Lewis Lounge, just behind the amphitheater where poets kept their coats and other personal belongings.

Silas was slated to read his poetry near the middle of the program. But now that was the last thing on his mind. He rifled through Obadiah's leather folder file, pulling drafts of his poetry and running to the administrative office to copy them. Work that Obadiah had yet to copyright or even share.

Silas had been Obadiah's college roommate and had also been in the school's creative writing program but enjoyed far less success.

Neither his college work nor writings since had received any favorable attention. No Golden Daffodil, no Orchid and Oak Award, and no interest from publishers.

He had dropped out of school and secured employment as assistant crematorium operator at Cousin Critter Cremation. Like everyone else at Crawford House, Silas was in awe of Obadiah's talent, but that admiration had turned to envy with the realization that it was just a matter of time before his success would grow far beyond Summerville.

An hour after Obadiah, it was Silas's turn to read his poem. Though he had dropped out of the writing program, Wellington Worth believed in second chances. And besides, they were short on poets that evening, in dire need of filler.

"Our next artist is Silas Brown, a former student in our writing program. Silas now works in pet memorial services and products, selling cremation scattering tubes, custom gravestones and urn pendant necklaces. And it's my understanding they're quite tasteful. I give you, Silas Brown!"

Silas walked on stage to brief but polite applause.

"Well, you could probably guess by now that I work at the pet crematorium over in Cousin. Now some may think that's morbid. But I see it as a place where people say their final farewells to their little loved ones. What most of the world doesn't realize is that a pet is the only family some people have. This poem is a tribute to them. It's called, *Fluffy Bear's Furry Requiem*."

Murmurs and gasps spread over the audience as people looked at each other bemused, unsure what to expect.

Fluffy Bear bounded across the soft grass
Her furry fluff flew as her little paws passed
With a joy in her heart which no one could rob her
Her kiss met my face with a mouth full of slobber

I picked up her stick and threw it up high
And Fluff quickly followed to catch on the fly

But I threw it too far and as Fluff's fate would have it
She'd catch a Ford Taurus in oncoming traffic

The rush hour crowd had no time to bide
Its horns would not silence as I kneeled by her side
So, I took her back home and laid her on down
Dressed her up fine in a bath-towel gown

We rode to the furnace on that one final drive
I bid Fluff farewell as they laid her inside
You'll never know death or the depth of despair
Till you smell the hard stench of yo dog's burnin' hair

Other than an animal lover in the front row who was almost inconsolable, Berry's response to *Fluffy Bear's Furry Requiem* was muffled and something less than affirming. But that mattered little to Silas. He had gotten what he came for. Now all he had to do was to sit and wait for Obadiah to make the big time.

25

ATOP THE LITERARY WORLD

J*une 2015*

Just as Silas Brown and everyone else in Summerville had predicted, Obadiah's big break would come, and sooner rather than later. Just over three and a half years after Obadiah moved to New York, *Hidden Letter Publishing* released his first commercial literary compilation, *Every Life a River*. It was a collection of his best work since graduation, refined in the artist's crucible, where forces of brilliance and ambition grind against life's struggles and hardships to produce the sublime.

It would be Adam's magnum opus, receiving critical acclaim from some of America's most respected poetry reviews: *The Wandering Road, Attic Door, Uncaptured Verse* and *Sublime Reveal* hailed the arrival of Adam, describing him as poetry's new superstar, the 21st century prince of rhyme and versification.

The work's impact on the poetry reading public was immediate and dramatic. At the age of 36, seemingly overnight, Obadiah Adam had scaled the summit and was now sitting atop the literary world. He was an aberration, the rare combination of writer who was well received not only commercially, but also by the literary public which viewed work through the lens of artistic value.

He moved into a penthouse on Manhattan's upper east side overlooking Central Park. His newfound star power suddenly got him a place setting at the city's finest restaurants and as a guest on the late-night talk show circuit. A national reading and book signing tour followed and with it, a lucrative seven figure deal with *Hidden Letter Publishing* that would give Obadiah financial security for life. Or so he thought.

Obadiah's book signing and reading tour would be received with great enthusiasm from coast to coast, and he would kick it off at none other than Crawford House to a packed amphitheater reading, *Every Life a River*. The crowd erupted with applause as Obadiah finished reading each of just few of the pieces in his new collection. When he was done, they followed him to Frost Foyer, hundreds of them, standing in line waiting for a signed copy of his book. But tucked away in the corner was none other than Silas Brown and his lawyer, Harlan Parker.

Just months earlier, Parker had read the poetry drafts Silas brought him, and even he recognized that one day they'd be very valuable. He also knew that Obadiah was their author. But, for Parker, being bound by the facts was something losers did.

With copies of Obadiah's yet to be copyrighted manuscripts now in his clutches, Parker directed Silas to copy each poem in his handwriting. He then enlisted Tori Stevens to register copyrights with the Library of Congress under the name of Silas Brown. She filed the collection under an obscure title which was unlikely to be detected by the copyright office when a publisher or lawyer later registered the work in Obadiah's name.

So, when Hidden Letter published *Every Life a River*, Parker would sit back and allow the book to be released into the marketplace without the cloud of litigation hanging over it. Then the poetry reading public would flock to bookstores and online sites pushing it to the New York Times Best Sellers List which, in turn, would send book sales higher still, maximizing the value of a future lawsuit.

∾

JULY 2015

Silas watched impatiently as the swell of Obadiah's fans grew larger and larger as they clamored for a copy of *Every Life a River*, quickly exceeding the capacity of the foyer to then flow out into the street. Silas could wait no longer. He had the litigation itch, and only his lawyer could make it go away.

"See all that money standing in line? We need to file suit now and cash in, Harlan!"

You could almost see dollar signs flash in Parker's eyes as he watched Obadiah personalize one signature after another on the front leaf of each book.

"Not yet, Silas. Let him sell our book for a few months so he can put a few million in the bank. Then we'll just walk across the street and take what's ours."

Silas does a double take. "Our book? What you talking about? The copyright was in my name last time I checked. It's all mine, mine, mine. And don't you ever forget it!"

In two and a half decades of his sordid legal career, Harlan Parker had learned how deal with the idle threats and real ones. He was a con's con, someone who instinctively knew what buttons to push to get unruly clients back in line. He'd done so with cold blooded killers, kingpins of redneck marijuana trafficking organizations and any number of much more intimidating characters than Silas Brown. He almost laughed.

"Sure would be a shame if your Obadiah file folder shuffle got out. You'd have to go back to gassing cocker spaniels and hugging blue-haired ladies the rest of your life."

Parker's staccato jabs put Silas on the defensive. The muscles in his jawline twitched as he clamped his teeth together, his back stiffened, and the bulging veins in his neck were now visible. He had no comeback and Harlan knew it.

He flashed a big smile. "Go right ahead. Just keep disrespecting your lawyer and that little birdie is going to go tell Adam all about it."

"Why... you mother..."

Like most of Harlan's angry clients, Silas's first and last recourse was profanity. For Harlan it was all about control and the only way to keep it now was to raise the intensity level. He grabs Silas's arm and pulls him close enough to kiss him.

"You don't know jack, Silas Brown! You're in way over your head. That's why you hired a lawyer. You don't cash out a deal like this overnight. You wait for it to build into something. So, you're going to do it my way or get nothing. Do you understand me?"

Silas immediately changed his tune. "Got it, Harlan! You're the boss."

∽

November 3, 2015

Five months after the release of *Every Life a River*, Parker sent a cease and desist letter to Hidden Letter Publishing claiming Silas Brown was the author and rightful holder of the copyright to *Every Life a River*, directing them to immediately stop publishing it.

When Hidden Letter received it they viewed it as a hollow threat that Parker and Brown couldn't back up. Fraudsters always came out of the woodwork attempting to extort money out of publishers, crying copyright infringement over the latest hugely successful commercial release. To Hidden Letter it was nothing usual and wasn't about to slow its release in the middle of the holiday season. The promotion and sale of *Every Life a River* continued unabated. Its in-house counsel's response was predictable. *Let them file a lawsuit if they think they can prove it.* So Hidden Letter gave its standard response, which was no response at all.

But Obadiah didn't view the letter so routinely. Growing up in Crawford County, Obadiah knew Parker well. He was the lawyer who represented an oil company that fabricated oil and gas leases to try to steal the Adam farm in a heated mineral rights dispute twenty years before. Even though Judge Renfro found the leases fabricated and threw out the lawsuit, defending it had cost Earl Adam over $20,000 which put the family in dire financial straits for years. So, Obadiah knew that whatever hand Silas Brown played in this letter, he was just the puppet that Parker was using to cash in on his success.

For three hard years, he washed dishes, waited tables and continued to hone his craft in Greenwich Village, biding his time in anticipation of his big opportunity. The life of the poor, struggling artist only enriched the texture and depth of his verse. Finally, his big opportunity had come, and now Harlan Parker threatened to take it all away. Obadiah wasn't inclined to respond with lawyer-speak to get his feelings across.

26

THE GLUTTON'S PUNISHMENT

arch 2016

M Harlan Parker grinned ear to ear as he examined the pig laid out spread-eagle over the roof and hood of his seven series BMW. In size, the feral hog rivaled that of Hogzilla, the record setting behemoth swine killed by a hunter in North Caroline in 2014. It approached 8 feet in length and had to weigh over 400-pound lbs.

Even if it wasn't quite as massive as Hogzilla, it was just as dead. Its colon was tied around the pig's neck like a tunicate, and the rest of its guts and bodily fluids draped and dripped over the windshield and top of the luxury sedan like frosting on a cinnamon roll. Tucked inside the beast's mouth was a bored-out apple. Filling the space of its hollow core was a rolled-up note.

Anyone else's response to such a scene would be to immediately call the police. Then the police would come over and photograph the animal as Parker had found it, preserve the evidence and do a complete investigation into the matter. But Parker already knew who did it. And he didn't want Obadiah to be charged by the police. He didn't even want Obadiah to be interviewed. He had something much grander in mind.

He called his private investigator, Milton B. Shake. "Shake, you're going to need your pickup truck and camera, and to be sure and wear some latex gloves along with some spandex pants and a long-sleeved shirt. And you're going to need to wear some old clothes over that after you're done, or you'll muck up the inside of your truck. You're about to get some foul creep all over you."

Parker's comments stirred Shake's curiosity. "What are we talking about, Harlan? If it's a death scene you need to call the coroner."

"It's a death scene alright, just not the humankind. We won't need anything of that sort. It'll be obvious when you get here."

During his 30 years as a special agent with the Bureau of Alcohol, Tobacco and Firearms Milt Shake had been the mortal enemy of Parker, at least in the courtroom. They'd worked on opposite sides of some of the county's highest profile arson cases. Parker had cross-examined Shake as lead investigator for the prosecution. One of the examinations had gotten so intense that Judge Renfro had stopped it and sent the jury out of the courtroom. He had to privately admonish both lawyer and witness before resuming testimony.

But that all changed when Shake retired from federal service. Now with time on his hands with little to do, he decided to do some private investigative work for local attorneys. Then he interviewed some witnesses for Parker who immediately saw an opportunity. Shake's ability to sound like he knew what he was talking about overcame any deficit in his experience or training.

Between the two of them, they usually found some case in Shake's career that touched on an issue Parker needed expert testimony about. The fact that Shake had absolutely no training in several of his so-called areas of expertise was secondary.

Parker began using Shake as an expert witness on a wide array of disciplines, claiming that his background as a federal investigator for 30 years made him eminently qualified to do so. Whatever Parker needed in a certain case, Tori Stevens researched the field of expertise and drafted well-reasoned and clearly worded opinions for Shake to pass off as his own. Then all Shake would have to do was commit it to memory and testify.

Shake's first expert opinion was a psychological profile of a defendant who had confessed to a murder. Shake opined that the accused had made it all up because of an overwhelming need to be accepted by an authority figure, acceptance he had never received as a child.

In this case the authority figure was the investigator who interviewed him. The investigator decided the accused was guilty, so the accused said he was. It all went back to the accused's childhood of never being able to please his father. The jury bought the nonsense and acquitted the defendant.

Then Shake held himself out as an expert in the physics of handgun design, testifying as to how many pounds of pressure per square inch needed to be applied to the trigger of .45 Ruger. In his opinion, that made it all but impossible for Parker's female client to have had the strength to fire the murder weapon.

Shake had become Parker's best friend, his courtroom whore, his interchangeable, all-in-one expert who could be whatever and say whatever Parker needed. Like all prostitutes, Shake only performed for the right price, but the client always paid.

Shake was the best counterfeit expert around. Parker and Shake developed a nefarious symbiotic relationship in which the two worked in tandem to scam the system. And it lasted far longer that it should have.

When Shake arrived on the scene of Hogzilla II, Parker directed him to photograph everything and retrieve the note from the pig's snout. Shake stood on his toes and stretched him arm as far as he could over the vehicle, now encased with ooze and gump of the feral hog. He pulled out the apple and read the note.

The Glutton's Punishment

His pink head was bare with sparse brittle hair
He'd root with a gruffy round snout
I thought he some swine just taking his time
But that wasn't what he's about.

It wasn't acorns or earthworms he sought
But words that I wrote and rhymes that I wrought
The pig couldn't read, much less hope to write
Just took what was mine and went out of sight

It wasn't some boar that slipped through my bog
But some portly lawyer that looked like a hog
With blood-sucking teeth set inside his jaw
His five-toe hooved feet were nothing but claws

But now he can't grunt or bandy about
His outsides are in. His insides are out
The swine who dare dine with head in my trough
Will pay for his supper at much higher cost

SHAKE IMMEDIATELY WENT into investigator mode.

"The author of this note thinks you're bald, overweight, and poorly manicured, Harlan."

SEPTEMBER 18, 2017

Eighteen months later, *Silas Brown vs. Hidden Letter Publishing and Obadiah Adam* were in trial in federal court in a copyright infringement action and Shake was Harlan Parker's expert witness. Shake's area of special knowledge was now forensic writing. The climax of the trial was Shake's testimony.

After studying the sentence structure of some of Brown's known creations and comparing it to the writings in *Every Life a River*, Shake testified that they were written by the same person, Silas Brown. After he gave his opinion on direct examination, it was time for Robert Bloomberg, counsel of Hidden Letter, to cross examine.

"Good morning, Mr. Shake."

"Morning, Mr. Bloomberg."

"You don't have a degree in English, do you, sir?"

"No."

"And you don't have one in creative writing or any other kind of writing, either?"

"No, sir."

"In fact, you got a C- in English class in high school, didn't you?"

"We were graded on a C curve, sir."

"And in 30 years of testifying in federal court, you've never been qualified or testified as an expert in the area of forensic writing, either. Have you?"

"No, sir."

"When did you become an expert in forensic writing, Mr. Shake?"

"About two months ago, sir."

"And what inspired you to suddenly do that at the age of 59?"

"Harlan asked me to be one while we were having coffee one morning."

"You've been an expert for Mr. Parker before, haven't you?"

"Yes, sir."

"In fact, you've testified for him in areas of false confessions, quantum physics, how to barbeque with a microwave oven, and finally, a condition known as 'acute audible sensory deficit for husbands when asked to help around the house'. Is that correct?"

"Yes, sir."

"Does that last one come from your education or personal experience, Mr. Shake?"

Harlan Parker calmly intervened. "Objection."

"Sustained," Judge Branch ruled.

Shakes answered. "Yes, sir. I've been fortunate to have a vast knowledge and expertise in a wide array of disciplines, Mr. Bloomberg."

"Just no particular training, experience or prior expert testimony in writing, language, sentence construction or grammar?"

"I'll let my credentials speak for themselves, Mr. Bloomberg."

"I think they do quite well, Mr. Shake."

Parker adopted a stern countenance. "Objection. Move to strike."

Judge Branch replied, "Sustained. Strike comment of counsel from the record. Continue."

A muscle in Bloomberg's cheek twitched. "And you conclude that Silas Brown wrote *Every Life a River* after comparing it to *Fluffy Bear's Furry Requiem*?"

"Yes, sir."

"Can you tell me how a poem describing the agony of someone watching his dog getting trucked and then cremated has anything in common with *Every Life a River*?"

"They both have the common theme of nature and death, sir."

"Did Mr. Brown provide you any other work to compare?"

"'Fluffy Bear was enough. His unique way of phrasing in each poem is unmistakable, sir."

"Didn't you find it unusual that Mr. Brown didn't provide any other poems before or after 'Fluffy Bear'?"

"The sample size was sufficient."

"Wouldn't you need more than one sample of someone's work to evaluate his writing style?"

Parker spoke up once more. "Objection, you honor. Asked and answered."

However, Judge Branch saw some sense in this line of questioning. "Overruled! You may continue, Mr. Bloomberg."

"Mr. Brown hasn't written any other poetry the past two years that he could give you to compare with *Every Life A River*?"

"I can't say he hasn't written anything else."

"Well, if he did write other poetry, he certainly didn't show it to you, did he, Mr. Shake?"

"No, sir."

"No further questions, your honor."

Things went from bad to worse for Silas Brown when Judge Branch allowed Obadiah stand in the place of his lawyer to do the closing statement, reciting, *The Glutton's Punishment*. Overwhelmed with Obadiah's awesome display of literary talent, the jury quickly ruled in favor of Obadiah and Hidden Letter Publishing.

But the whole episode had still been very costly and embarrassing. After the jury verdict, Obadiah walked up to Parker with a fore-boding message that and everyone in the courtroom heard.

"One day, maybe tomorrow, maybe five years on, I'll be coming back around to pay you a visit, Harlan. We're gonna have us a time down on the Blackacre. Now don't bother looking for it on a map because Blackacre's not a place you go to physically as much as spiritually. And I promise you that it will be spiritual for both of us. So, until then."

27

WELLINGTON'S BIG REGRET

M *ay 24, 2018*
Wilt decides to take Ms. Sweet up on her advice and go pay a visit to Wellington Worth, Crawford House's Curator. Worth has known Wilt through the years, calling on him from time to time to investigate periodic acts of vandalism wrought upon Crawford House, usually college kids getting out of hand after drinking too much. However, Wilt has never been to Mr. Worth's residence.

In the 19th century, Barret Park, today referred to as "Old Summerville" or "Old Town" was where the county's well-to-do called home. Families steeped in railroad, coal and tobacco money spared no expense building residences that lined its avenues and sidewalks cut twice as wide as the rest of town. As passersby strolled down its thoroughfares in horse and buggy, one could readily see one architectural wonder after the other built in original but varied iterations in Colonial, Neoclassical or Tudor styles. But most of Barret's homes were Victorian, painted in vibrant colors, each anchored by a sweeping front or wind-around porch and topped with roofs filled with gables, turrets and towers.

However, by the 1950s, with its original inhabitants having died out and many of those remaining deciding to opt for newer and more efficient ranch, postmodern homes in the suburbs, much of Old Town had fallen into disrepair. But that would change in the 1970s when Wellington Worth moved to Summerville. He bristled at the notion of living in a rectangular, brick and mortar home in neighborhoods where every house looked like the other.

Then he happened upon Sinclair and immediately saw the vast potential hidden within its once blossoming grounds, rusted gates and tattered exterior. Because suburban flight sent the Old Town real estate market to rock bottom, Worth bought the Sinclair mansion for a pittance before giving back whatever bargain he achieved by spending over $200,000 to restore it. His vision would prove to be the spark that would usher in a preservation movement that brought Old Town back to a glimpse of its former glory.

When Detective Wilt arrives at the front gate of the Sinclair mansion, Worth is waiting for him, sitting at a table on his front porch, wearing a white collared shirt with matching pants and shoes, complete with a Panama straw hat.

"Welcome, detective. Always good to see you. Please have a seat and make yourself comfortable. Would you like a refreshment of some sort? Perhaps a snack?"

Worth quickly summons Harrison, his live-in butler, who emerges from the house in black pants and a white serving jacket. He carries a tray upon which a pitcher of water and two glasses rest.

Wilt, not accustomed to being in such grand surroundings, just sits in wonder at the wrought iron table, glancing up and about the porch before realizing Worth was speaking to him. "Uh, no thank you, Mr. Worth. Very of kind of you to offer, though. Water will be just fine."

"Are you sure you don't want something a bit stronger? Something to take the edge off. Perhaps a Vodka Lemon Spritzer? Harrison makes a divine rum punch."

"I'm afraid not while I'm on duty. Chief Justice might frown on that."

"Oh, Henry wouldn't have much room to complain. A fish of the first order. Never met a decanter 'he didn't take a shine to." He laughs.

"Agreed, Mr. Worth."

Wilt chuckles and nods his head.

"The reason I called you is that I'd really appreciate your insights on something."

Wilt pulls out a photograph of *Gum Pond Road* written on the menu board from the Lovely Bean and places it on the table. Worth pulls his spectacles out of his shirt pocket and picks up the photo. The resolution of the photo is such that it makes the poem easy to read. During poetry nights, Worth is generally effusive in his praise, not only to encourage beginners but to create enthusiasm for the program that evening, though he usually isn't so generous with compliments in a one-on-one setting. But as he glances over *Gum Pond Road* it clearly catches his interest. Worth smiles as he works his way through it.

He places the photograph back on the table, removes his spectacles and looks back at Wilt with astonishment.

"Well, I never imagined you had a penchant for dark romanticism, Detective! It's one thing to deal in matters of the mysterious and macabre for a living, but your obvious talent to express it in rhyme and verse is exceptional. Well done! Bravo! I'm sure Julia Sweet and the patrons at the Bean are quite pleased you've chosen its menu board as a canvass to share your gift. This is all I need to extend an invitation to you to render at our poetry night. It would be an honor to have you!"

Wilt is slightly embarrassed that Worth had misread his intentions and grossly overstated his literary abilities.

"I wish I could take credit for writing something like this, Mr. Worth. But I'm afraid the author of this poem wouldn't be a good fit for your program. We strongly suspect whoever wrote this murdered Harlan Parker."

"Oh my! That would be rather awkward for the audience, if not terrifying, wouldn't it? Rendering poetry in leg irons and an orange jumpsuit. Although it certainly would be a thrilling evening! But no. I agree with you completely. Not a good fit. Not at all!"

"I'd hoped you might recognize the writing style, Mr. Worth. We're thinking that the writer may have been a student at Crawford or someone reading at your poetry night. Does anyone come to mind?"

Worth suddenly appears uncomfortable. Quickly reflecting over his 40 years at Crawford House, he can recall only a handful of students that could write poetry of such quality, and one in particular. He also knew Parker and quickly surmises that if one of his former students did it, the revelation would be more disturbing than surprising. Worth has no intention of making any of them suspects without corroborating information.

With one hand clenched and held to his mouth and the other tapping the table, he pauses for several few moments, choosing his words carefully.

"No one comes to mind, Detective. We've had hundreds of students come through the program or read poetry at Crawford."

"Did Harlan Parker ever frequent Orchid and Oak?"

"Harlan has an inglorious history at Crawford. He was actually enrolled in our creative writing program his freshman year, but he couldn't cut it." He pauses for a moment. "No, that's too harsh. Let's just say, he simply didn't have the gift."

"I'm not sure I understand what you're saying, Mr. Worth."

"When Harlan wasn't plagiarizing someone else's work, he mixed metaphors like a bad gin and tonic. But, despite it all, I'll hold you to the strictest confidence in telling you that Harlan's leaving the writing program is one of my deepest regrets."

"You felt as though you judged him too harshly?"

"Quite the contrary. I'd been more than generous in giving him a D in English composition, but during our year-end, student-teacher conference I inadvertently said something that will encumber my heart to the sarcophagus."

"What was that, Mr. Worth?"

Worth pauses for several moments, biting his lip, looking up, down, anywhere but at Wilt. It is as if he were on the verge of confessing to some heinous crime. Seeing that Worth's struggling to share his secret, Wilt tries to encourage him.

"Now, Mr. Worth, whatever it is that you said to Harlan, it can't be that bad."

With a hand on each leg, Worth takes a deep break and then exhales. Suddenly, the pace of his words quicken as his pitch surges from tenor to soprano.

"I told him not to be discouraged...that lots of failed writers go to law school."

Wilt is stunned. Initially, he just sits in shock, without words. As the revelation begins to sink in, he locks down his lips trying to keep the words from escaping. Struggling mightily to contain his disgust, Wilt's head begins to shake frantically as if were swiveling on the spring of a bobblehead doll. But it's just too much. His tone instantly intensifies from conversational to accusatory.

"Well, well, well. So now the horrible truth is finally revealed! For years, I've wondered who in the name of God would give Harlan Parker the idea of going to law school. And now we finally know!"

Wilt stands and points a finger at Worth.

"Wellington Worth is the reason Harlan Parker became a lawy..."

Worth stands in his defense.

"Enough! Not a word, Detective! I swear by God and Queen that you've made it all up and have clearly gone mad. They'll be feeding you tapioca pudding in the home within a week!"

Realizing he's lost his cool and unfairly judged Worth, Wilt immediately tries to make amends.

"Mr. Worth. I apologize for upsetting you. Believe me when I tell you that I completely understand. I'm so very sorry! Please be assured your confidence will go no farther than this porch."

Clearly embarrassed, Worth retakes his seat, pulls out a handkerchief and dips it in his water glass before dabbing it about his face and neck. "I don't know what came over me, Detective. It is I who should apologize."

"Not at all, Mr. Worth, May I continue?"

"Please do."

"When was the last time you recall Parker being at Crawford?"

"In recent years, I don't recall."

"Do you recall Parker ever coming to poetry night to hear Obadiah Adam?"

Worth pauses again, then exhales slowly while shaking his head, acknowledging a fact he had hoped to avoid. Obadiah was the first person that came to mind when he read *Gum Pond Road* and now he had no choice but to talk about him.

"Yes. Now that you mention it, I do recall Harlan at Crawford on one occasion. Forgive me. I must have erased that from my memory bank."

"Was there anything special going on that evening?"

"Harlan came with Silas Brown when Obadiah Adam opened his book tour at Crawford House. I'm sure you've heard of Obadiah's nationally bestselling compilation, *Every Life a River*?"

"Yes. Certainly. Haven't had the pleasure of reading it. Not really my thing, but of course, everyone's heard of Mr. Adam. Do you know if Parker was a friend or follower of Mr. Adam?"

"I wouldn't say they exchanged fruit baskets or cheese balls, Detective. But really, at this point I think I've said quite enough. I see where you're going, and I find it highly unlikely that Obadiah would do violence to Harlan Parker. He's a poet, not a killer."

"He was in special ops, wasn't he?"

"He's a patriot, Detective. He did what he had to do for country in the line of duty. There's quite a difference between killing the enemy and killing for revenge."

"Did Obadiah have a reason to feel vengeful about Parker, Mr. Worth?"

"You'd have to ask him. But good luck finding him. He's been in seclusion for several months. Since that unseemly copyright trial."

"Yes, I'm aware of that case, Mr. Worth." Wilt has already interviewed Milton Shake and knew about the threats Obadiah made to Parker, before and after the trial.

"Does Obadiah write about, as you say, the mysterious and macabre? Would he write something in the genre of *Gum Pond Road*?"

"Lots of writers who've come through Crawford fancy themselves as the next Edgar Allan Poe, Detective. I wouldn't say that would be unique to Obadiah."

"You seem rather fond of him, Mr. Worth. I'm not sure you're the most objective person to be asking these questions to."

"Precisely! Just hearing these questions makes me feel like I'm consorting with the enemy. No disrespect intended, of course."

"None taken, Mr. Worth. Thank you for your time."

28

DON'T ASK, DON'T SMELL

By the time Obadiah was a teenager, his father Earl had amassed so much land in the northeastern corner of Crawford County that the western boundary of his farm ran for over one mile along a ridge which overlooked the Kentucky River. When Earl's widow, Easter passed away just months after him, the children decided to keep the family farm together and continue to work the corn, tobacco and soybean fields together as they always had. Each of them had built homes on the farm and were raising their own families there by the time Obadiah returned from military service.

The family farm arrangement worked well for over a decade, that is, until brother Cletus decided that he could make considerably more money growing weed than what he made off his take of the family soybean, corn and tobacco crops. Although Crawford County law enforcement had taken a laissez-faire attitude toward the cultivation and use of marijuana for two decades, the rest of the family wasn't as confident that some state or federal drug task force officer eventually doing a flyby over their farm would feel the same way. If Cletus was caught growing marijuana on his tract, the entire farm would be at risk of being forfeited to the government. The rest of the family wasn't about to take that chance. They decided to subdivide the 1300-acre farm into nine separate tracts.

Because Obadiah had no family to support and his livelihood didn't depend on farming, he selected a densely wooded, uneven terrain wrought with sinkholes, steep ravines, and jagged sandstone outcroppings that meant certain death for any tractor, plow, or harvesting combine that dared trying to cultivate it.

Most anyone else would consider the landscape unwelcoming, even hazardous to tread upon, but to Obadiah it is ideal. He sought seclusion and quietude, hoping to find his creative light again. His world had gone pitch black from the anguish and humiliation of being portrayed to be a fraud and thief by Harlan Parker.

Though he was vindicated by the jury in the copyright trial, the entire farcical ordeal had left him disillusioned, bitter and on edge, capable of going off on anyone at any moment. Not one to opt for counseling or prescription medication to manage his anger, Obadiah determined the only way to keep himself from losing it in public or in front of family was to isolate himself in the backwoods until he resolved his anger issues.

He built the cabin himself, framed with notched oak beams, a thatch roof and poplar floor. He killed or grew what he needed to sustain himself and pulled water through an iron cast pump that drew from a well he dug below the cabin's foundation. Though the front of the structure had all the appearances of a cabin, the rear was left open and affixed around a cave entrance, so the back of his home was a cavern one could easily walk about and lounge comfortably in for several hundred feet.

There was no phone, television or any other means of communication with the outside world, and that was fine by Obadiah as there's no one he desired to talk with. If you want to reach him, you must go find him, which means negotiating a perilous landscape to an unknown location looking for a former Navy Seal under duress where the only thing more dangerous than the search is succeeding at it.

There are no children to drive to school or wife to have friends over. There is rarely a reason to leave his homestead and he hardly had since returning to Kentucky. Obadiah gave his agent, publicist and siblings strict instructions not to disclose his location, but Detective Wilt suspects that someone in the family knows Obadiah's location, and he knows just who to squeeze to find out.

~

June 12, 2018

Cletus is in his back yard admiring his marijuana crop when Wilt and Andrews pull onto his driveway and approach. "Good morning, Cletus. Those are some fine-looking leaves you've got there. Looks like several hundred plants."

"Well, thank you, Mr. Wilt. That's quite a compliment coming from a man of your knowledge and experience. To what do I owe the pleasure of your appearance at the Adam farm?" Cletus knows Wilt as the home plate umpire when he was a little leaguer, and, a few years later, as the patrol officer who arrested him for drunk driving.

"We need to speak with Obadiah. Thought you could tell us where we might find him."

"Wish I could help you, detective, but your guess is as good as mine. Haven't seen him in a coon's age."

"How long have you been growing that wild tea, Cletus?"

"Now—you don't expect me to answer a question like that, do you? No disrespect to you, Mr. Wilt, but I don't think you call the balls and strikes on the power parsley round here no more! Don't ask, don't smell is the law of the land!"

"It's not law, Cletus. It's an unwritten policy promoted by the Garden Party running City Hall who just want an excuse to smoke weed. As far as you're concerned, don't ask, don't smell is only in effect if you're cooperating with us. It's not a constitutional right. Your brother has been keeping a mighty low profile around here, and you know where he is. It's your moment of truth, Cletus!" Wilt motions to Andrews, who walks to the trunk of the police cruiser and retrieves a sickle.

"Now, come on, fellas. You don't want to harvest Mary Jane before her time, as pure and undefiled as she is. Oba doesn't like anyone knowing his business, Detective, including me. That's all I got. Straight up!"

"Alright, Cletus. Don't say I didn't give you fair warning." Wilt nods to Andrews, who walks over to the first row and starts chopping.

"Surely, you're not gonna...Wait! No! Alright! Alright!" He nods in the direction of the river. "He's over yonder. Please, just stop whacking the plants!"

Wilt looks to Andrews and makes a cutting motion across his neck, suspending the chopping. "So, where's your brother, Cletus?"

"Now, I've never been to his cabin, but I know he has one. Couldn't even tell you where he's at, not exactly. Oba doesn't entertain, other than to visit with his—hmmm, concubines; I mean his admirers." He coughs, holding his hand to his mouth.

"His property is over there." He points. "Runs from this big oak right here, all the way to the ridge overlooking the river. They all park in my driveway and pass through here and into that gap in the tree line, right there."

Still struggling with subtlety and nuance, Andrews probes further. "How can you be so sure what they're doing down there, Mr. Adam?"

"Because I've seen most every sweet thang who scampers through that tree line before, at that place Oba goes to tell his little story rhymes, and they're usually on the front row, most of them getting very emotional, gently weeping and such."

After another eye roll, Wilt takes a deep breath, then exhales. "Okay, how much is he down there, Cletus?"

"At first, he came out every few weeks. Now it's less often. But I could count on one hand the times he's stayed out longer than a few hours. I've picked him up at the airport in Louisville when he was coming back from New York a couple of times, but that's been at least 6 months. Has a funny name for the place—Black Ridge?" He ponders. "No. Black Holler— Blackacre? That's it. He calls it Blackacre, whatever that means."

Wilt and Andrews look at each other. They know the significance of the Blackacre reference.

Cletus continues, "You have no idea what you're getting into, fellas. You best let go of what brought you here. Just trying to get real with you."

Wilt again is skeptical. "What're you trying to say, Cletus? Has he threatened anyone?"

"No. Nothing like that. Oba doesn't threaten people, that is, when he's himself. But since he's moved back from the city; his fuse is just real short. One second, he's as calm as a summer brook, the next..." Cletus winces. "You don't want to know."

"Does he have weapons down there?"

"I hear shots down there now and again. I know he hunts for food. It wouldn't matter if he had one or not. Oba don't need a weapon to put both of you down. If you get too close and startle him, then you could be in big trouble."

"Well, his admirers obviously don't spook him. If he doesn't have a phone, how does he know they're coming?"

"Big difference and you know it, Mr. Wilt! He's happy to see them. Expecting to see them. I'm not supposed to be telling anyone this stuff. Oba's gonna kill me!"

"You're making the right choice. Just think of that power parsley, Cletus. How does he know they're coming?"

"Each one has a special signal they give as they approach his place. Calls of nature, he says. At least he's told me as much."

Wilt and Andrews exchange a humorous glance and a smirk as Cletus continues.

"Like I'm trying to tell you. When the bear says to leave him be, then you leave him be. I don't know what kind of information you want, but I promise you that it's not worth it. You could be hiking out there for hours and never even find him."

"Great point, Cletus. We're going to need a tour guide. Go get your duck call. You're hired."

Cletus has no idea what information Wilt and Andrews want from of Obadiah, and for the time being it's clear he's not going to find out. But it doesn't matter. He has no choice but to help them find Obadiah, even at the risk of alienating his brother. His livelihood depends on his cooperation and he has a family to support. To avoid hiking around for hours in the punishing summer heat, the three agree it's best to meet at dawn the following day to set out in search for Obadiah's cabin.

29

NEAR FATAL ATTRACTION

J*une 14, 2018, 6:45 am*
Cletus is waiting outside his house when Wilt and Andrews get out of the patrol car. Wilt swings the driver's side door shut with a casual flick, then removes his sunglasses. "Good morning, Cletus."

"Good? I don't know about that," Cletus mumbles.

As he was instructed, Cletus has retrieved his handmade duck call, and just in case Obadiah's admirers don't use that particular one, he also brings along a digital game call which contains the sounds of over 100 female animals in the throes of heat. As the three men side-step and lumber over the inhospitable countryside, Cletus explains the versatility of his high-tech device.

"My Burning Love Predator X-57 is without question the number one game call device on the market today. This puppy comes with two remote swivel speakers, the recorded sound capacity of over 1000 animals, realistic surrounding wildlife sounds, and even a moon phase indicator, which set me back a little extra, but well worth it!"

Wilt is starting to regret bringing Cletus along, but at this point they are well into the hike, and Cletus is the only one who knows how to get back to Blackacre. Even so, Wilt's patience is beginning to wear thin. "I'm sure the moon phase feature is very helpful, Cletus, especially now that it's 7:30 in the morning."

Now that Wilt has Cletus's full attention, he continues to pump him for information as the hike crawls on. "How does he get down there, Cletus? Does he drive an off-road vehicle?"

"Oba's only owned one car in his life. A big Lincoln. A Continental, I think. Tinted windows. Piece of junk. Bought it in high school but rarely drove it after that. When he moved to New York he left it here rusting in the field near the access road." He points, "With the old tractors and such."

"Does he drive it to his cabin?"

"Never. That's not even possible. Anyway, it's been missing for a while, at least since last fall. Someone hot-wired it and permanently borrowed it."

"Did Obadiah report it stolen?"

"Of course not. Oba laughed about it. Said the guy did him a favor. Said he couldn't have given it away." Wilt and Andrews exchange glances again as Cletus keeps talking. As soon as they get back to the station, they're going to have the records of Obadiah's Lincoln pulled up in the system.

Some 50 yards ahead, the men observe a metal pipe sticking out the side of a rock formation pouring spring water onto the ground. Cletus knows the area well, had camped there with his brothers as a teenager, and hunted it with his children until the farm was divided a few years before. It is the first time he'd seen the pipe and is certain Obadiah had put it there. He thinks it a sure sign they are close to his brother's cabin. The makeshift watering hole is also the perfect spot to stop and rest a few minutes.

As Cletus fills everyone's canteens, Andrews picks up the carrying case containing the call device and pulls out the instruction manual, flipping through it with considerable fascination. He'd finished in the top ten in his police academy class, primarily on the strength of testing the highest on the written portion of the exam, that measured technical aptitude and memory.

In other words, Andrews is what baby boomers refer to as a nerd or geek. Generation X might call him a dweebcake. But their status had risen significantly in the age of the Millennial, who dubbed him as a propeller head or brainiac. He's the guy who can readily process the technical verbiage of an instruction manual in one reading and build a 300-piece apparatus without the need to even glance at the illustration in the assembly chart. The one who drives others to homicidal thoughts at a real estate closing by reading every letter of fine print at the bottom of each document. Within ten minutes, Andrews has every detail in the manual committed to memory, being especially impressed with the index on the back page listing the entry code for each animal call.

"Will you look here. There's one for a begging swine, a hairy woodpecker, wild turkey, whitetail deer, even a caribou. Really cool."Cletus nods his head in agreement. "Yes. And there's a good chance Oba would recognize anyone of those you mentioned there and believe it was coming from one of his special friends."

"My lord! How many women does this guy have coming around? And why is he so depressed?"

"If I told you how many, then you would be depressed, Mr. Andrews."While Cletus and Andrews continue to discuss the features of the X-57, Wilt notices a message etched in the rock on the side of the hill. He takes off his glasses and wipes them before putting them back on to read it.

Five miles from Summersville, just south of town
Lee Ann stole the moonlight in a red evening gown
Kept men that sail on a steamboat that won't
The life that she chose was lovin' men that she don't.
Beware of her ballroom of stone and desire
Where breath on her kiss breeds unending fire
For all wretched souls that aren't worth a'saving
Dance for a chance with the River Queen Maiden

Wilt calls his understudy over to look at yet another cryptic message. "Andrews, look at this and tell me if you're thinking what I'm thinking?"

"Well, that depends on what you're thinking, sir."

Taking a deep breath, Wilt waits for Andrews to read it, then tries again. "Okay, Andrews. Let's do this another way. Does this poem remind you of anything?"

"Well, yes. It sort of reminds me of *Gum Pond Road*. You get the same feeling anyway. Like they may have been written by the same person?"

"Exactly! Excellent Andrews! What's that called in our line of work?"

"That would be what they referred to at the academy as, *modus operandi*. A suspect's particular way of doing things. This is getting very interesting."

The two men look at each another, do a fist pump, and nod.

For the first time, Wilt is starting to think that maybe, just maybe, he has been wrong about Andrews. That his sidekick actually has the right stuff to do this after all. Cletus is just standing there, having no idea what they are talking about. Wilt sees another opportunity. "Cletus, do you recognize the writing on this rock?"

"I surely do. That would be my brother's handiwork. Another one of his little story rhymes. Except in this case, the story is true. The River Queen Maiden is real. She's an apparition that resides in a cave not far from here, at the bottom of the holler we're approaching. But, believe me when I say, you don't want to go there!"

Cletus goes on to tell one of Crawford County's epic tales of tragic love; the forlorn apparition of the River Queen Maiden. In the 1840s, Lee Ann McClain was a beautiful young woman betrothed to Zachary Logan, Captain of the grandest steamboat on the Kentucky, the River Queen. One fateful night, Logan and Lee Ann were aboard the Queen headed down river to be married the following evening, but sadly would never get there.

It was a thunderous, stormy night, turning the normally placid Kentucky into an angry, rolling torrent. The Captain lost control of his vessel and the Queen ran aground on a sandbar just a few hundred yards from what is now known as River Ghost Cave. The force of the wreck's impact caused Lee Ann to fall and fracture her leg. With the boat badly damaged and quickly taking on water, Captain Logan carried her to the cave where he built a fire and explained that he had to get to Summerville to find a doctor to come back and set her leg. Despite her tearful plea for Logan not to leave her, he would carry her no further for fear of causing irreparable damage. He promised on his soul to come back the following day and bring her much needed medical attention, then take her away to marry as they had always planned. She finally relented and agreed to wait there for him.

But when Logan reached town, he discovered the doctor a dangerously beautiful woman and immediately fell in love with her, completely forgetting his betrothed. Logan and the doctor ran away together, never to return to Summerville, leaving Lee Ann wanting and waiting, all alone, eternally a maiden. To survive, she was forced into the life of a madam, using the landlocked River Queen as a brothel for sailors traveling the river. And now her spirit resides in the cave that's named for her apparition, where she still waits for Logan's return, every night. Except now she no longer believes he will return to rescue her from her desolation and despair. Instead, she waits for him to exact her revenge. Whenever a man enters the cave, the Maiden initially believes he is Logan and lures him into her ballroom of decadence and deception. When she discovers the visitor is not her betrayer, her rage is unleashed, but even more so. Very few manage to escape, and many are never seen again. The Maiden has waited in Ghost River Cave for over 170 years, not only to avenge Captain Logan's betrayal of her but to collect as many souls as possible so she will never be alone again.

Cletus goes on to describe his own dark encounter with the River Queen Maiden. "My brothers and I used to camp and knock around in there growing up. To each of us, it was a magical place, in the beginning anyway. My dance with the Maiden is forever etched in my memory, like a curse that will never let me go."

Wilt smirks and turned to go relieve himself behind a bush.

Andrews continues to listen, hanging on every word. "Please continue, Mr. Adam!"

"If courtship's a dance, and love a dancer, then sometimes betrayal makes a convincing dance partner. I was drawn to her irresistible apparition, an hourglass figure draped in a scarlet, full-length, night gown. She extended her hand to me as the music began to play. I recall her words and the sound of her voice so clearly, as if she said them to me today. 'Come to me, my love. There is no one else in the world but us now. I knew you would never leave me. We are bound here together, forever in our embrace.'"

Andrews pulls out his handkerchief and wipes the sweat now pouring from his forehead. He feels his chest expand and contract as his breath is becomes heavier. He continues to listen as Cletus recounts his near fatal attraction.

"And then there's only music. We glide across the ballroom floor as everyone watches. Her piercing eyes and fetching face are what speak to me now. Her flowing brown hair swings softly around her neck. The fullness of her breasts presses against me. My hands run down the curvature of her back as she gently slides her face across mine. I draw upon the lavender scent of her long neck and soft cheek, as she gently feels my earlobe with the corner of her mouth, before sliding to mine. Suddenly, she pulls back, teasing me, drawing me further in. Her mouth opens and closes as I try to kiss her, moving to me and away, then closer and away again, almost but never touching as she breathes in my every breath. She looks into my eyes so deeply, it's as if she is love itself. But she is anything but love."

Wilt, who is now about twenty feet away, impatiently looks down at his watch, back to Cletus, and off into the distance as Cletus continues to relay his dalliance with the River Queen Maiden.

"At last, our lips meet, hers sliding across and into every crevasse of my mouth, consuming me, as if feeding upon me. Because she is feeding on me. She is far too alluring for any man to resist, much less a teenage boy yearning for his first, perfect love. Her final words to me; 'You are mine now, forever.'"

Cletus turns to Andrews with one last thought. "Most of us dance for love. But never forget. Betrayal dances with you for the sake of something else."

Wilt has moved several more yards up the ridge looking out into the holler and smoking a cigarette while Andrews is thunderstruck like an 8-year-old who was at the cinema for the first time, listening intently while eating popcorn and slurping his slushie in the front row.

"That must have been some kind a woman, Mr. Adam. How did you manage to escape? But, more than that, why would you want to?"

"I was one of the lucky ones. The Maiden of Darkness created the illusion of love and pleasure to seduce her impressionable young victims. Teenage boys, just coming of age, laden with testosterone and longing for a beautiful woman to share it with. She drew them into her apparition of erotica and lust so intimately, so completely, by the time they realized it was a grand deception created to feed upon their souls, it was too late! So, every night, the eternal dance of horror resumes, as those lost souls scream, wreathing in agony, arm in arm in the clutches of the River Queen Maiden. In other words, there's a whole lot of nasty ballroom dancing going on in dere!"

The search soon resumes with Cletus leading the way up a steep incline. As they reach the top, he looks out over a holler at something that immediately catches his eye. As he strains to make out the object in the distance, a sudden look of horror and dread comes over his face. "No—it can't be. Surely, my eyes are deceiving me. Oba would never have done something like—would he? Not there. Anyplace but there! We need to leave. Now!"

"Cletus, what in the world are you talking about?" Wilt then turns to look in the same direction. "Well, what do you know? There it is. Look Andrews, the cabin. Looks like it's up against a rock formation, there at the base of that ravine. See those oak beams. He blended the cabin in really well with the surrounding landscape."

But it isn't the camouflage aesthetics that Cletus is focused on. "That's not just any rock formation, Mr. Wilt. It's the front of a cave. Oba's done gone off and built the back end of his cabin over the entrance of River Ghost Cave. The haunted eternal ballroom of none other than Lee Ann McClain, the River Queen Maiden of Darkness."

Not about to suggest he is buying into the ghost story, Wilt continues to stare at the cabin in the distance, shaking his head. "I just don't get it, Cletus."

"Well it's all true, Mr. Wilt. I can assure you she's in there, waiting for her next victim."

"No. I'm not referring to your first, postpubescent girlfriend, Cletus. I'm speaking of your brother. He can afford to live anywhere he wants, and he chooses to live in a cave? That alone tells you he's clearly has some significant mental issues."

"Well, I don't know what you're trying to suggest, but, anyway, it's a very nice cave."

Seeing Cletus is offended, Wilt tries to back off his offhand remark. "Meant no offense, I was just…"

"River Ghost Cave is not your run of the mill hole in the ground, Mr. Wilt. It's a pristine, natural, high-end space. It has an unlimited supply of pure drinking water; it's bone dry and stays at a constant 71 degrees year-round. It would not be an exaggeration to say it's a mountain man's paradise, that is, if it wasn't haunted by the Maiden of Darkness."

"Then I stand corrected. My apologies, Cletus. Now how are we going to do this?"

After several more threats to destroy his marijuana crop, Cletus finally agrees to station himself with Wilt behind a boulder about fifty paces from the cabin. Andrews would place a speaker at the cabin door, then walk back up the holler, well behind the other two, and remotely engage the digital call device. If Obadiah answers the door, Cletus and Wilt would then appear out in the open and approach, explaining the purpose of their visit, hopefully to a calm and collected Obadiah. The only flaw in the plan was not discussing in advance what animal call to draw Obadiah out, an oversight which would prove to be disastrous.

It is the kind of attention to detail that for a non-hunter might seem insignificant one moment only to become life altering the next.

For instance, it would just be good sense to be aware of the selected animal's mating season. Best practices would also dictate not using a call that would attract a fast, large and highly aggressive animal that had the ability to easily outrun and maul humans. But neither of those considerations would matter at all if the animal selected isn't indigenous to and thriving in central Kentucky.

Unfortunately, Detective Andrews isn't a hunter, and less fortunate still, his vast knowledge of classic cars, science fiction trivia and video gaming would have no practical application in this situation. Nevertheless, he is supremely confident, having easily mastered the information in the manual. In his mind, he is overqualified to go it alone in operating the digital call device. And Wilt is trying to instill confidence in his understudy, thinking to himself, what could possibly go wrong by letting Andrews handle the technical end of things? That is his strong suit, after all. He certainly didn't need the assistance of a countrified simpleton like Cletus to connect dots for him. Andrews has this, or so Wilt thinks, as he watches his young assistant march back up the holler, device in hand, along with the second speaker.

But as things turn out, a rudimentary knowledge of hunting or even zoology would not only have been helpful, it was necessary to avoid the mayhem which was about to unfold. It is the middle of June, peak mating season for the American Black Bear, a species which made a miraculous comeback in Kentucky the last 25 years and roaming the countryside in numbers not seen in well over a century.

As Wilt huddles with Cletus behind the boulder, it suddenly occurs to him that Obadiah may not even hear the call, that is, if he happens to be way back in the cave somewhere. "Cletus, how far back does the cave go?"

"Quite a bit. Several hundred feet, with a couple of passages leading back out the other side. I'll say this. It goes back far enough for several adult bears to live in there."

Wilt feels a sudden tingle run up his spine and tightness in his chest. "I'm sure Andrews has the good sense not to pick a bear call."

He ponders. "Even if he doesn't, what are the odds he'd pick that one out of all the calls on that thing? 1 in a 100? Ha! No way!"

"Mr. Wilt. It would definitely not be a good idea to use the mating call of a female black bear at this time of year."

"Oh, I see what you're saying, Cletus. They're so common around here right now. Obadiah would probably think it was coming from a real bear and wouldn't even come to the door. And I'm sure he wouldn't put his special friends in harm's way by having them use a bear call."

"Well, that, and Mr. Andrews will very quickly find himself in the path of a very horny, then disappointed, then enraged bear."

"Oh! Just to be safe, I better get up there and tell him." Just as Wilt turns to go warn Andrews, the roar echoes throughout the holler. The mighty mating overture of the female black bear is now telling every male in the neighborhood that she is primed and ready for the first stud who could find her, and one of the beacons directing them to her location is the second speaker sitting right next to Andrews.

For maximum effect, Andrews had made sure to set the device's speaker volume function to maximum, making the call so loud it drowned out the screams of Wilt and Cletus, who are now waving in Andrews' direction trying to get him to turn it off. Andrews watches with bewilderment as both men charge up the hill towards him.

His first reaction is that the group's worst fears had come to fruition. Cletus and Wilt are running from Obadiah, set off by the bear call and fueled by the homicidal rage that consumed him, bent on destroying anything in sight.

However, as urgent as Andrews' first fears are, they would instantly be rendered meaningless compared to what was about to happen. The scene morphs into a slow-motion movie as Wilt and Cletus, still well away, continue to lumber toward him. Andrews quickly turns off the device and pulls out his service revolver scanning the countryside to locate Obadiah for a clear shot.

Then it comes. A second roar, but different from the first. Far louder and more realistic. That's because it's the kind of bear cry that doesn't come from a speaker or could even be replicated by technology, or man. But worst of all, it isn't coming from the cabin. It is directly behind Andrews, who turns slowly, continuing to hold out hope it is coming from the second speaker. By the time he turns completely, his hopes turn to prayer, seeing the bear is less than ten feet away.

He quickly jerks back the slide on his Glock to load a round into the chamber. Then, with both arms shaking uncontrollably, he lifts to aim it, only to watch the beast rise on its hind legs and tower eight feet over him. There is no more time for hope or prayer, but only one thing now.

Then, seemingly out of nowhere comes a third roar, the loudest of them all. But it isn't coming from the bear standing directly in front of him, but a second male, even larger than the first, standing a few feet away, ready to win the right to breed with a female that doesn't exist. The first bear quickly accepts the challenge, returning to four legs and lunging into its new rival. The Titan battle for naught is on!

Andrews immediately takes the opportunity to flee the scene, running faster than he ever had in his life or ever would again.

30

MEETING IN THE MAN CAVE

Not able to lure Obadiah out of his cabin, and just seeing to his sidekick barely escape a violent death, Wilt is done with Cletus dictating how to conduct his investigation. In his storied career, Wilt had interviewed hundreds of violent criminals, including the mentally disturbed and all other manner of loose cannons, many of them at their own residence. After making sure Andrews was okay, he immediately turns and walks to the front door of the cabin as Cletus remains well back, pleading with him to not go there. Wilt walks up and knocks on the door.

After a couple of minutes, Obadiah answers the door. Wilt doesn't get three words into his introduction when Obadiah nods and waves both detectives into the cabin. "Come in! Take a chair. Get with you in a second." He motions to an oak table in the center of the room.

Wilt and Andrews walk inside to take a seat as Obadiah steps just outside the door. He could still see the two bears fighting, now far too distant up the holler to pose a threat. That doesn't mean others weren't roaming nearby looking for love. "Cletus! What are you doing way up there? Don't you see what going on behind you? Get in here, now!"

"I'll be just fine, thank you very much, brother!"

"What's wrong with you, boy!" Obadiah thinks. "I've told you, she's not here anymore! It's all in your head!"

"How do you know? You could be under her complete control this very second in a grand scheme to ensnare me, again!"

"You've been popping those shrooms again, haven't you, Cletus! I'm going to tell Millie if you don't get in here, right now!"

Obadiah knows marijuana isn't the only earth born mood enhancer Cletus dabbles in. Though Don't Ask Don't Smell doesn't apply to psychedelic mushrooms and two members of the Summerville Police are now hearing details of his medicinal transgressions, it still isn't enough to get Cletus in the cabin. More concerning to Cletus is what his wife, Millie, would do if she learned he was yet again taking trips without ever leaving the farm. The prospect of her fury is so terrifying, Cletus would rather take his chances sitting at the doorstep of the Maiden of Darkness than face it. Obadiah knows the key to his brother's full and undivided attention.

Cletus holds his index finger to his mouth, trying to shush his brother as he begins his trek toward the cabin. Obadiah turns to the detectives to clue them on Cletus.

"The cave is kind of traumatic for my brother. It was where he was with his girlfriend for the first time, let's just let's say, in an intimate way. His first love, a beautiful girl named Lee Ann. Unfortunately, she also broke up with him a few years later in there as well. The night before they were to be married, in fact. Pretty tough stuff. Over 20 years and he's never gotten over it. So, if he seems a little flipped out in here, says some crazy things, that's why."

Andrews has no trouble unraveling the rest of the real story. "Let me guess. Her last name was McClain and she met a doctor the week of the would-be wedding and fell deeply in love. And they ran off together never to return to Summerville."

"Yes, so you pretty much know the story, then."

"In a matter of speaking, Mr. Adam. Thank you for the heads up, though."

Wilt suddenly stares at his understudy in awe, nodding to him with a respect one might imagine given to a Samurai warrior after a great victory. Then Wilt explains the purpose of their visit, about which time Cletus walks through the door. Having newfound faith in his understudy, Wilt defers to Andrews to start the interview.

"Mr. Adam, coming over here we came upon a poem carved on a rock. Something about a River Queen Maiden..."

Obadiah looks over at Cletus, shaking his head in disgust.

"Did you tell them I wrote that poem? You still don't want the boys to know you like writing poetry? Unbelievable!"

He turns to Wilt.

"You're 43 years-old, Cletus! You let Homer and Broughton get to you way too much. There just having a little fun with you. And nobody cares what Bone or Billy think! They're idiots!"

Cletus blushes like he's a 14-year-old just caught by his mother looking at porn.

Obadiah continues. "Cletus is afraid our brothers will ride him to the end of the earth if they find out he writes poetry, like they did to me growing up. But as you can see, he has some ability. He's an even better storyteller, if he'd just focus on developing it instead of worrying about what our brothers thought, he could do something with it. At least it would be good for him mentally, instead of smoking that weed and popping shrooms."

He looks at Cletus. "And all of it behind sweet little Millie's back!"

Andrews nods his head, acknowledging Cletus's vivid imagination.

"Yes, we've heard the gift, firsthand, Mr. Adam. To say it is gripping, spellbinding, enthralling, would not be overstating it."

Cletus just sits and stares at Andrews, then moves his eyes back to his brother and back to Andrews, not quite sure whether Andrews is complimenting him or insulting him.

"He's so terrified they'll find out, he won't even say the word, poetry. He calls it something else: rhyming stories, or some nonsense. It's all a big act," Obadiah says.

Cletus has heard enough.

"Oh, so now I'm acting, and afraid of what other people think?

Profound personal insights coming from a guy whose longest intimate relationship is just under 12 minutes!"

"Leave my poetry students out of this, Cletus!"

"Which one, Oba? The Swooning Mallard? The Yearning Warthog? Or perhaps, the Furry Woodpecker! Obio, Obio, where art thou, Obio?"

"Cute Cletus. Real cute."

Cletus isn't done. "That's all I need. A life coach who hides in a cave! You don't have to put up with them. You can just hold up here or hop on a plane and fly back to the big city and do your little story rhymes where everybody claps and lights up to you. Well some of us have to stay here and do the suffering and the dying so primadoners like you have something to write about!"

When the brotherly spat dies down, Will resumes the interview, first asking about Blackacre. Obadiah tells them that's how the place has been referred to for decades, named after the Black family, who owned the land before his father bought it. Obadiah admits to saying it when threatening Parker after the trial but says that was the last time he saw or communicated with him.

When they ask about the Lincoln, he says he has no idea who stole it, but that he very much appreciated it. Though he denies writing *Gum Pond Road*, he is impressed when Wilt shows it to him in the photo of the menu board.

"That's strong. Sounds like something I could have written. As I'm sure you know by now, my poem about Harlan wasn't quite so flattering."

The other three laugh loudly.

"I can see why you'd suspect that I took him out. I loathed him. Couldn't be happier if I never see him again. He tried to steal my work, and years ago, he tried to steal our farm. You've got me with a solid motive, and I threatened to kill him not once, but twice. Once in front of half of Summerville. The other time, with a ghoulish poem delivered by a butchered hog! What else do you need?"

As everyone just sits silently for a few seconds, Andrews is starting to think the same thing.

Wilt is already convinced Obadiah isn't the killer. Obadiah's reactions are too genuine, too casual to be coming from somebody trying to hide something. Wilt decides to be direct. "What I need next is to establish your whereabouts."

"I was in New York," Obadiah says.

"Do you remember where you were when you first heard Mr. Parker disappeared?"

"Cletus told me about it, in Louisville, when he picked me up at the airport about a week after everyone else in town first started talking about it."

Cletus nods enthusiastically in agreement.

"I'd been in New York working at a writing workshop at NYU and doing some public appearances, book signings, stuff like that. I'd been in the city for at least two weeks before that. Just check with my publicist. She has all my airline records. I've got hundreds of people who can verify my location during that period."

"You're from here, who do you think did it, Mr. Adam?"

"Somebody he sued."

The interview concludes with Wilt and Andrews thanking Obadiah for his time. As they walk back to the farm, well behind and out of earshot of Cletus, Wilt goes over the interview with his apprentice. "I had a strong sense he didn't do it, even before he mentioned New York."

"Why was that, sir?"

"He didn't lie about any uncomfortable details that guilty suspects usually lie about, though he had several opportunities to do so, and he didn't hide that he still has disdain for Parker. The guilty ones often feign subtle remorse, at least initially, try to appear a little somber to convey at least some concern. He was cracking jokes about the guy. If his alibi checks out, we're checking him off our list."

As it turned out, Obadiah's Lincoln Continental would prove to be a different make and model than the Lincoln which had been sunk to the bottom of Quarry Lake, and a review of Obadiah's flight records and credit card expenditures confirmed his New York alibi.

31

EVERY LIFE A RIVER

ugust 4, 2018

A The site of Parker's final resting place is a matter that would ordinarily be reserved for his family, but Harlan Parker has no surviving relatives. So, Judge Renfro takes it upon himself to select one. He immediately rules out the local cemetery as an option. He knows there would most likely be more than a few in town, either out of resentment or anger, who might vandalize Parker's gravesite if it is in some location away from public view. This would likely impact others who came to the cemetery to pay their respects to loved ones buried nearby. For them, Parker's gravesite would only be a nuisance and uncomfortable distraction.

Instead, the judge decides to have Parker's ashes interned at the courthouse. If any mischief making were to be done there, it would be captured on video surveillance and the perpetrator would be brought to swift and certain justice. Renfro selects a relatively remote spot, just off to the side of the first step leading up to a seldom used side-entrance at the west wing of the building. Parker's ashes would be placed in a sealed urn and set underneath a square foot brick, engraved with the inscription, *Harlan Henry Parker, 1967-2017. One Confident Lawyer.*

Believing himself to be almost immortal, Parker had no will. So, Renfro appoints Tori Stevens executor of his estate, so she takes it upon herself to also plan the memorial service. Understanding Parker's complex legacy throughout the community, she only contacts attorneys in Summerville, sending a group email to membership of the local Bar Association.

> *Please join us for a brief memorial service honoring*
> *the life of Harlan Henry Parker, this Wednesday,*
> *noon, at the west wing of the Crawford County*
> *Courthouse. Judge Mackenzie Renfro presiding.*
> *Gestures of appreciation and sympathy can be made*
> *by donations to: Clients Without Lawyers, George*
> *Handlon. 212 Main Street, Summerville, KY*

It rains heavily the day of the service. Scores are huddled underneath umbrellas and standing out in the pouring rain. Renfro waits for the last of the visitors to gather as he stands under an awning on the steps in front of the entrance. It is a challenge, even for someone with the oratory skills of Renfro, to prepare remarks sincere and fitting for the occasion. What could he really say that wouldn't evoke an emotional response from someone from a crowd, especially one this size?

Renfro understood that holding a memorial service for Parker came with some risk. What if an angry husband or businessman bankrupted by Parker became unruly at the ceremony? No one could blame them. Renfro ultimately decided that they were the strongest reason to go forward with a service.

But neither Renfro nor Stevens had anticipated so many would attend. But, as it turns out, they had badly underestimated the cathartic effect celebrating Parker's demise would have for those who needed a sense of finality, of closure, to put the memory behind them once and for all. People who needed to be there and see it for themselves, to see Harlan Parker finally put in the ground, even in pouring down rain. Lawyers and non-lawyers, trench coats and rain pullovers, of all colors and styles, professionals and working class alike have shown up for the event. Some onlookers hold umbrellas, but many do without, standing motionless, expressionless, almost oblivious to the steady onslaught of drenching rain. If anything, the downpour is symbolic, something that would finally wash away some outrage, injustice or indignity that Parker had wrought upon them. For them, this would be no wake, moment of silence or celebration of life. Only a commemoration of regret.

Renfro steps forward to address the crowd. He begins the service with a piece from one of his favorite writers.

Every life a river
Searching for the sea
Longing to discover
How it came to be

Some with sounds of children
Playing in their stream
Some in ancient forests
Rarely touched or seen

Runs of raging beauty
That lure for lover's sake
Devouring all her suitors
Souls lost in each heart's wake

Some with jagged rocks
Too often in their path
Too brief their still cool waters
Their peace not meant to last

Some waters flow abundant
Give life to all they touch
While some dry up and wither
When much is not enough

Every life a river
Searching for the sea
Longing to return
To that which made it be

THEN RENFRO BEGINS his prepared speech. "Welcome friends, as we pay our final respects to Harlan Parker. And I'm certain that I speak for Harlan when I say thank you being here. He would be quite moved by this sight, and somewhat surprised, I think. As many of you know, Harlan had no family, but I guess you could say that, in a sense, we were Harlan's family, the legal community. And if such is true, then it's also fair to say that this courthouse was his family room. And like every family room, it saw division and passion, and those who left with some satisfaction and some not. But it's always been a place Harlan and the rest of us came to and hopefully learned something and even grew from the disagreements we had here. May God bless Harlan Parker and all those who serve justice, and all who will walk past him through these doors seeking it. Anyone else who would like to step forward and say a few words feel free to do so."

After waiting a couple of minutes with no one coming forward, Renfro thanks everyone for coming and the crowd begins to disperse.

Detective Wilt is off to the side, on the steps of the county jail, with a clear view of the courtyard and everyone attending the service. Next to him, standing under an umbrella, is Julia Sweet. They weren't there as much to pay respects, but to see who was there and just as importantly, who isn't. In Wilt's experience, sometimes the killer comes to the funeral to display feigned sorrow, or they just show up fearing their absence might draw suspicion. And he could see that almost everyone who had been at least suspected at one point in the investigation was present: Ridley Barnes, Brock Braden, Christa Collinsworth, Greg Lantham, and Wally Martin. Only Obadiah Adam and Kenny Martin were absent.

And none of them look particularly upset or out of character for someone at a funeral, that is, except Wally Martin. He is holding a handkerchief up to his face and slightly dabbing his eyes, clearly trying to appear grief stricken and looking around to see if anyone was noticing. During Renfro's remarks, he'd closed his eyes briefly and nodded rapidly as if agreeing with the sentiments expressed.

As the crowd disperses, Wilt and Sweet approach him. "Hello, Mr. Martin. So thoughtful of you to come by and pay your final respects, and with such feeling at that. Didn't you tell me the last time we spoke that you'd never met Harlan Parker?"

Wally is immediately on the defensive. "Mr. Wilt. I've never swung a golf club. Hell, I can't even read. If I'm incontinent, how can I write poetry!"

"Very quickly, Mr. Martin!" Having interviewed him before, Wilt now has no difficulty translating Wally-Martin-speak, but he can't resist getting a jab in.

"If you're saying that I'm here for any reason, except out of a sincere respect for Summerville, then you'd be wrong. Mr. Parker was famous in this town. This is a historic event. And how could anyone not be moved by the Judge's words, saying we're one big family and all?"

Wally then walks up to Wilt and wraps his arms around him, laying his head on the Detective's shoulder. Wilt stands there, visibly uncomfortable. He looks at Sweet with a nauseous look on his face. Wally unlatches.

"Have you heard anything from your brother, Mr. Martin? We're going on a couple of months now, aren't we?"

"I wish I knew. I haven't heard from him. Hasn't answered any of my messages, either. But it's not the first time he's disappeared for a while. He has a way of checking out all the sudden for a month or two, sometimes. I'm still holding out hope he'll show back up before long. But if you happen to hear anything, please let me know."

"I was going to ask you the same thing, Mr. Martin."

"Yes sir. Sure will. Good day to you, Detective, and the missus." Wally nods at Sweet.

Sweet pretends not to take offense at being called a sidekick.

Wally excuses himself and walks away.

Sweet is less than impressed with Martin's feigned sympathy. "His behavior is just odd. There's no other explanation other than he's acting like someone's who's guilty. You have him near Parker's car the weekend he disappears. Shortly thereafter he upgrades to a very nice trailer and RV park without saying how he could afford it, and his Critter Crematorium story can't be verified."

Wilt counters why Martin wasn't their man, yet. "He has no violence in his background. He has no criminal history at all in fact. The people at Critter could neither confirm nor deny Martin took his dog there because last fall they had a dead doggie walk-in promotion where bereaved pet owners could pay in cash. We need more."

In the weeks following Parker's service, traffic on the west side of the courthouse picks up considerably. In fact, almost every lawyer in town and most other people begin to enter the courthouse from the west side of the building. It gets to be such a problem, that court security must move their metal detector machine there from the main entrance to scan most of the people coming into the courthouse. Renfro wants answers. It's his job to make sure that the facility is safe and secure, so he directs security to figure out what is going on. And when a deputy sheriff watches the camera surveillance closely, he discovers the problem.

Every lawyer in town and half the rest enter and exit on the west side of the courthouse so they could get a chance to step on Harlan Parker, some doing it with considerable enthusiasm. No age group, race or station in life decline to participate in the ritual. Little old ladies find a sudden skip in their step to give ole Harlan a good pop, and one man in a wheelchair even stands up to do a sidestep to give the marker a healthy stomp before sitting back down to enter the courthouse. The high step parade would continue for months. Parker's internment at the courthouse has so dramatically changed the traffic flow in and out of the building, the County would eventually renovate its front to make the west side the main entrance.

32

HEARTTHROB IN AN ORANGE JUMPSUIT

eptember 12, 2018

S   A month after Parker's memorial service, the state crime lab produces its forensic analysis on Parker's smartphone. It was able to lift one partial print on the glass screen which has five markers in common with the right index finger of Brock Braden. Because fingerprint experts can require as many as twenty common markers to confirm an exact match, only five common markers on a partial fingerprint can't definitively prove that it belongs to Braden, but it narrows the odds significantly. By dividing 50 million, the number of people in the FBI fingerprint database, by the number of persons in it who shared five common characteristics with the print on Parker's phone, the mathematical probability that it belongs to Braden's was roughly one in five. Together with the other evidence Wilt had developed in the investigation, District Attorney Lesousky believes it is enough to charge Braden and the Martin brothers.

The next morning, Granville Pearl, with a gigantic cigar in his mouth, is on the square passing out free copies of the morning edition of the Summerville Songbird, celebrating as if he's announcing the arrival of his newborn child. The headline at the top of the front page confirms what he's been saying for almost a year.

Brock Braden Charged With Murder of Harlan Parker

W-MART AND K-MART ALSO CHARGED IN MURDER CONSPIRACY.

K-MART STILL AT LARGE.

The judge sets Braden's bond at one million dollars, which Braden posts with no difficulty. In addition, Judge Renfro sets several conditions, ordering that he be confined to Lonesome Pine and wear an electronic ankle bracelet to monitor his movements. He also directed Braden to have no contact with potential witnesses in the case, including any contact with Kenny or Wally Martin.

Having no means to post bond, Wally Martin is ordered held in the Crawford County Jail pending trial. But interest in the case spreads quickly as Wally's jail photograph was posted online. The website *Doing Hot Time* showcases mug shots of attractive inmates across the country. When it discovers Wally's photo, the website selects him as its cellmate of the month. The exposure transforms Martin's image to one of the antihero hunk who vanquished the evil lawyer, making him the object of fondness and attraction by scores of misguided, lovesick women. They send Wally care packages with fine chocolates and other assorted treats and personal, handwritten notes of encouragement, marriage proposals even prom invitations from outside Crawford County, of course.

Wally receives so much attention, it almost makes it worth living in the county jail, at least for a while. One woman who is particularly smitten, whom Wally "sort of" agreed to marry if he ever was released, starts a Go Fund Me campaign called, "Free Wally Now" to raise enough money for him to make bond. And although it falls well short of $200,000 needed, it is more than enough to hire a private attorney.

But because of the intense media interest in the case, Wood Williams, known as "Hollywood," Williams, probably would have done it for next to nothing. If there were ever a lawyer made for the telegenic age, it is Williams. Like most every trial lawyer, he's a flower who thrives in direct sunlight, except Williams takes profile to a completely new level. Williams is the guy who puts the 'high' in high profile, best known for defending the wrongly accused and widely misunderstood in the sensational murder case.

The more gruesome the facts, all the better for Williams. It just means that more people will be tuning in to watch Hollywood. His movie star good looks and deep, slow Tennessee brogue are the ideal fit for Jury Trial TV. The channel always receives its highest ratings when Williams is giving another riveting closing argument in a silk tie that's perfectly coordinated, with a hand-tailored pinstriped suit in hues and tones that rarely dare to tread across a courtroom floor.

But he's far more than a show pony. He could recite the law with the best and is a skilled cross examiner. His ability to get a hostile witness to tell his version of the truth is legendary. For Williams, it's about how to use your skill and gravitas to get the other guy's witnesses to tell your story. And when the lights are the brightest, Wood Williams does it better than almost anyone. His eloquence and penchant for the dramatic are truly a throwback to the golden age of trial lawyering.

For much of the 19th century and first part of the 20th, a murder trial at the county courthouse was the best show in town. Spectators came from miles around to see the great lawyers of the age try cases to packed courtrooms built with seating capacities now seen at movie theaters and concert halls. It was a time when a courtroom gallery felt more like an opera house, when the floor and witness stand seemed more like a stage.

When the oratory of lawyers like young Abe Lincoln, William Jennings Bryan and Clarence Darrow echoed off a pressed tin ceiling to reverberate to every corner of the courthouse, it meant to do more than to merely persuade twelve men and women on the issue of guilt or innocence. It resolved to change all who came to hear it, and in so doing, raised the craft of trial lawyer to an art form.

But with the advent of radio and television, public interest in live courtroom drama gradually waned to a trickle. So contemporary courthouse galleries have been scaled back significantly. With rare exception, the only people attending a trial today are lawyers, their clients, the judge and his staff. Few rarely go to the courthouse out of curiosity or to be entertained.

When charges were filed in the Parker case, Judge Renfro realized immediately the trial would attract far more spectators than the new courthouse could accommodate, so he decides to hold it at the old courthouse. One of Summerville's last remnants of the Gilded Age, Crawford County's first public building was spared the wrecking ball of shifty real estate developers in the 1980s when the Summerville Preservation Society successfully petitioned to have it placed on the National Register for Historic Places.

Though trials are no longer held there, it continues to serve as offices of the Sheriff, the County Judge Executive and Department of Deeds and Licenses. And its grand courtroom remains virtually intact, though it is used sparingly, usually when a town hall meeting or investiture of a county official was expected to attract more people than usual. Otherwise, the magnificent space has become an afterthought, left vacant, locked away and closed to the public.

When Judge Renfro's staff and the county clerk moved to the new workspace some years before, Colton (Colt) Roswell, the head of maintenance at the old courthouse, also planned to move with them. But he would only stay a few days. To him, there would never be another Crawford County Courthouse, other than the one both he and his father before him stood watch over for more than a half century.

Recognizing Colt was out of place in his new surroundings, Judge Renfro ordered him to return to his former station where he would remain for two more decades. "I've been thinking about this for a while, Colt. That old building still needs you. I'm afraid it'll just fall apart if you're not around."

October 10, 2018

And as things turned out, Colt would see one last trial at his courthouse before retirement. When Judge calls and explains what he is thinking about doing for the Parker case, Colt eagerly ambles upstairs to the second floor and waits with keys in hand. A few minutes later, Renfro appears, limping up the marble staircase to meet him at the courtroom's main entrance.

Colt unlocks its Gothic, dual wooden doors, twelve-feet-high and ornately appointed in a style one might have seen in ancient Rome. Each one moans angrily, as it's opened as if its sleep hadn't been disturbed in a millennium, ushering in a view of the grand courtroom. The vast expanse of woodworking majesty puts most any contemporary courtroom to shame by comparison. The bench, jury box, and the stairwell leading to a balcony are all detailed with unique, intricate carvings hewn a century before by workers who were more artisans than carpenters.

Only the railing which separated spectators from the litigants needs repair, short a couple of balusters which could be replaced with little difficulty. A cathedral ceiling, 32 feet high, keeps watch over thirty rows of seating in the gallery and seven more in the balcony bringing total seating capacity to 350. Other than the buildup of about five years of dust and some paint that had peeled off the walls, the courtroom is amazingly well preserved.

When Renfro inquires whether the space could be put into form to host the Parker trial in three months, Colt's response is as certain as enthusiastic. "Nothing a couple of weeks of elbow polish and touchup paint can't fix. I will have her ready, beyond a shadow of a doubt, your honor!"

33

THE HOTTEST TICKET IN TOWN

J*anuary 9, 2019*

On the first day of the trial, one could have easily mistaken the neighborhoods around downtown Summerville for those near Churchill Downs on Derby Day. Parking space is in such demand, residents living as far as a half-dozen blocks from the courthouse are charging $10 a day to eager trial spectators more than happy to pay such a price for front lawn parking. Nothing better than an infamous lawyer being bludgeoned to death with a 7 iron to create a mini-economic boon for the locals.

Judge Renfro begins the day as he does every other weekday and Saturday, sitting at the counter at Carletta's Starlight Diner, built in two modified R-46 Manhattan subway cars found at a scrapyard in Queens, New York in the 1970s and hauled to Kentucky by Carletta's first husband. A couple of years later she would relegate him to the junkyard. The popular dining spot is located about a mile from the square and on the way to the courthouse for the judge.

The proprietor, Carletta Fant and Judge Renfro are lifelong friends, each born in Summerville having known each another since before grade school. They even dated for a short time in high school, which their friendship managed to survive, outlasting fourteen Presidents, the Vietnam War, four marriages, three divorces (two for Carletta), eleven children, five judicial elections and the passing of Renfro's second wife five years before.

Starlight is also a mainstay for members of the local Bar and business community. One by one, they file in the door saying good morning to the Judge as he nurses a cup of straight black coffee, working through the same breakfast he had the day before and every other day his colon could remember: four eggs (over medium), two white toast with grape jelly, spicy hash browns with mushrooms and a little Vidalia onion with three sausage links. Several regulars approach him with well wishes presiding over the trial. Otis Strode asks if he really thinks Braden and Martin are guilty.

But Carletta is right there with coffee pot in hand to shut him down. "Now Otis, you know better than to ask Judge a question like that. Now, let the man be. He's got a big week ahead."

But most just inquire as to the best day to slip in and watch the drama unfold. Never needing a robe and gavel to command attention, Renfro is always good for a quick comeback. "If you're lucky enough to find an extra seat, please let me know. I could use one!"

Dan Jack Gray still has thirty minutes before he must be in Judge's chambers, so he is in his office with Brock Braden reemphasizing some final points about courtroom appearance and decorum. Gray is most concerned about snap impressions the jury could take from a loose cannon like Braden, who is unpredictable at best, and that's when he is stone-cold sober. Gray had spent weeks with him, emphasizing the importance optics play in front of the jury. It is critical to always present a picture of a stable, responsible, professional, and the only way to create that impression is for Braden to never show emotion during witness testimony or argument by the prosecutor. Dan Jack explains there would be at least one juror looking at him at any point in time throughout the trial, watching for a flinch, grin, a frown, anything that might give them a reason to judge you unfairly.

And it is especially true in Braden's case. There will be testimony from two ex-wives about threats he made against Harlan Parker during their divorce cases. There will be graphic testimony from the medical examiner and coroner describing the manner of death, including photos of Parker's corpse pulled from Quarry Lake, complete with bashed in skull. Even the slightest hint of approval or levity from Braden during such testimony means a certain lifetime membership at the state penitentiary.

Dan Jack takes some solace in that at least Braden had followed his advice on what to wear. His client walked to the office donning a blue blazer and white dress shirt with a conservative red and blue striped tie. But there is one glaring red flag Dan Jack detects the moment he saw him. "Morning, Brock. Nice Rolex. But too nice to wear

to court. Hand it over. It'll be in my safe deposit box until the end of the trial. Other than that, you look perfectly average."

A jury's suspicion, or even worse, its' envy of a wealthy client is always an issue to be aware of with a defendant with Braden's net worth. He is going to be judged by a group who couldn't afford such an item even if they'd pooled their money together. It is going to be hard enough to present his client as a rags-to-riches, regular Joe without the flashy timepiece.

Then Dan Jack goes over how Braden will communicate with his lawyers during witness examination. While Braden is encouraged to suggest questions, it must be done subtly. No whispering in his lawyer's ear. No waving at his lawyer to summon him over to listen to his question. Braden is to write his thought on a notepad and pass it to Savannah. If she thinks it's a good question, she'll slide it to the edge of counsel table so Dan Jack can look down and see it. If not, she'll explain why during the next break. Savannah has tried enough cases with her father that he has come to the point that he not only trusts her judgment but relies on it.

Dan Jack explains to Braden why he shouldn't take it personally if his lawyers decide not to ask one of his questions. "One of the reasons you hired me was to know what questions to ask, Brock. And more importantly, what questions not to. I've seen guys convicted because they hounded their lawyer into asking a bad question. Don't be that guy!"

Savannah would also serve as a buffer for her father during trial, sitting between Braden and Dan Jack, not only to answer questions of the client but to help keep him under control. It not only allows Dan Jack stay focused on witnesses and legal argument, it makes the prospect of lawyer and client bickering in front of the jury far less likely.

Three blocks away, Wood Williams is in a holding cell at the old courthouse with Wally, going over courtroom dos and don'ts. He hands his client a backpack containing some regular clothes he'd picked out at a men's clothing store the day before. A light brown sport coat, blue dress shirt, dark slacks and dress shoes. If the jury sees Wally in jailhouse clothes, there will be virtually no chance he will be acquitted. But Wally fails to see the connection between what he wears and the perception someone might have of him in the courtroom. It is as if he is a twelve-year old boy fighting his mother about dressing up on his sister's wedding day. After twenty minutes of his lawyer screaming at him to *put on the blasted clothes*, Wally finally relents. But when Williams pulls out the tie, Wally steadfastly refuses to take it from him, saying, *no freaking way* repeatedly shaking his head. He'd never worn a fancy jacket before, much less a tie, and doesn't have any idea how to put one on anyway. He thinks wearing a shirt with a collar and a sport coat are major concessions which should have made his lawyer happy. Even though Wally feels more than slightly uncomfortable, business casual looks very nice on him.

Outside, eager trial watchers form a line that extends halfway around the block which moves at a snail's pace into the main entrance. There, a walk-through metal detector awaits, scanning for firearms, knives and any other kind of weapon that was detectable. Each time the machine's sensor goes off, the person walking through was politely asked to step to the side where they are also checked with a hand scanner and frisked from shoulders to shoes. Most visitors cooperate patiently without comment and some even thank the court security officers for the job they are doing in keeping everyone safe.

But there are always one or two who show disapproval. It is

usually no more than a huff and puff, acting as if they are put through some intolerable indignation, even though they are treated no differently than anyone else. And less frequently the disapproval could appear as dramatic as an apoplectic seizure. Most of the security personnel from the Crawford County Justice Center had been reassigned to work the Parker trial for the week, and they are excited for the change in pace. No one could recall seeing a trial in Crawford County that received so much attention.

With notepad in hand and a ballpoint pen wedged in the top of his right earlobe, the Courier Journal's Donald Norton walks up and down the line scouring the crowd for quotable quips describing the sensational mob scene and upcoming trial, and there's no lack of spectators ready to oblige him.

Production trucks from Jury Trial TV and all four of Louisville's network affiliates are camped outside the courthouse, each doing clips about the trial to come. Some standing in line are even asked to answer a few questions on camera about what they think about the spectacle and why they had come there to watch. Some of the answers are not what you'd typically expect to hear at a murder trial.

> "I'll be the first to thank Mr. Braden
> and Mr. Martin if they really did it.
> Personally, from what I've read,
> I have my doubts!"

Two dozen women, making up the *Real Women for Wally* fan club, wear blue t-shirts with Wally's photo on the front as they inch forward in line chanting, rhythmically clapping and stomping in unison as if they are in a pep club.

> "Free Wally Now!"

In the courtyard on the right side of the courthouse, a dozen or so alums of Summerville high's marching band play tunes you'd hear in the 1980s at a prep basketball game. Food trucks across the street offer slushies, funnel cakes, pork sandwiches, burgers, and brats to scores of the hungry true crime enthusiasts.

Harlan Parker's murder trial hasn't even started, and it had already turned into a twisted festival where the accused are victims for a murder that seems to inspire more celebration than cries for justice.

34

BEHIND CLOSED DOORS

At 8:30 am, lawyers gather to argue pretrial motions in Judge Renfro's chambers just behind the courtroom, more than close enough to hear the rumble of footsteps across the hardwood floor, the hum of dozens of conversations echoing off it and wooden benches in the gallery creak and bend as members of the jury panel take their seats.

In every criminal trial, the court rules on dozens of issues in trial as lawyers object to questions or the answers they would invite. And there's evidence that's especially important which the defense identifies in pretrial filings that the court often rules on just before the trial begins. And there were several raised beforehand in this case.

Judge Renfro starts things off with his court reporter of twenty-five years, Thelma Duvall. "Good morning counsel. Thelma. Let's go on the record. We are on the record in *Commonwealth v. Braden et al.* Counsel, state your appearances."

"Jim Lesousky for the Commonwealth, your honor."

"Dan Jack Gray and Savannah Blue for Brock Braden."

"Wood Williams for Wally Martin. Good morning, your honor."

The first piece of evidence Dan Jack seeks to exclude is any reference to the whereabouts of co-defendant, Kenny Martin, who went missing the day the Summerville Songbird first broke the news that Parker's body was located. The Commonwealth attempts to link the timing of the newspaper article with Martin's disappearance, arguing that it strongly suggested that Braden had Kenny Martin killed to prevent him from cooperating with the police. Dan Jack argues that the Commonwealth had produced no proof that Kenny had been killed or silenced, and it was just as likely that he had fled the jurisdiction, neither which made Braden or Wally Martin's guilt more probable.

Renfro grants Dan Jack's motion, excluding it, holding that the danger of unfair prejudice substantially outweighed any probative value of such evidence. No reference to Martin's absence would be made during the trial by the Commonwealth and the jury would be instructed that it wasn't material to the issue of guilt or innocence of either defendant, and that they were not to speculate about it or even consider it during deliberations.

After all pretrial issues are ruled addressed, the attorneys and defendants enter the courtroom, which is now packed with spectators, and take their seats at their respective counsel tables. Jury TV cameras are set on opposite sides of the courtroom in addition to a sky cam which moves remotely on a cable to follow the action and capture shots anywhere in the courtroom at any given time. The show's director is stationed in a production truck outside the courthouse where he would give instructions to the camera crew as action in the courtroom developed.

Suddenly, crowd chatter gives way to a sharp cracking sound as the head bailiff Jessie Hogg opens the door to the judge's chambers and steps just inside the courtroom. With a silver badge pinned on his chest and three bars on each sleeve designating his lofty rank, Hogg belts out the clarion call to begin public proceedings.

"All rise! Hear ye. Hear ye. In the matter of Commonwealth vs. Brock Alton Braden and Wallace Presley Martin. Judge Mackenzie Beauregard Renfro presiding."

Everyone stands as Renfro entered the courtroom and takes his seat at the bench. "Welcome to all who have come to watch this trial.

The court has taken notice and takes much pride in the public's interest in this case as it's our right as American citizens to watch this public proceeding. I only ask you to please be mindful and respectful of the seriousness of the matter in keeping conversations to a minimum during arguments of the attorneys and witness testimony."

The court then asks everyone to rise and face the American flag standing behind him for the Pledge of Allegiance. Although such a gesture is rarely performed as part of a public trial, Renfro always does so, believing that it was important to emphasize the public service aspect of the proceedings. No one is about to argue with him. It is time to select the jury.

35

THE CHOSEN ONES

On day one, the first four rows of the gallery are reserved for the 120-member jury panel from which fourteen jurors would be selected. Twelve who would make up the main jury, in addition to two alternates if one or two of the main group couldn't complete their responsibilities, usually due to illness or some other unexpected issue. Ordinarily, a criminal trial in Crawford County would only require a panel half as large. But there would be many candidates disqualified because of strong feelings about Harlan Parker, so Judge Renfro called for twice the usual allotment.

In some cases, attorneys hire firms to do background research on every person on the panel to learn about their background, opinions related to crime and punishment, and any other information that might suggest bias in favor of one party or the other. The inquiry could include anything as basic as internet searches for criminal records, newspaper articles, social media posts, and as intrusive as hiring a private investigator to interview neighbors, coworkers and friends. There would be no such background research necessary in Summerville, where most everyone prided themselves in knowing everyone else's business.

The jury selection process, known as voir dire, is intended to discover opinions, experiences or relationships from those on the jury panel that might suggest bias's in favor of or against a party. But sometimes lawyers use the process as an early opportunity to ingratiate themselves to the jury or promote their theory of the case. Judge Renfro isn't going to allow such nonsense. He always asks the preliminary questions before permitting the lawyers to do limited follow up. Renfro burns through the basics:

- *Does anyone here know Dan Jack Gray?*
- *Does anyone know Brock Braden?*
- *Has anyone ever sat on a jury before? What was the result?*
- *Has anyone or a family member been party to a lawsuit before?*
- *Does anyone have a close friend or family member who's been charged with a crime?*
- *Does anyone here work in law enforcement?*
- *Does anyone have a family member who works in law enforcement?*
- *Has anyone seen or read any news coverage of this case?*

If the question is personal in nature, panelists approach the bench, where they're immediately converged upon by lawyers for follow up questioning. Some people are reluctant to divulge any opinion whatsoever, which makes it impossible for lawyers to get a sense for their perspective. But others welcome the attention, raising their hands and going to the bench at every opportunity to share their story.

When Lucinda Rogers received notice for jury duty in the mail, she immediately called friends and family with the news. She was finally going to meet her idol, Hollywood Williams. Her bookshelves are overflowing with true crime novels which included two of William's legendary trials. And, of course, her favorite TV show is none other than Jury Trial TV.

When she got to the courthouse, it was all she could do to contain her erogenous zones. "Oh, my word!"

She held her hand to her chest.

"Just look at that vison of a lawyer. And what might his name be? Hollywood Williams, you say? I may just have to commit a felonious offense in the great state of Tennessee to require the services of a lawyer the caliber of Mr. Williams."

When the panel is asked if anyone knew Harlan Parker, Lucinda jumps at the opportunity, being the first one to approach the bench. Renfro's questioning gest more specific.

"Good morning, Ms. Rogers. Always nice to see you. So how did you know Harlan Parker?"

Lucinda turned and addressed Williams as if he were the only person in the room.

"Well, Mr. Parker asked me to go to Compton Movie House a couple of times. I politely turned him down. He was considerably older, of course. The problem was, he just wouldn't take no for an answer. I suppose he learned that I'm not currently seeing anyone and just spend my evenings keeping to myself, reading true crime novels, cooking and of course, working out, which I do religiously six days a week. I really have no life other than volunteer work and making the ones I love feel very special. I think that's what it's all about, wouldn't you agree, Mr. Williams?"

Williams smiles back, politely agreeing with Lucinda and then asking if she could set aside her very unpleasant experience with Harlan Parker and render a verdict solely based on the evidence. Without hesitation, Lucinda promises to do so.

"Why yaess! I do. I do. All the days of my life. I mean, I give you my solemn word that I will be fair if selected to serve on your jury, Mr. Williams. It would be such an honor!"

After Lucinda returns to her seat, Jim Lesousky addresses the Court.

"Judge, I think it's obvious that Ms. Rogers is not only incurably predisposed in favor of Mr. Williams, she clearly wants to have a drink with him. Did you see the way she looked at him? We're talking double coconut, white hot mocha eyes, Judge. I move to strike for cause!"

Williams tries mightily to keep Lucinda in the panel.

"Judge, Ms. Rogers clearly stated that she could be fair, and she exhibits the kind of enthusiasm that's sorely lacking but greatly needed in our juries today. And besides, in case you didn't notice, she's a total smoke show. The viewing audience will absolutely love her. The producer thinks she's destined to be a Jury TV sensation."

Williams looks around to the other lawyers continuing to make his case for Lucinda.

"Guys, if we can just find some common ground here, the exposure of this trial could mean big things. I mean, no TV judge I've seen has anything on his honor!"

Renfro just grins, shaking his head slightly. He isn't about to keep someone in the panel based on TV ratings, but with a line of people who know Parker extending out the courtroom and down the stairs to the first floor, he isn't eager to start striking people so soon.

"We'll keep her for now and see how many people are remaining at the end of voir dire. I'm sure Ms. Rogers' star will continue to shine brightly whether she's on this jury or not."

As expected, eighteen people have either a family member or close friend who had been on one side of a case in which Harlan Parker was the lawyer, saying their feelings are so strong they would have a difficult time returning a guilty verdict against anyone who murdered him. All are stricken for cause. Eight are stricken for a work hardship or illness in the family, and one woman is excused due to the personal trauma sitting on the jury would cause her, as her husband had died in a drunk driving accident, on a golf course no less, after driving his cart into the lake.

After two days of questioning, the defendants and the prosecution each exercise twelve peremptory challenges to remove individuals they object to but couldn't manage to strike for cause. As expected, District Attorney Lesousky uses one of his challenges to strike Lucinda Rogers. The clerk then calls out the names of twelve jurors, five men and seven women: Three farmers, two stay-at-home mothers, a high school English teacher, a postal worker, mechanical engineer, an accountant, a manager of a fast food chain, an insurance company executive and a retired fireman. As their name is called, each juror walks from the gallery and takes their seat in the jury box.

When each is seated, the court clerk directs them to raise their hands.

"Do you swear and affirm that you will impartially try the case between the parties and give a true verdict according to the evidence and the law?"

The jury responds in unison. "I do."

Four jurors had not answered as much as one question in voir dire, which is concerning for both the defense and the prosecution. Judge Renfro thanks the rest of the panel for their participation and dismisses them. Seeing Lucinda is dejected, the judge asks Colt to make sure she has a seat for each day of the trial. It is no small gesture, as there would be many the Fire Marshal would have to turn away once the seating capacity of 350 was reached. Lucinda heartily accepts the judge's kind gesture and would take her place in the balcony to listen to opening statements the following day.

36

INCONVENIENT TRUTH

S pectators file into the courtroom as Jim Lesousky goes over his opening statement one final time. But no matter how many times he reads through it, the thoughts won't go away. In fact, they hadn't left him since the day Harlan Parker's body was found; joy, gratitude, even bliss. He has a sense of inner peace he'd never felt before. And though he was never one to go to church, except on holidays or when someone got married, what he is experiencing now is unquestionably spiritual. Still, the contradictions wouldn't stop running through his head. The men sitting across the courtroom who eradicated the sole source of his misery the last twenty years are cold-blooded killers. He'd taken an oath to enforce a law which he is grateful had been broken.

As much as Lesousky tries to conjure up some guilt about his genuine appreciation for what Braden and Martin had done, even a respect for them on a certain level, he just can't do it. No matter how brutal and abhorrent the murder of Harlan Parker, it had dramatically and suddenly improved Jim Lesousky's quality of life. He actually enjoys going to work again. His blood pressure had dropped to healthy range for the first time since he'd passed the Bar. It had saved his marriage and his relationship with his children, now that he isn't so irritable anymore after coming home from work reeling because of another humiliating acquittal at the hand of Parker.

Although he fully intends to perform his responsibilities to the best of his ability, that doesn't mean he has to feel good about it. The lawyers across the courtroom sure don't have to feel good about the miscreants they represent, but they somehow manage to get to that place Lesousky now finds himself.

Judge Renfro takes the bench and gets right to the matter at hand. "Good morning everyone. It's now time to hear opening statements. You will first hear from the Commonwealth. Mr. Lesousky."

Lesousky rises and acknowledges the court and opposing counsel as he walks to the center of the courtroom, standing directly in front of the jury. "Brock Braden had everything that money could buy. The finest cars, the nicest home, a 120-foot yacht and more than enough money to build one of the finest golf courses in America. But there was one thing Brock Braden could never buy, and that was a wife that would put up with his bad behavior. Each one of Braden's first three marriages would devolve into a not so marry-go-round of liquor, dysfunction and abuse. But then Braden thought his luck had finally changed when he met Christa Collingsworth. But the proof will show that Christa's interest in Braden would eventually fade into deep disappointment and heartbreak, leading her to seek comfort in the arms of another, and then another, and several others."

"And it was Christa's search for happiness that would lead to a love triangle of betrayal, treachery and, ultimately, the murder of Harlan Parker."

"The proof will show that, the week of October 2nd, 2017, when Christa Braden filed for a divorce, Brock Braden also learned that she planned to run off with golfer Percy Ridge, and the only thing they were waiting for was for Percy to earn his PGA tour card later in the week at the qualifier at Lonesome Pine. And if that wasn't enough, Christa had retained Harlan Parker as her divorce attorney. This would prove to be the last straw for Brock Braden."

"So, what did Brock Braden do? He devised a sinister plan to get rid of both Percy Ridge and Harlan Parker in one stroke. He went to the bag room at Lonesome Pine and pulled Percy's best club, his 7 iron, to not only sabotage Percy's efforts to make the PGA tour, but to keep him from running off with his Christa. But Braden was far from done. He then gave the club to the Martin brothers and directed them to use it to kill Parker, to frame Ridge for Parker's murder. And in so doing, Braden would not only save his marriage, he would finally get rid of the divorce lawyer who had been the bane of his existence for over twenty years. The proof will show that he paid the Martin brothers $100,000 to do the deed, in a contract signed and sealed with the blood of Harlan Parker."

Lesousky also contends that it was Braden who wrote the poem, *Gum Pond Road,* and he did so to lead investigators to Parker's body and the murder weapon to frame Ridge. The prosecution would call Gia Goodnight, an exotic dancer at Cork and Cleavage Gentlemen's Club, who would testify Braden admitted to it in the middle of a lap dance.

The evidence would also show that Braden made a $100,000 cash withdraw from his checking account at Summerville Savings and Loan the week of Parker's disappearance. There would be testimony from the owner of Rebel Yell Prefabricated that Kenny Martin paid him $50,000 cash for a mobile RV for himself and a modular home for Wally two weeks after Parker was murdered. There was the Compton Movie House surveillance video showing Kenny Martin's bizarre Bill Clinton moon dance near Parker's car while Wally idly sat by on the evening of October 6th. And Wally's statement to investigators about his dog, Bo, was nothing but a cock-and-bull Cockweiler story made up to conceal his role in the murder conspiracy. There are the fingerprint markers that matched those of Brock Braden lifted from the phone of Harlan Parker. Lesousky finishes, contending the proof would show that both defendants had ready access to the murder weapon that went missing from the bag room the weekend of October 6. Lesousky holds the golf club up to the jury, pointing to the tree sticker on the shaft.

"Braden and Martin are each tied to the murder weapon by the

Lonesome Pine, where defendants worked together daily and planned the murder conspiracy."

Next up is Hollywood Williams. As always, the production crew has briefed him beforehand on the best place on the floor to capture his sharp jaw line and bring out the vibrant colors and texture of his magnificent pinstripe suit and matching tie. Williams enters center stage and introduces himself to the jury and television viewing audience at a decibel level that would stir the near dead.

"May it please the court." He nods to the judge, then the lawyers. "Esteemed counsel. Good morning! Wood Williams for Wally Martin! If the tale of our lives were told by the hands on a grandfather clock, what would they say about us? They would say that some of us are born into this world five minutes early. We get a head start on everyone else. We see them every day. Hopefully you're among them. Those blessed with intelligence, beauty, or the support and tender love of caring parents with the means to provide opportunities to enjoy a life well lived. It's much easier to get ahead when you're born ahead, isn't it?"

As everyone on the jury nods their heads in agreement, Williams knew he had immediately made the all-important connection so necessary to present his client's defense. He continues.

"But in the tick tock of life, not everyone gets a jump on the clock. For his first five years of school, Wally Martin was never in his seat when the morning bell rang at a quarter after eight. And by the fifth grade, his home room teacher's patience had run out. So, one day she got the kids in class to do something that to some might seem innocent, even funny, that is, if you didn't understand where Wally was coming from. As he walked into class, late once again, the entire class, already seated, greeted him with, 'Good morning, Wally'. Imagine the humiliation of that ten-year-old boy, as tears welled up in his baby blue eyes, standing there as all the kids in his class laughed at him. Everything moving as if were in slow motion. Wally just looked over at his teacher and said, 'How can I be late every day when it's only 8:20 and school doesn't even start till a quarter after eight? I'm five minutes early.'"

Williams pauses a few seconds to let the picture of the pitiful young Wally sink in.

"Ladies and gentlemen of the jury, that, as well as anything, sums up the life of Wally Martin. A guy who's always tried to get there five minutes early only to end up five minutes late."

One man on the jury swallows hard. Another blinks to fight off the tears. Still another pulls out a tissue and begins dabbing her eyes. From the balcony, Wally's sort-of fiancée stands and stomps her feet. She claps her hands and yells, "Free Wally Now! Her chant is joined by the Real Women for Wally fan club and the rest of the gallery. The Wally-cry thunderclap grows to such intensity, the courtroom shakes beneath it. People walking by the courthouse at the time likened the commotion to a well-choreographed prison riot.

Renfro is quickly losing control of his courtroom. "Order, order in the courtroom! Order! Any further displays of this sort will result in immediate removal from the courtroom, an order of contempt, and free room and board at the county jail!"

It would take several minutes before order is restored. But it doesn't bother Williams in the least. He's already managed to get the gallery behind his client, but he also knows that could change in an instant. He continues, saying the proof would show that committing such a horrific crime was inconsistent with Wally's true nature as someone with a reputation for being peaceful, kind and no criminal record.

He attacks the prosecutor's description of Bo's tragic death calling it a cold and callous mischaracterization, saying the proof would show that Bo is real and that he was cremated in Cousin, just as Wally had told the investigator. That the prefabricated modular home was a gift from his brother, and the evidence would show Wally had no idea how much it cost or how Kenny could have afforded it. Williams takes another opportunity to emphasize Wally's impoverished upbringing.

"And considering the conditions Wally had lived in his entire life, he wasn't about to question it."

And as for the Bill Clinton mask, Kenny wore it the evening of October 6th just trying to make his brother laugh a little after losing his beloved Bo earlier that week. The evidence would show Wally grew up a huge Bill Clinton fan because his mother told him when he was a child that he looked like a boyhood version of the 42nd president.

Williams concludes by saying that Wally just didn't have the wherewithal to carry out a scheme as sophisticated as the Harlan Parker murder plot.

"The proof in this trial will show that Wally Martin doesn't have the attention span to conspire with a billy goat, much less one to participate in a scheme to kill Harlan Parker."

Judge Renfro turns to Braden's lawyer. "Now, for the final opening statement, you will hear from Daniel Jackson Gray."

Dan Jack walks to the center of the courtroom and stops to face the jury box, making eye contact with each juror along the back row and then in the front before beginning.

"The Irish poet, Oscar Wilde once said, 'True friends stab you in the front.' The proof in this trial will show that Parker had few friends but many enemies. Show me someone who was truly upset the day the news broke that Harlan Parker's body was found at a rock quarry in Bitty, Alabama, and I'll show you somebody angry they didn't get there first."

Gray goes on to briefly discuss the burden of proof. "Now, as we stand here today, you may think that Mr. Braden and Mr. Martin are on trial, but the court will instruct you that it's the government that has the burden of proof here. So, as we move forward, I ask you to remember that it's the government that's actually on trial. Its credibility, its diligence, its judgement, the evidence investigators pursued and evidence they did not pursue. All of it on trial the next several days."

He goes on to rebut several pieces of evidence mentioned by the prosecutor. He says the proof would show that the $100,000 withdrawal was not blood money but was used to promote the golf tournament held that weekend at Lonesome Pine. Gray says the proof would show the money went to pay for door prizes given to spectators to encourage them to come out to the course. As strong attendance was important for Lonesome Pine to attract future events. The finger-print evidence would prove not to be exclusive enough to conclusively identify anyone, and particularly not Brock Braden. As for the testimony of Braden's ex-wives, Gray rhetorically asks, "Who in this courtroom would not be convicted if ever tried for their lives on such evidence?" Raucous laughter roars throughout the courtroom.

Gray then discusses the disparity in the number of witnesses his client would be calling compared with the government, indicating several witnesses Braden intended to call will be called by the prosecution, and that he would examine them at that time. Although the court instructs the jury not to consider how many witnesses are called, it's something Gray always addresses in opening.

Gray always attempts to create a personal connection with the jury by describing the coming trial as a conversation that will take place between him and them.

"Now I won't have a chance to talk to you again until the closing statement, at least directly." Gray turns and points to the witness stand. "But please know that as I ask questions to each witness, it is you who I will be speaking to."

"Lastly, please keep in mind that what the government has just told you is only their version of the truth as they expect the evidence to show. But what they failed to mention is their own inconvenient truth, the one that will not go away, which is, there are at least four people who had a stronger motive and better opportunity to kill Harlan Parker than Brock Braden. You will hear from each of them in this trial, and it is that inconvenient truth that will prove to be the dominant theme of this trial, rendering the government's professed version of the truth incapable of convicting anyone. Thank you."

Throughout opening statements, Braden appears attentive and engaged without reacting, following his lawyers' instructions perfectly. But the jury and the television audience hardly notice, as the TV camera and all eyes are far more focused on Wally, especially as his lower lip quivered when Williams related stories of Wally's painful childhood and his fondness for Bill Clinton.

37

FOR THE PROSECUTION

The first witness for the prosecution is Hanley Oldfather, who testifies to discovering the poem written on the menu board at the Lovely Bean. He is followed by Captain Clint Wallace of the Alabama Emergency Response Scuba Unit, who authenticates photos and video taken by his dive unit showing the discovery of the Lincoln, Parker's body and the 7-iron. Next is the medical examiner, Dr. James Grimm, who testifies Parker's cause of death was a result of blunt force trauma by a metal implement consistent with the golf club located at the bottom of the quarry. He came to the opinion after measuring the width and 37-degree angle of three entry wounds on Parker's skull which were identical to the loft and width of the 7-iron.

On cross examination, Wood Williams establishes that Dr. Grimm is also a scratch golfer. Despite the vehement objection of Lesousky, Judge Renfro allows Williams to qualify the medical examiner as a golfing expert. Grimm then opines that, after examining the imprint of the club face on Parker's skull, the golf club's position at point of impact indicated the killer was, to a reasonable degree of golfing certainty, a passable duffer, having somewhere between a twelve and sixteen handicap.

Next up is Percy Ridge, who testifies that his caddie kept his clubs in the bag room at Lonesome Pine, and that his 7-iron went missing the weekend of October 6th as he played in the PGA qualifier. The last time he'd seen his golf club was Thursday, in the first round when he used it on the final hole. When handed the broken club found at the bottom of Quarry Lake, Ridge confirms that, it indeed is his. Ridge's testimony turns dramatic when asked how he knows the broken club and his missing 7-iron are one in the same. After pausing several moments, Ridge's facial muscles contort as he fights to hold off a flood of tears. It being too painful to look at his broken 7-iron, he stares at the floor pointing to the sticker on its shaft, struggling mightily to find the words. He would need only one.

"Lonesome."

Ridge also acknowledges that he had an affair with Christa Braden, and that the two of them had planned to run away together, but he broke up with her the first week in October just before the tournament. Lesousky finishes his direct examination of Ridge, dispelling any suggestion that he is the killer.

"Mr. Ridge, did you have time to travel to Alabama the weekend of October 6th?"

"No, sir."

"What were you doing?"

"I was kind of busy, trying to win a golf tournament at Lonesome Pine."

"If you intended to kill Harlan Parker, would you have risked breaking your best club to do it?"

"If I was going to kill Harlan Parker with a golf club, I would have used a driver!"

"No further questions."

Dan Jack is first to cross examine Ridge. "You don't know who stole your 7-iron, do you, Mr. Ridge?"

"I have my ideas, but no, not really."

"It could have been any number of people?"

"It was obviously somebody who had access to the bag room."

"Anyone who kept their clubs at Lonesome Pine could walk into that bag room get them whenever they wanted, couldn't they, Mr. Ridge?"

"I suppose."

"There were over 100 golfers who kept their clubs at Lonesome Pine, weren't there?"

"Yes."

"Christa Braden was one of them, wasn't she Mr. Ridge?"

"I've seen her in there frequently, yes."

"You gave Christa Braden private lessons, didn't you?"

"Yes. She golfed in college and wanted to pick up the sport again when she moved out to Lonesome Pine."

"Isn't it true that she filed for a divorce because the two of you were planning to run away together?"

"Just what are you suggesting, sir?"

"You were deeply in love with Christa, weren't you Mr. Ridge?"

"I'm still in love with her. She really liked my 7-iron!"

"Isn't it true that you complained to Christa that she was spending way too much time with her divorce lawyer, Harlan Parker?"

"That's absolutely true. I didn't like it. Not one bit."

"And in fact, you told her as much?"

"I told her several times!"

"And that you were so angry at her you broke off the relationship the week of the tournament?"

"Yes, I did! What kind of a sleaze bag lawyer meets clients in his condo?"

"In fact, Christa told you she was going to make you pay for dumping her right before you were about to make the big time, didn't she, Mr. Ridge?"

"She told me that she would never let it happen."

"I'll pass the witness."

It's Wood Williams' turn to cross examine the witness.

"Good morning, Mr. Ridge. Wood Williams for Wally Martin! You know Wally Martin well, don't you?"

"Well, I've known Wally as one of groundskeepers out at Lonesome Pine."

"Have you ever seen Wally swing a golf club?"

"Wally wasn't a golfer, but I've seen him sort of swing a club. Yes sir."

"And when was that?"

"One time there were some beavers building a dam across Moss Creek, chewing up little trees and such. Brock wanted Wally to go out there and take care of it."

"What did you interpret Brock to mean?"

"He wanted Wally to whack the little varmints into next week."

"Did Wally do it?"

"Oh, no. Wally would never harm an animal. He just waved a club at them and spooked them into a steel trap and took them off course."

"Thank you, sir. No further questions."

38

LAP DANCE CONFESSIONS

On day three of the trial, the prosecution calls Gia Goodnight, an exotic dancer at Cork and Cleavage Gentlemen's Club. On direct, she testifies that Braden is a frequent guest in the VIP lounge. On one night, during a lap dance with Gia Goodnight, Braden began talking about his love for poetry, saying that he is the one who wrote *Gum Pond Road*, and that he did so to lead investigators to Parker's body and Percy's golf club.

But the impact of Goodnight's testimony would fall flat on cross examination when she admits Braden has a history of trying to impress the girls at the club by telling whoppers. She acknowledges, that on previous occasions, Braden had also claimed to know the whereabouts of Jimmy Hoffa, Amelia Earhart and even went as far to claim that the second gunman on the grassy knoll at Dealey Plaza was a member at Lonesome Pine.

Next, Ridley Barnes testifies to receiving a text message from Parker's phone on Sunday evening of the weekend of October 6th, asking him to cover a court appearance the next morning in Cousin, Kentucky. On cross, Dan Jack establishes that Parker had never asked Barnes to cover a court appearance in the twenty years they had known each other, that Barnes traveled to Cousin the next morning only to find there was no court scheduled, and that he was greatly relieved as he didn't have the slightest idea what to do anyway. Gray also establishes that Barnes had profited handsomely from Parker's disappearance, having doubled his income in the past year after finally taking the initiative to learn how to practice law upon inheriting two of Parker's better corporate clients.

Then comes the testimony of two of Braden's ex-wives, both who testify that Braden was furious that they had chosen Parker as their divorce attorney. Each state that Braden had told them, that one fine day, he would own a magnificent golf course and one of its holes would be known as Harlan's Gulch.

Christa Braden acknowledges that she was heartbroken after Percy Ridge ended the relationship the week of the tournament, but vehemently denies poaching Ridge's 7- iron. "It wasn't even my favorite club!"

When asked why she spent so much time at Harlan Parker's condo, Christa testifies she was thinking about going to law school and that Harlan was just showing her common mistakes attorneys made blurring professional and personal lines with their clients. Lesousky would later argue in closing how unfair it was to consider Christa as a suspect, as Parker's murder had been particularly tragic for her, as she had lost her husband, sugar daddy, and sugar baby all in the same week.

Next comes the state crime lab's fingerprint expert, Russell Grant, who testifies that one print lifted from Parker's phone shared five common markers with Braden. While 20 common markers are typically required to establish a definitive match, the findings are enough for the expert to opine that the mathematical probability that the print belonged to Braden is one in five.

On cross examination, Dan Jack neuters Grant, establishing that ten million other people in the FBI database also shared five common markers on the print found on Parker's phone, and that the Grant's one in five odds go up to 1 in 25 when considering that his analysis conveniently excluded over two hundred million other adults in the United States whose prints are not included in the FBI's database.

On cross examination, Wood Williams continues to reinforce the primary theme of Wally's defense. "Mr. Grant, you also compared Wally's prints to those found on Parker's phone, didn't you?"

"Yes."

"And you didn't find any matches, did you?"

"That's correct, sir."

"You have no forensic evidence that Wally Martin ever touched that phone."

"No, sir."

"Did you know Wally Martin's so clueless that he doesn't even know how to use a smartphone?"

"No, sir. I wasn't aware of that."

"Did you know when I asked Wally about his browsing history, he thought it was the houses he walked by at a neighborhood yard sale?"

"I'm very sorry, sir."

Having heard three days of Wood Williams talking about how stupid Wally was, Lesousky has had enough.

"Objection your honor. I fail to see the relevance of Mr. Martin's smartphone aptitude. And besides, I think it's well established that stupidity isn't a defense to the crime of conspiracy to commit murder in the Commonwealth of Kentucky."

But Williams is ready. He postures toward the camera lens and clears his voice.

"If stupidity were a crime in the state of Kentucky, then Wally Martin stands before this court a condemned man!"

The fingerprint evidence would prove to be of little benefit for the prosecution. Not only was its emphasis on it misplaced, its' failure to have the state crime lab examine Parker's phone for other valuable information would end up being a glaring oversight. But Dan Jack Gray would not make the same mistake. In pre-trial discovery, he had requested a cloned copy of the hard drive of Parker's phone and had its data forensically examined by his own expert. The findings would be valuable information for Gray on cross examination.

"The Commonwealth next calls Tori Stevens."

Stevens testifies on direct examination that she received at text from Parker's phone at 7:42 pm on the evening of October 6th, when she was working late in the office preparing binders for a trial Parker had scheduled the following week. The text indicated that Parker had met a friend at Deadwood Rose and wouldn't need his BMW for the evening. As she'd been directed at least a dozen times before, she retrieved his car and drove it the carport of his High-land Park West condo. She then walked six blocks back to the square to retrieve her car and went home for the evening. She also testifies that Braden had left a threatening message on Parker's office voicemail during one of the divorce cases Parker litigated against him.

On cross, Williams would only ask Stevens one question. "Do you know how dumb Wally Martin is?"

At this point in the trial, the gallery was fully indoctrinated to the theme of Wally's defense and responding to Williams' questions about Wally's intelligence in unison. "How dumb is he?"

Williams would then answer his own question.

"Wally Martin's so dumb, he thinks the Ark of the Covenant is a boat!"

"Oh. How unfortunate for Mr. Martin."

"No further questions."

Dan Jack approaches the podium for cross. "Good afternoon, Mrs. Hughes."

Caught off guard, Tori looks over at the judge and smiles. "I've changed my name. I've recently gotten married."

"Well, isn't it a fact that you've been married for over two years, Mrs. Hughes?" Dan Jack asks.

"Yes..." Tori makes a show of thinking. "I'd say that's fairly recent."

"But you didn't take your husband's name until two weeks after Harlan Parker's disappearance, though it was over a year after you were married, correct?"

"That's true, but I fail to see the significance of your question, Mr. Gray."

Gray hands Tori a copy of her text messages to Harlan Parker. "I want to direct your attention to the texts you wrote to your boss the week prior to and after you got married and show me where you referred to it?"

Tori looks through messages for twenty seconds before looking at the jury. "I may not have mentioned it to Mr. Parker. I can't recall."

"Is there any reason you would not tell your boss that you got married?"

"I keep my personal and professional lives separate, Mr. Gray. It had nothing to do with my job performance."

"Would it be because you didn't want him to know you were in a relationship with another man?"

"If you're suggesting I had an intimate relationship with Mr. Parker, you'd be mistaken, Mr. Gray."

"Well, you and Harlan went riding on your motorcycle together, didn't you?"

"I've never owned or ridden a motorcycle in my life, Mr. Gray, and certainly not ridden on one with my boss!"

"Does your husband own or ride a motorcycle?"

"Never!"

"Were you aware whether Harlan owned a motorcycle?"

"That would look rather awkward, I'd think. I've never seen or heard that, Mr. Gray."

"I'm handing the witness an email dated December 16, 2016. Now, you'd been married a couple of months by December of 2016, correct?"

"Yes," Tori says very slowly as she looks out to her husband, who's sitting in the front row of the lower gallery.

"That's your email address, isn't it?"

"Yes."

"That is an email you sent to Harlan the week you'd been out of the office for a week taking final exams, correct?"

"It appears to be, yes."

"Move for admission of Braden exhibit 17, your honor."

"Admitted."

"Permission to publish to the jury."

"You may publish," Renfro rules.

"Can you please read to the jury the email you wrote to Harlan that day, Mrs. Hughes?"

Tori Hughes reads the email to the jury so softly no one can hear her.

Judge Renfro interrupts. "Mrs. Hughes, could you please read significantly louder so the jury may hear you!"

Tori nods to Renfro affirmatively. She reads the email aloud, quickly.

"I've missed you so much, Harlan. Can't wait to get back to Summerville and ride my Harley."

Lesousky exclaims, "Objection to relevance, your honor!"

The gallery explodes in laughter. Renfro bangs his gavel several times to calm the storm.

"Order! Order in the courtroom!"

After the raucous laughter subsides to the hum of a hundred whispers and then silence, Renfro rules on Lesousky's objection.

"Overruled! You may continue, Mr. Gray."

"Thank you, your honor. Mrs. Hughes, so the Harley you referenced in that email isn't a Harley Davidson motorcycle, is it?"

"I told you I don't own a motorcycle! This is a misprint, Mr. Gray! I didn't ride Harlan!"

"Thank you, Ms. Hughes. That goes to my next question. If you've never owned or ridden a motorcycle, can you tell this jury what you're referring to when you say you can't wait to 'ride my Harley'?"

Tori sits in silence, shaking her head in disagreement as she looks at the email and then out to her husband.

Renfro again intervenes. "You may answer, Mrs. Hughes."

"This must be a misprint. I have no idea, Mr. Gray. What does this have to do with anything!"

Mr. Hughes stands up, glares at his wife and walks out of the courtroom.

Dan Jack refers Tori to seven text messages before and after she marries, where she tells Parker that she loves him.

"Mr. Parker taught me much and gave me the opportunity to finish college and go to law school. Yes, we were very close, but as I've stated here several times there was nothing physical, Mr. Gray!"

"You changed your name, October 19, 2017, less than two weeks after Parker disappeared and ten months before his body was discovered, didn't you?"

"I suppose, I was so busy with school and work, I just hadn't gotten around to it."

"Ms. Stevens, forgive me, I mean Mrs. Hughes. If you were in fact keeping your marriage from Mr. Parker, and you waited to change your name just after he disappeared, it could suggest that you knew he wasn't coming back before anyone else, couldn't it?"

"The two events have no relationship, I can assure you, Mr. Gray."

Gray then shows Tori a copy of the forensic report of Braden's computer expert, detailing the movements of Parker's phone the evening of October 6th, which indicated that the phone traveled from Summerville Square to Parker's condominium, then traveled south to Bitty, Alabama before returning the morning of the October 7th, where it remained for another 38 hours in an area near Tori's home in Summerville.

"It appears that, on the evening of October 6th, Mr. Parker's phone arrived at his condominium around the same time you drove his car there, and after returning from Alabama, remained in an area that included your residence, Mrs. Hughes?"

"The area which you are referring to would also include the homes of several hundred people, Mr. Gray."

"Your husband's a golfer, isn't he?"

"Yes."

"He has a membership at Lonesome Pine?"

"Yes."

"And he volunteered to help with the tournament on the week of October 2nd, didn't he?"

"Yes, he's very generous with his time to help others, Mr. Gray."

"And he appears to have lots of time on his hands. What does he do for a living?"

"He's a fitness expert, Mr. Gray, and a motivational speaker."

"Who does he motivate? You, so he can golf every day, Mrs. Hughes?"

"Objection, your honor," Lesousky puts in.

"Overruled! You may continue, Mr. Gray."

"I am handing you a copy of Mr. Parker's personal and business account."

Tori identifies Parker's bank records.

Dan Jack asks, "You handled Harlan's payroll, including your own pay, correct?"

"Correct. I did many things for Mr. Parker."

"You were making quite a bit of money working for Harlan Parker, weren't you,

Mrs. Hughes?"

"Mr. Parker appreciated my skill set and work ethic, Mr. Gray."

"In fact, as a paralegal, you were making more money than any lawyer in the firm, except Mr. Parker?"

"I don't know what other lawyers made at the firm, Mr. Gray. Most of those transfers were personal loans Mr. Parker made to help me with tuition and school expenses."

"Three hundred thousand dollars for school, Mrs. Hughes?"

"A law school education is a lot more expensive today than when you went, Mr. Gray."

"And how much of that loan have you paid back, Mrs. Hughes?"

"I've only been a lawyer for a few months, sir."

"And now that Mr. Parker's out of the way, you and your husband don't have to worry about paying him back, do you, Mrs. Hughes?"

Dan Jack doesn't wait for Tori to answer.

"No further questions."

After the close of the government's case, the only witness the defense calls is Silas Brown, a childhood friend of Wally, who testifies that Wally had indeed brought his beloved Bo to Cousin Critter Crematorium to be cremated and have his remains collected into a scattering tube. When asked on cross how he could remember such an event with no record of Bo ever being there, Brown is emphatic.

"The stench of burning Cockweiler with that Betty Bake Double Cream all over her is something I'll take to my grave. It took us two weeks to get rid of it!"

Taking advice of counsel, neither Brock nor Wally take the stand. After closing statements, the court reads instructions to the jury on the law and what they are and are not to consider during deliberations.

The court pays for the jury's lunch and dinner, takeout from the Lovely Bean the first two days of deliberations. But after three days pass without a verdict, Renfro secretly asks Bailiff Jessie Hogg to eavesdrop to find out what was holding things up. As it turns out, the jury had reached a verdict the first day, but was enjoying the Bean's fine cuisine so much they didn't want to say they'd reached a verdict. Renfro promptly directs Colt to turn down the heat on the second floor and begin ordering carryout from Buck's Diamond Grill, the culinary armpit of Summerville.

Upon being served lunch from Buck's, the jury knows the gig is up, and without a bite immediately decide to advise the court they have reached a verdict. The packed courtroom stands as the jury files into the courtroom. Renfro begins the verdict protocol. "Has the jury reached a verdict?"

"We have, your honor."

"Please provide to the Court Clerk to publish."

Jessie Hogg retrieves the verdict from the foreman and hands it to the clerk, who reads the verdict.

"In the case Commonwealth of Kentucky vs. Brock Alton Braden, we the jury find the defendant, not guilty. In the case Commonwealth of Kentucky vs. Wallace Presley Martin, we the jury find the defendant, not guilty."

The courtroom explodes in cheers and applause upon hearing Wally's verdict. Positioning himself perfectly before the camera, Wood Williams wraps his arm around his client and shakes his hand. Wally's sort-of fiancée works her way through the crowd onto the courtroom floor to embrace her dreamboat, only to not be recognized by Wally. Stunned by the rejection, she becomes hysterical and must be ushered from the courtroom. The court then orders that Martin be released from custody and Braden released from his bond, and the matter of *Commonwealth of Kentucky vs. Braden and Martin* concludes.

39

THE CHARMS OF A VICTORIAN TIME CAPSULE

After his acquittal, Wally signed a six-figure endorsement deal with a golf club manufacturer promoting irons guaranteed to kill it (referring to golf balls) on every shot with a shaft so durable it was guaranteed to not to break under the most extreme conditions. Brother Kenny would live the rest of his life under an assumed name in Alaska working in the oil and gas industry. Although Kenny would deeply miss his twin brother, Brock Braden had made things just comfortable enough for him to never return to Kentucky.

Christa would eventually find her eternal summer by moving to Cabo San Lucas with her boyfriend, Colin Barnes. They would live happily ever after, renting jet skis and other watersport gear out of their surf shop.

Tori Stevens would be indicted and convicted of 173 counts of wire fraud and sentenced to nine years in federal prison. Even though she'd be disbarred, she would become the greatest jailhouse lawyer in the history of the Federal Bureau of Prisons, writing habeus corpus briefs for fellow inmates in exchange for not getting the stuffing beaten out of her.

Tori's husband immediately filed for a divorce and decided that the secret to true happiness was to forever avoid stunningly attractive sociopaths and only pursue honest women without law licenses who possessed becoming yet understated beauty.

Although Pearl was furious Braden was acquitted for Parker's murder, he was more than impressed with Dan Jack's courtroom abilities and would hire Blue and Gray as his law firm, not only personally but for his amusement park.

Despite the absence of Harlan Parker, Greg Lantham couldn't cut it in Summerville as a lawyer eventually leaving the practice of law altogether. However, his fortunes would change one 4th of July afternoon as he wandered about Summerville Square when a six-year-old girl approached him. Mistaking him for a sad clown, she asked him to make her a twisty doggie balloon. The chance encounter would prove to be a defining moment for Lantham, who would triple his income making appearances at children's birthday parties and other special events as Lanthy the Clown. The career move enabled Lantham to reconcile with his wife.

After the unexpected death of Hank Justice, the Mayor ignored Marshal Wilt's mandatory retirement and appointed him Chief of Police where he would serve eight years before retiring. Detective Andrews would leave the force within a couple of years for the FBI where his investigative achievements would one day become the stuff of legend.

Julia Sweet would have to hire someone to manage the Lovely Bean full-time after Chief Wilt made her lead homicide detective for the Summerville PD.

Obadiah Adam eventually returned to New York where his star continued to rise, being awarded the Pulitzer Prize for Literature, two National Book Awards and named America's Poet Laureate.

Because Dan Jack and Savannah had spared Braden from living out the rest of his life in the state pen, they would be rewarded by serving as legal counsel for all his commercial interests. Braden Contracting and Lonesome Pine National created so much legal work for Blue and Gray it fulfilled Dan Jack's dream of building a law practice worthy of passing on to his daughter.

Within six months of the verdict, Dan Jack and Savannah would move out of their modest two-person law office into the more spacious and elegant surroundings previously occupied by Parker, Barnes and Jeffries, or at least what was left after the Lovely Bean had annexed it. The nicest office space on the square would prove to be the perfect fit for the fastest growing law firm in Summerville.

JUNE 8, 2009

One Saturday evening, while Savannah is finishing up the move to the new office, she clears out the last of what remained of the firm's old file room and runs across a folder containing some old newspaper articles her father had saved. There's one clip that catches her eye because of an image that seems strangely familiar to her. She looks at the top of the article, now torn, brown and faded, seeing it's a 2001 story from the Lynnville Bee, in Bethune County, Alabama. Then she realizes where she had seen it before. It's a photograph of Quarry Lake, set underneath a headline:

Kentucky men convicted in Quarry Lake Murder

Savannah begins to read the article, initially thinking what an amazing coincidence it is that two men from Kentucky had traveled to Alabama 18 years before and murdered someone and tried to dispose of the body in Quarry Lake.

A sickening feeling falls over her. With her back to the wall, she slides down to the floor as she continues to read.

The article goes on to describe how the van had gotten stuck at the quarry's edge because the killers made a fatal mistake. Instead of driving the vehicle into the lake, they put it in neutral and tried to push it in.

Savannah feels her heart pounding in her chest. Beads of sweat suddenly surface on the back of neck.

As the front wheels rolled over the quarry's limestone edge, the van's undercarriage dropped to bedrock, bringing the van to an abrupt halt. The killers frantically tried to push the van in, but it would move no further. Fearing authorities were in route, they flee the quarry, leaving the van hovering over the lake. A deputy sheriff discovers the van next morning. When authorities pull if from the edge of the water and open the back door, they find a 71-year-old woman, still alive but badly beaten and the body of her husband. The article details how the woman identified her husband's killers at the trial, leading to their conviction.

Three quarters through the story, Savannah suddenly drops the article and plunges her face into her hands, trying to unsee it. But it's too late.

"Assistant United States Attorney, Dan Jack Gray told the jury the defendants would have gotten away with murder if they hadn't made the mistake of trying to push the van into Quarry Lake. 'If they had just driven it in, Joe and Helen Roberts would have never been found.'"

Across town, Dan Jack is at home in his favorite leather chair, reading beneath the dim lighting of a stand-alone lamp. On the nightstand next to him is a photograph of him giving his 12-year-old Savannah a golfing lesson. He laments how rarely he gets out to Lonesome Pine anymore to play a round. Work at his firm had just gotten so busy.

But he thinks how fortunate he and Savannah are to have such a problem now. Every few minutes a smile flashes across his face as he flips page after page of one of his favorite books, a bound collection of poems written some 30 years before by a promising young writer in Summerville College's creative writing program. The author's name, once written in bold white print on the book's spine, has long since faded. But if you look very closely, you can still see the outline of the letters just enough to make out who it is; *1988 Orchid and Oak recipient, Daniel Jackson Gray.*

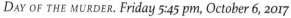

DAY OF THE MURDER. *Friday 5:45 pm, October 6, 2017*

Within a minute of leaving the office of Blue & Gray, Parker receives a call from Dan Jack. He picks up smugly and holds up a finger to the court reporter, silently requesting her to wait. "Already seeing reason, Dan Jack?"

Dan Jack said, "Harlan, come back to the office for a moment, I was meaning to tell you that I came across something you'll be very interested in. Some old photos of you and Annabelle at Jamboree, sophomore year."

"How'd you come across photos of me and Annabelle?"

"I handled her mother's estate. They were in a box of records Annabelle brought to me."

Without hearing Dan Jack's side of the conversation, the court reporter proceeds to her car.

Harlan quickly does an about-face and starts walking back to Blue and Gray. Parker loved anything that involved reminiscing about his glory days when he had thick flowing hair and a chiseled frame of 190 lbs. Thirty-plus years later, he was north of 300 lbs., with a waist-line at a robust 46'. So large a man, he shopped only at a big and tall shops, that is, until he became successful enough to have his clothes custom made to mask his rotund form. For Harlan, the present could never compete with the past.

"Annabelle kept pictures of her and me?"

"She sure did. Go figure."

Harlan chuckles. "See you in a second." He hangs up and tucks the phone back into his pocket.

Harlan and Dan Jack were never what you'd call friends, but they had graduated together from Summerville High in 1984. In those days Dan Jack had a couple of friends but mostly kept to himself and wasn't really into sports. But even after the school cancelled football, Harlan was still the big man on campus. And of course, he also dated the prettiest girlfriend in school, Annabelle Larkin. She broke up with Harlan the day after the principal found him and her best friend in his Camaro during lunch break. Over the years, he had forgotten the momentary indiscretion, like all the others, and still had fond memories of Annabelle.

Harlan walks up the stairs to the second floor of the Victorian building and enters Blue and Gray. Dan Jack is standing at the secretarial station waiting for him with a big smile on his face.

"Come with me Harlan. The photos are in my desk. They really take you back. Annabelle's still lovely, but back then—whoa!"

Dan Jack turns to walk to his office as the two continue the conversation. Harlan nods and flashes a smile.

"Yeah, I'd love to see her again."

"She's still married, Harlan."

"Some women are more married than others, Dan Jack."

"And Annabelle's one of them, Harlan."

Harlan follows Dan Jack down a long narrow hallway to the last door on the left. As they walk in, Dan Jack closes the door behind Harlan, nodding at the tarps which covered the desk, floor, and hung on scaffolding throughout the room.

"Please excuse the mess, Harlan, we're painting the office yet again. Ever since Savannah has come to work with me, she wants to redecorate every couple of years."

As Dan Jack walks around to the back of his desk and opens the middle drawer, he points to the chair in front of the desk.

"Take a seat for a couple minutes while I dig out these pics. You're really going to love them, a lot."

Harlan, a self-styled bourbon aficionado, notices a bottle of fine Kentucky bourbon whiskey and a couple of shot glasses sitting at the front of Dan Jack's desk. Still on his feet, Harlan picks up the bottle to check out the label. And he's impressed.

"Dan Jack! I had no idea you had such a fine taste for bourbon. This stuff goes for about $2,200 a bottle, last time I checked."

Dan Jack grins as he fumbles his hands inside the drawer, as if searching for photos. As he shuffles paper, he imagines how lovely Annabelle would look if the photos actually existed. Instead, there's an empty opioid bottle from a prescription Dan Jack had filled a couple of years before, after knee surgery. The nausea the pills caused made him more miserable than the pain, so he only took two of them at the time. Dan Jack looks back up to Harlan.

"I wish I could take credit for affording something like that, Harlan. It was a gift from Tommy Thompson after I walked him out of federal court for tax evasion. Take a shot or two if you like. I mean, it's Friday after all!"

"Well, don't mind if I do. Thank you very much!"

As Harlan picks up a shot glass and begins to pour himself a drink, he notices a golf club leaning against the front left corner of Dan Jack's desk and begins to laugh loudly.

"You're still trying to hit the golf ball, I see. Last time I saw a club in your hand I think it was the scramble at our 30th high school reunion a couple years ago. You dropped three in a row in the lake on the 6th hole!"

Harlan's obnoxious laughter fades to a faint chuckle as he lifts the glass to his mouth and throws it down. A low gravely hum of pleasure moans from Harlan's closed lips as he looks the label again, nodding with approval at the smoothness of the whiskey. He points the shot glass in the direction of Dan Jack as a show of appreciation, before pulling it back to his chest to pour himself a second shot.

"It's not polite to let a guy drink alone!" He puts down his glass and picks up the second glass to pour one for Dan Jack.

Harlan's words begin to slur as he holds out the glass now filled to the rim. He closes his eyes and opens them trying to correct his vision which is suddenly blurry.

"Here ya go!"

Dan Jack reaches out to grab the shot, nodding in appreciation.

"Thank you, Harlan."

Harlan picks up his glass throws down the second shot. Within seconds, he sways side to side, then turns to look for the chair behind him to steady himself. He reaches back but catches only air and falls to the tarp beneath him.

Directly below Blue and Gray's 2nd floor office is Maggie's Beauty Salon. Maggie usually closes up shop at 5:30, but her last appointment was a cut and color, so she's shutting down about twenty minutes later. Suddenly she hears a loud thud overhead and looks up to see dust blow through cracks in the pressed tin ceiling, worn and frayed from too many years and too little attention.

"Hmm. That one's louder than usual. Hope Dan Jack hasn't fallen down." She quickly redirects her attention to checking out her customer. "Oh well, just one of the charms of working in a Victorian time capsule."

Upstairs, Dan Jack slowly walks around to the front corner of his desk. He stops and looks down at Harlan, now flat on his back and looking back up at Dan Jack. The expanse of Harlan's torso is too wide for his arms to reach across and push himself up, and he's not happy.

"Well, are you going to help me up or just stand there!"

Dan Jack just stares at him without expression. He's spoken his last words to Harlan Parker.

Downstairs, Maggie walks toward the alley-side entrance of the salon to leave for the evening when she hears an almost rhythmic creak and crackle above her. It's a sound she's familiar with, one she's heard many times before, except it's longer this time; wooden beams bending and bowing in the subfloor underneath Dan Jack's office. As she opens the door to leave, she freezes for a moment still holding onto the doorknob. Turning an ear slightly upward, she tries to make out the source of the muted, mysterious rumble coming from above.

Sounds like Dan Jack is helping a mare give birth up there.

Shaking her head in bewilderment, Maggie backs out into the alley, closing the door behind her.

EPILOGUE

As time passed, the public's interest in finding the killer would wane. No one would ever be brought to justice for the murder of Harlan Parker, and for most everyone in Summerville that was just fine.